The Kimbo – Stop the Presses! – Series

Book 1

Mystic Seer

S.L. Kotar & J.E. Gessler

Ahead of The Press
St. Louis, MO

Library of Congress Cataloguing-in-Publication Data
The Kimbo – Stop the Presses! – Series Book 1 Mystic Seer
/ S.L. Kotar and J.E. Gessler

ISBN KINDLE Mobi 978-1-950392-61-2 (ebook)
ISBN PAPERBACK 978-1-950392-60-5

Ahead of The Press Publishing
St. Louis, Missouri

Table of Contents

DEDICATION

For Darren McGavin and Kathie Browne, two of the most talented and nicest people who ever lived.

SLK

And JEG, always

CHAPTER 1

"Kimbo!"

As opening lines go, that was not a Pulitzer Prize winner.

It was not on a level with "Call me Ishmael."

Not even, "It was the best of times, it was the worst of times, it was the age of wisdom, it was the age of foolishness, it was the epoch of belief, it was the epoch of incredulity, it was the season of Light, it was the season of Darkness, it was the spring of hope, it was the winter of despair, we had everything before us, we had nothing before us, we were all going direct to Heaven, we were all going direct the other way – in short, the period was so far like the present period, that some of its noisiest authorities insisted on its being received, for good or for evil, in the superlative degree of comparison only."

Which made one hell of a sentence.

A modern-day editor, used to novels being under two-hundred double-spaced pages, would cut that down to twelve words.

He (or she) wouldn't pay Dickens by the word, either. We lived in a world of percentages. In case you're wondering, it never favors the writer.

Sort of like *1984*.

Actually, not sort of like: it *was* 1984. Although I'm narrating this from my notes many years later, so there may be some slip-ups along the way.

In 1984 I was 39 years young. (I was going to say 40, which also isn't true, but there's a huge generational gap between being in your 30s and reaching the advanced old age of forty-something. I look like I'm thirty-ish so I can get away with it.)

"Kimbo!" was not a recommended beginning to anything. In truth, it sounded more like an ending.

For me, at least.

I had heard that tone of voice before. Lots of times. More times than I can count, and I'm known as a whiz. At least the guy in my bathroom mirror tells me so. And he's never been known to lie. Welsh on a few bets, maybe; run down the back stairs while the repo men were knocking on his apartment door. But never lie.

Not anything worthy of, "Forgive me, father, for I have sinned." Nothing that big.

If you believe that and you're a big city editor, then you're in the wrong job.

"Kimbo!"

That's me, by the way. A. Kimbo. That's how I'm known around newsrooms, crime scenes and animal pounds: as "Kimbo," but drop the "A." I don't use the initial unless I have to. There's a particularly good reason for that. It doesn't stand for anything. Just a letter of the alphabet. Don't get me wrong. That's not what's on my birth certificate. It was expected the temporary one issued by the hospital would be changed by the orphanage and so it was. I never considered it – excuse the pun – legitimate, and therefore refused to acknowledge it. I wanted a real name: one that belonged to me. Unfortunately, my parents neglected to give me one. No one knew who they were or what they were called. They just dumped me on the steps of a church. They used to do that with kittens, too. Unless the river was closer, in which case they dropped the litter – pun intended – or the unwanted kid in a sack and flung them/it overboard.

Sometimes, it's kinder that way.

Which doesn't make it any less murder.

The name they gave me at the "Home" was generic. Soulless. Not that I'm a religious fanatic but I'd like to think my name stood for something. As a kid I was an avid reader. You know how some words just stick to you? "Akimbo" was that word for me. I didn't know what it meant at the time, but I picked it out, separated the "a" from the "kimbo" and made myself a name. I insisted they use it at the state school we were sent to. It caused confusion at first because they thought there were two kids: an A. Kimbo and the one with the generic name. I persisted on being called by my real name and they went along with me. I always suspected they got to charge New York for two students. I figured the state could afford it. When I was old enough, I changed it legally and scrubbed my old name off the record books. Since that orphanage is long closed I suspect no one could ever tag me with it. I hope not because it would make me feel like a nobody. Which I was.

At least this way, I'm the only Kimbo I know.

When I sign my name on legal documents – that would be paychecks, when I occasionally receive one – I'm forced to write "A. Kimbo." Most people assume it stands for Andrew, long for Andy. I don't know why. There are lots of names that start with the first letter of the alphabet.

"Adam" comes to mind, for no apparent reason. I don't mind being called Andy. At least when it's enunciated in anything under a low roar. My last name, however, has that certain ring to it. It seems to inspire higher octaves, giving it a knife-in-the-ribs- quality.

"Kimbo!"

See what I mean?

Three "Kimbos" in a row. Third time's a charm.

"Coming," I dutifully replied.

I pasted my best nonchalant smile over my freckled face, straightened my tie and crossed myself.

Figuratively speaking, of course.

The last time I was in church was for some guy's wedding. I had forgotten his name before the ink was dry on his divorce papers. I think I bought the couple three bottles of scotch; one to share and one each to drown their future sorrows in.

I always like to be ahead of the game.

"Yes, sir?" I asked, pushing open the door to my editor's office. It was built of solid oak with a thick glass window. It was a throwback to the olden days when desk chairs were wooden and weighed about two-hundred pounds. They tilted back with springs that inevitably squeaked. A chair like that had personality.

Once you got used to it, you could fling yourself at that chair from any angle and land your posterior exactly in the depressed, un-cushioned seat. Anybody else trying nothing more exotic than resting themselves down in it either tipped backwards when the springs gave too much, or fell over sideways.

The kind of chair a man has says a lot about his character.

I have a chair exactly like that at my desk. It's an old railroad castoff. I think Casey Jones once owned it, and he was the greatest railroader there was. I read a book about him once when I was a kid. Never forgot it.

It didn't make me want to grow up and be a railroad man, but it did give me an appreciation of all things railroad.

Which was fortunate, for I've been railroaded more than a time or two.

"What story are you working on?"

The man sitting down was settled into a Lazy Boy recliner.

My editor was a big man. Not tall, as men go, but he had an inch or two on me and had the bulk of a Sumo wrestler. He was a gentle giant who never raised his voice. Except at me. We had an understanding, Mr. Sweet McGraw and I.

We were friends. I had never been to his home and he had never been to mine. I had breakfast with him once when he offered to buy. I was younger in those days. Also naive. After the eggs, hash browns and two cups of coffee, he gave it to me straight.

I was "the best damned reporter he knew," and I was "going to tone it down a bit, or be reassigned to setting typeface for the classifieds." The order, he said, "came from the top."

Publishers hate me.

The feeling is mutual. Anyone who has the audacity and the connections to make it up the career ladder all the way to newspaper publisher has to know a lot of people. Translated, a lot of people own him. I never had any respect for a man who would sell his soul for a house on the Hill, a swimming pool and the right to call the mayor by his first name.

Sweet, on the other hand, was just an editor. He was lower management, bottom- rung supervisor. Translated, that meant he took all the crap and received none of the glory.

He started out as a beat reporter, just like I did. When he forgets his roots, I like to remind him. But only when I'm standing between him and his window. If he threw something at me, I could leap aside, and the book, or paperweight, or coffee mug would strike the glass, breaking it.

I always figured that's why doors had windows in them – to save poor sods like me.

"Sods" is an English cuss word. It is short for "sodomy." It's etymology is Middle English, corrupted from the Old French *sodomie.* The French apparently took it from Late Latin, *sodoma.* It's used in Genesis 19:1-11. You know that story. It broke about two-thousand years ago. In the Business – capital "B" – we call it old hat. You probably know it by another name.

I love words. Words are my stock and trade. You can learn a lot from a dictionary.

No one uses dictionaries anymore. People talk in sound bites, now. I wouldn't be a writer for a TV news program to save my bank account.

"Sod" is not a word I normally use. It's a late addition to my vocabulary. If I were still working in St. Louis, Missouri, I would have said, "to save poor bastards like me." But I, along with the entire newsroom of our pitifully small wire service, had been transferred, kit and caboodle, to London.

England. You've heard of it. The country you always wanted to visit and never will. Home of crumpets, the Queen and the Beatles.

Not in that order.

We now represent the "foreign" component of the Cover-All News Service. They pay us like we wear "coveralls," too. Janitors. Or whatever they call them these days. It's like Personnel. In our politically-correct society, "Personnel" was changed to "Human Resources." Now it's "People Management."

Everything has to be international these days. We even have a computer in the office. No one knows how to use it. I don't think it's even plugged in. But we're here and it's there and that's all that matters.

I guess "close" counts for more than horseshoes after all.

"I'm not working on any story, sir."

That was the established answer. If I told him what I was really working on, he would take me off it. It was a matter of principal.

"Good. I have a hot little item here I want you to investigate."

In most lines of work, the expression "hot little item" would refer to the pretty woman the boss was dating. She was always "hands off." To a reporter on a Big City rag, it might mean a socialite who had gotten herself murdered, kidnapped, or who was seen slipping out of the incumbent's private back entrance. For me, it always meant down and dirty.

My shoulders sagged. I should have lied. I should have told him I was onto the biggest story since the Hindenburg. We in the News Business always speak of Big Stories which occurred before we were born as though we covered them personally. It's an ego thing.

"Yeah?"

Not exactly the Queen's English, but it adequately expressed my enthusiasm.

"Yeah."

Between us, we talked like we were the bad guys in a Dave O'Brien "B" Western. You remember Dave. When he wasn't a singing cowboy – yes, there was more than one – or punching cowpokes, he starred in *Reefer Madness,* the greatest hoot since Adam gave Eve 3:1 odds the Lord would never throw them out of Paradise. Dave also did some pretty darned good grade zilch films with Bela Lugosi. I can quote them, chapter and verse.

I think all reporters are frustrated actors.

We're also frustrated novelists. The fastest way to get on our bad side is to tell us Random House just optioned your novel, or that your writing has been compared favorably to that of John Steinbeck.

The second fastest way is to remark in that oh-so-smug-tone, "I coulda been a writer."

Yeah. Right. It starts with putting pen to paper.

You note I didn't say it began with talent.

"Sit down."

When your editor tells you to sit down, that means the story is a turkey. I sat down. The chairs were all upholstered. None of them made a noise when you leaned back in them. A poor recommendation, right off the bat.

"OK. Give it to me straight."

There was no point beating around the bush. I was stuck with it and that was that. It didn't mean I would ever write the story. I might fuss with it a bit, then alphabetically deposit it in the proverbial Round File. Or, if I did write it, none of the clients who subscribed to our news service would pick it up.

You learn a lot about humility being a writer.

But then, I came by mine early. Before I was out of diapers. In England, by the way, they call those nasty necessities of infancy "nappies."

Now, you've learned something today.

"It's big."

My heart sank. Don't let anyone tell you hearts don't sink. They go down faster than the *Titanic.*

"Big?"

Sweet nodded. When he didn't try to soften that kiss-of-death word with a smile, I perked up somewhat. Maybe there was hope, after all.

Hope springs eternal.

Just ask Ponce de Leon.

There was a lot to be said about a liberal education.

Today, schools teach television, ecology and computer science. That's so the kids can justify absorbing their history by watching "Cleopatra" on the small screen, then reading the abridged version (Cliff Notes; 20 pages), or buying a ready-made term paper. The earth- awareness course is to inform them the damage they're doing to the planet when they throw a Pepsi can out the car window.

It takes three-million, four-hundred and sixty-two years for an aluminum can to biodegrade in a land fill. I learned that on a nature program about why there are no more lions in Africa.

It was sponsored by the San Diego Zoo and they had a name-actor narrate it. I'm just cynical enough to believe he did it for the tax write-off.

Well, I've written a few pieces, myself, which look good on a resume, so don't mind me.

I've never won any major awards, although not from lack of trying. It's always held over a reporter's head if he hasn't won a Pulitzer. You'd think they handed those things out in paper bags along with your cheeseburger and fries.

Which I'd be selling, if I wasn't a news hound. That's what liberal arts degrees are good for these days.

The starting salary for that new creature called a "computer programmer" is ten times what I'm making now and I've been in this business since I was out of nappies.

Graduated young.

"It has to do with the stock market."

What I know about the stock market you could fit into my personal 401K portfolio. The last time I looked, it held two U.S. savings bonds in twenty-five dollar denominations. They would mature about the time my grandchildren were getting ready to retire. And I don't have any. Get the point?

"I'm not a financial writer, Sweet."

"It's more complicated than that."

"Tell me."

I'm a glutton for punishment.

Sweet got up, no small feat, and perched on the top of his desk. He stared down at me with those round, hazel eyes of his. He looked fatherly. I loved him like a son.

He has all his hair and I have most of mine. We have a lot in common.

His hair is black when he remembers to dye it; otherwise it's tinged with grey – that's the British spelling, by the way – Americans spell it with an "a," and yes, we're back to that, again. My hair is red and my eyes brown. That's where the similarities ended.

People called me "Red" when I was young and I always hated it. They called me "Carrot-top," too. I had the freckles which went with that sort of hair, but my color was a lot lighter than what's commonly associated with a vegetable. I tolerated it because it was better than what the orphanage put on my birth certificate.

It's a funny thing about birth certificates. The mother can put anything she – darned – well pleases on it. That includes the last name. In my case, of course, I was disowned right from the get-go. The other thing that bugs me is that the law shields the parents' real names from the kids they dump on paid strangers to raise. It's one of the last cruelties *homo sapiens* cling to. It's right up there with walking upright and possessing a sense of humor to prove we're superior beings.

"Andy, you know and I know that the stock market is a melting pot. Hundreds of millions of people invest their hard-earned savings every day."

"So they tell me."

"We also know it's really controlled by a few big wigs."

That I could agree to without doing any research at all.

Sweet and I speak the same language. We come from the same Old School. Where we went, however, they didn't hand out neckties so we could identify each other at the local watering hole. We earned our diplomas from hard work and even longer hours. I put myself through night school in New York City. I worked a day job as a waiter, cab driver and even as a respiratory therapist. The hospital promoted me from Central Supply and trained me in-house because they were desperate. I liked the pay but I couldn't stand the mucus.

Even worked as a gumshoe until I got the piss scared out of me one night when some bozo came at me with a gun. I hate guns. Guns don't kill people. People kill people. People with guns kill a lot of people. I'd like to see some jerk with a knife try and slaughter a school full of little kids.

Sweet put himself through day school by performing gigs playing the violin. He was a classical musician by trade but he never got the Big Break. What he did get was a sweet nickname, which, in the scheme of things, was better than nothing. He also took a few parts off-Broadway. I used to attend the theatre a lot because with my degree in journalism I figured if I wasn't qualified for anything else, I might be a talent scout. Once, after a play in which he had a small part, I waited outside in the alley. When he came out, I asked for his autograph on the playbill. He signed his name on his picture with a blue-ink Bic pen, right over his forehead. I figured he hadn't had much practice.

We never met again until he hired me as a reporter about a dozen years ago. That was when we were both on the downside of our careers.

We've been inseparable ever since. It's an office relationship. They're the best kind because when one gets fired, the company takes care of the severance pay.

"There have been rumors for months, now. Maybe years, for all I know."

"These big wigs aren't paying their taxes?"

There was hope in my voice, despite myself.

He shook his head and sunk my boat before she had been properly launched.

"No. Nothing that... plebeian."

My eyes squinted, drawing my eyebrows together. A girl once told me I look like a red herring when I did that. I try not to do it too often.

Although, as I joked at the time, I'd rather be the red herring than the guilty party.

I think she had been reading Agatha Christie. I fascinated her because I was a writer. When she discovered – at three in the morning when I got a call from one of my stringers, giving me a tip on a hot murder – that I covered real crime instead of making up implausible stories, she left.

I guess Hercule Poirot kept her warm from then on.

"OK, Sweet. I'll bite."

I found myself going from boats to aquatic creatures. Not good.

"Some select few men – the movers and shakers – have all been hitting the mark, lately. Whatever they speculate on has risen, increasing their wealth tremendously. They buy stock at ten dollars a share –"

"Pounds," I corrected. Sweet hated to be corrected.

"Pounds?" He was on the heavy side and tended to be sensitive on the subject. "You trying to be cute?"

"Who me? No. Never." Which wasn't too far off the mark. No one my age wants to be cute. Devilishly handsome, but not cute. Cute was for stuffed toys, babies and Garfield heads bobbing up and down in the back of car windows.

"Oh. I get it," he said with a slight tone of resignation in his voice. "Pounds, as in dollars."

"Two-to-one, at the going rate of exchange," I agreed.

When we were shipped to England, the salaries had sounded astronomical. We had wondered at the time, but being good ol', red-blooded Americans, knew nothing whatsoever about our English cousins. We thought the "Old Man," as publishers, wire service owners, pimps and sugar-daddies are invariably called, was finally being generous with us.

We should have known better.

I think the expression is, "When hell freezes over."

Our great salaries and "expense accounts," when adjusted for the currency exchange, amounted to exactly what we had been making in St. Louis.

To the pence.

And it's a – expletives deleted – lot more expensive to live in London than it is in the Gateway To the West.

And London doesn't even have an Arch.

"So, what's your point?" I asked. "The rich are getting richer. Happens every day."

"It's *how* they're getting richer which has raised a few eyebrows."

"How?" Now I was feeling like an Indian. "Come on, Sweet. I imagine they have a stable of very clever boys and girls fresh out of Yale who calculate odds and trends and all those sorts of things. It's the age of the computer, for Cripe's sake. Anyone who really understands these things ought to do pretty well for himself."

"They're never wrong."

There was the sound of a death knell in his voice.

"Never?"

"Never."

"How many big time investors are involved?"

"Make it half a dozen. Maybe more. But we've honed in on five outside the U.S."

"How are they doing it?"

There was that word again.

"Word around town is that they're getting advice from a mystic."

If I had been chewing gum at the time, I'd have spit it in Sweet's face.

"Advice from a mystic? You've got to be kidding."

He regretfully shook his head.

"That's what rumor has it."

"Assuming what you say is true, getting financial advice from a mystic, or a Gypsy, or having Bela Lugosi read your palm isn't illegal. Not too bright, but not against the law. And if it's working, then I'd say good for them."

Sweet squinted, placing his hands akimbo. I hated that posture. For obvious reasons. I was first informed of the meaning when I was about ten years old. *Akimbo.* Before that, I hadn't given it any thought. It was no stranger to me than "Dumbo" or "Snow White." It was a teacher who told me. His name was Mr. Redman, which he wasn't. He placed his hands in the classic rendition and said, "Akimbo. That's you. A. Kimbo: a boy with his hands on his hips. Fits you because you're always questioning things." It wasn't a compliment. By "things," he meant "authority."

When I graduated from the State Home for Orphaned Persons – SHOP, for short, as in "sweat shop," another word I learned early – I discovered any number of people knew the meaning. It was embarrassing. When I went to school – real school, not that place of detention New York State ran for unwanted kids – the admissions officer refused to accept my name as written. "It sounds made-up," he said. "And besides, no one has an initial for a first name." He demanded I fill out the form properly.

I refused. That's another reason I ended up in night school. There, all they care about is if you show up. It has something to do with state reimbursement.

"There's a story here, Andy."

"Could be," I agreed.

"Could be?" His face exploded into righteous indignation. "Where's your nose for news, Kimbo? Have you got a cold or something? Ask yourself: who is this mystic? Is he legit or not? If he is, what's he getting out of it? What's his angle? And if he isn't, how is he always giving good advice to these notoriously skeptical people?"

"I'll check it out."

"Is that all you can say: I'll check it out?"

"I'll check it out, sir." Early training tells.

Sweet rolled his eyes. It was one of the things they teach you in editor's school. It's supposed to make a reporter contrite and jump for joy at the idea for a story which had just been dumped in his lap.

I got up and turned to go, then remembered something.

"You got the background info? Names, ranks, serial numbers, that sort of thing?"

He handed me a manila envelope. The same sort of manila envelope editors have been handing reporters since the printing press was invented.

1521, by the way.

I have a head for numbers.

"How soon do you want to see a preliminary, and who's been down this road before?" I inquired, accepting the envelope and, by the way, the commission.

"I think a week is enough time for you to come up with something," he mused as if the idea had never occurred to him.

When he did not answer the second part of my question, I put it to him again.

If I had a middle name, which I don't, it would be "Stubborn."

Which, now that I think of it, wouldn't make a bad set of initials: ASK. I can see it embossed on my business cards now.

"Well," Sweet fudged. "There have been several stories on the phenomenon."

"I knew it. It's a dead duck."

"No, no, it's not, Andy. It's as live as Barbara Stanwyck."

I let that one pass. I always liked her pictures, but my favorite role will always be Victoria Barkley. Now, there was a woman who could put down an orange-grower's uprising, raise a daughter, three sons, tolerate her husband's indiscretion and accept his bastard without losing her dignity. She also had all the pithy lines in *The Big Valley.*

When you never had dignity as a kid, it's something you always admire in others.

She was also a damned good looking woman.

Which was taking me away from the point of the conversation.

"What conclusions did these Sunday supplements draw?"

That was an insult. No true news hound appreciated his work being compared to the hack jobs put out in the Entertainment sections of newspapers. That would be any day of the week.

Knocking the competition was also another tried-and-true right of the crime reporter.

"It's all in there," he said, nodding toward the manila envelope.

The hair on the back of my neck rose.

"Since when did you start doing background research for me?"

"Since Mr. Harold Poxie, the owner of this news wire, asked me to look into it."

He was "Mr. Poxie" to Sweet and the "Old Man" to me. When I was feeling generous.

"Asked you?" I queried in surprise.

Sweet's eyes narrowed in anger.

"Yes. Asked me. What's so strange about that? I was beating the pavement digging up scoops before you were born. And had more than my fair share, too."

Which was actually true – the part about scoops, not his age difference on me – and almost made me sorry I had asked. I hadn't really meant to insult him, but something didn't smell right.

"What's his interest and does he know you're giving the story to me?"

Another sentence containing two questions. I ought to know better. Never overload the boss.

"He's just interested, that's all."

"What's the matter? The mystic won't give him any tips?" I joked. Sweet was not in a joking mood.

"Mr. Poxie is heavily invested in the stock market. Which ought to mean something to you, inasmuch as his fortune is what keeps this wire service afloat. If he goes down, we all sink."

My boating analogies were apparently contagious. If he threw in a reference to keeping a schedule as tight as a railroad line, then I knew we were up a creek without a paddle and tied to the tracks as the 9:15 came roaring down on us.

It was a sickeningly familiar feeling.

And true as far as it went. CANS hadn't made a dime in years. With initials like that, what do you expect?

Excuse me: hadn't made ten *pence* in years.

"He's afraid there's a mysterious conspiracy involving this mystic. Get to the bottom of it, prove to him it's all nonsense and we can all sleep better at night."

Sweet was a chronic insomniac.

So was I for that matter. It goes with the territory.

"Does he know you're giving the story to me?"

"I told him I was busy so I was giving it to my best reporter. So, yes, Kimbo, he knows."

Which meant he knew nothing of the sort.

"I'm counting on you, Kimbo."

Which meant, don't blow it or my neck will be on the line.

There. I had made the railroad reference for him.

All ends neatly tied up.

I saluted, tucked the manila envelope up close to my chest and left, a patented smile decorating my face.

Which meant I was thrilled to death.

Not.

CHAPTER 2

Crossing the newsroom, I nodded pleasantly to my co-workers. It never paid to let any of them suspect you have just been given a royal headache. They would gloat. Reporters always gloated over one another. If it was not over a big story, it was over the assignment they got and you didn't.

No matter how many times you kick the waste can in bitter jealousy, only to discover the bum had a ticket to Peoria and not an exclusive interview with the President, you're always fooled.

Such is the nature of the beast.

Other trades have the same sort of professional jealousy. Like the neurosurgeon who brags he got the call for the emergency trephining case of a famous author. What he doesn't say is that it came at three in the morning and the guy was in heaven before he got there.

Doesn't stop the television reporters from interviewing him, though.

You lose some, you win some.

"What's in the envelope, Andy?" Rita shot at me as I walked by. I shrugged and put on a long face. That would convince them I had a real barn burner.

"Oh, nothing." I paused long enough to scuff my foot across the floor, the way the Dead End kids used to do when they were hauled up before the principal.

Remember the days when grade school principals were your greatest fear?

We grow up fast. Too fast. And the Lone Ranger is dead. A million childhoods just went with him.

And a few tears, too.

Me, I never cry.

"What's in the envelope, Andy?" Jimbo inquired. He was too young to know the Good Guy in the white hat never shot to kill.

"Just a recipe." I lied badly. It was part of the ritual. "Sweet gave me his brother-in-law's recipe for barbecue sauce."

"You? Cook?"

"Why not. I eat, don't I? A man who eats ought to know how to cook."

I wouldn't know one end of a spoon from another. I wasn't someone born with one of those silver implements up my derriere.

"I'm glad to hear you're improving yourself, Andy," Rita enthusiastically nodded.

She wouldn't know a kitchen from a petrol station.

I had been a grease monkey one summer after I ran away so I was one up on her.

"He's lying." There was doubt in Jimbo's voice.

Good. I had them on the run.

Shaking my head in dejected wonder, I retired to my desk. I hadn't had one decent story since we came to this foreign country and needed a break. A big one. I was pulling down the largest salary in the office and had to justify my exalted position. If I didn't, I'd be swimming home.

Don't ever let anyone tell you "home" isn't a four letter word.

Slipping into my worn old oak chair, I felt the familiar excitement steel over me. Couldn't help it. News was in my blood. Every assignment had the potential to be the Big One.

Well, strike that before that poor slob with a ticket to Peoria hears me.

They don't even have a baseball team in Peoria. The fans there are pretty evenly divided between the Cards and the Cubs. Everyone likes to make a rivalry out of it, but the Cubs haven't won a World Series since the goat was banned from Wrigley. On the other hand, the Cardinals are on the up-and-up. They're legitimate winners. All because of that guy they imported from Kansas City who knew how to put a team together. Did I mention he's the best darned manager in baseball?

The manila envelope wasn't sealed. There was a reason for that. Sweet would expect it back. It had seen good service and would do, again.

Waste not, want not.

Yogi Berra might have coined that phrase if someone else hadn't gotten there ahead of him. I used to be a Yankees fan until I discovered small ball. In St. Louis, it's called Whiteyball. There's no baseball in England. Maybe I'll buy a ticket to a rugby game while I'm here.

I think I mentioned I wasn't born in St. Louis. Everyone else who lives there was. When you meet a stranger, the first thing they ask is, "Where did you go to high school?" I tell them, "New York. That's how you know I can read." That's an insult. I asked a fellow once why anyone cared where you went to high school and he said because it tells you where someone grew up. South St. Louis. North St. Louis. South County, North County, West County. There isn't any East County because the city lies on the banks of the Mighty Mississippi. There is an East St. Louis, but it's across the water in Illinois. They tell me it was nice, once.

From what I've gathered, most of the la-de-da high schools are Catholic. St. Louis University is there, too. The first establishment of higher learning across the Mississippi. It belongs to the Jesuits. They insist everyone spell the name *Saint* Louis, rather than use the shorter, St. Louis. Out of respect for the saint who the city is named after. I make a point not to. What's interesting is that the city's name is always spoken of as Saint Louis, pronouncing the full word, "saint," and then "Lou-is," accent on the "lou," and then "iss." Over here, they say, *San Louie,* from the French.

You go where the jobs are. Most news services are anchored in Big Cities. New York. L.A. Chicago. I suppose the Old Man found rental property cheaper in the Show Me State.

Columns of numbers jumped out at me as I stared at the ream of pages Sweet had given me. They made my head spin. Acceding to the dictates of middle age, I slipped my half-moon glasses out of my jacket pocket and shoved them on my face. They didn't help much.

Maybe I needed a new prescription.

What I really needed was some inspiration, some way to forge through all this gross money-making and get to the root of the problem.

A clue, Sherlock. Something all the schmos before me had overlooked.

I tossed the papers down on the desk and leaned back in my chair. Closing my eyes, I let my mind wander. Stock market. Money-making schemes. Mystics. Sweet was right. It didn't make sense. But it worked. Logic dictates that men, no matter how gifted, cannot foretell the future. That was part of the Divine Plan. If we all knew what was ahead of us, no one would bother.

It just wouldn't be worth the effort.

If this mystic were to tell me I'd win some major prize, however, I might reconsider. *If* it came with a million dollars and a certificate suitable for framing.

I reapplied myself to the papers and didn't find what I was after. This mystic, apparently, had no name. No real name. Join the crowd. He was called the "Mystic Seer." Had an upscale London address. Well, he was making the money. No sense dying and letting the Inheritance Tax people get rich.

I supposed dying was the last thing on his mind.

And he ought to know.

Which brought me back to another conundrum. Why had Sweet given the assignment to me instead of keeping it for himself? If the Old Man had asked him to investigate it, there was no reason why he shouldn't. He had obviously started the legwork. What did he see that turned him off?

As far as I know, he wasn't afraid of anything. Except, perhaps, unemployment. And he had a nose for news. As dumb as this story was, it had an interesting hook. Black magic always caught the public's attention. The Mystic Seer couldn't be real. Look for the guy in the séance who does voice impersonations of the Dearly Departed without moving his lips and you've nailed him.

Could it be that Sweet was superstitious? He was an Italian Catholic, after all.

Pass up a story because you're afraid of spooks and crystal balls? Nah.

Well, maybe. I'd have to work on it.

Grabbing my hat and coat, I made a big show of leaving the office. I actually smiled. It brought tears to Rita's eyes and acrimony to Jimbo's. I didn't see Sweet. He was probably in the loo.

He had a private bathroom, too. Rank hath its privileges. Forget corner offices. The guy with his own – I was going to say "head," but changed my mind – toilet, really has it made. Open the window and he can sit and puff away to his heart's content. Flush down the butts – pun intended – to make it sound right, and who's to know?

Speaking of "butts" – the other kind – remember the story over the Big Tobacco kerfuffle? That was when the government forced them to start printing warning labels on cigarette packages? I covered it out of STL. People were suing the crap out of them, so they had to do something. Tobacco Conglomerates figured if they capitulated by placing some fine print on the packaging of their cancer sticks they could get out of future billion-dollar law suits. And guess what happened? By announcing their products were "dangerous to your health," their stock prices soared. Why?

Smoke screens.

This is how I see it: eventually a bunch of greedy lawyers will assemble some lung cancer sufferers and claim the warning came too late to save their clients. A judge will let it morph into a class action suit. That means a few attorneys will make a ton of money, while the many will get ten dollars and a coupon for a buck off a carton of Marlboros.

Delays, delays, delays. That's the name of the game. Don't pay today what you probably won't have to pay tomorrow. It's a sound business principle. I follow it myself. On a smaller scale, of course.

I walked five kilometers to the parking garage. Everyone over here uses the Metric System. The U.S. is the only civilized country that refuses to go along. The government figures the right to maintain our own distance and temperature measurements are as American as apple pie and Mount Rushmore; our answer to stone tablets. I calculate the real reason we don't convert is because no President or senator is smart enough to learn the proper exchange. Most of them are lawyers, don't forget.

There's no place to park in London. Petrol costs about three-pounds a gallon (sounds funny, doesn't it?) and they still don't have any parking. Everyone takes public transportation. When I was doing background, prefatory to coming over here, I discovered the Underground was filling with water. They bail it out with buckets, or something similar. Doesn't work. One day the entire system will be washed away.

I told the Old Man I wouldn't go unless I got my own "motor." There was one waiting for me when I got here. It was made in the Czech Republic. It's put together with rubber bands and runs on hamster power. I walk a lot.

I thought about calling ahead to make an appointment with Mr. Seer but changed my mind. I was sure to be refused. That would make my appearance at the office door look ungracious.

Never warn the enemy. That's one thing you learn up front. Catch him off guard. But then, I had a sneaking suspicion the Mystic Seer was seldom caught with his pants down. He was probably staring in his crystal ball right now. Having my license plate checked. They spell license with two c's in England. They use a lot of "u's," too. They all sound like they come from the Appalachians, although it's actually the other way around. When English settlers colonized those mountains they became isolated from those who went on to celebrate Manifest Destiny. Therefore, they tended to keep the accent of the Mother Country. Especially when they sing. I heard a tape some researcher made of locals belting out some olde-tyme songs and you'd swear they came from across the Puddle.

Driving on the wrong side of the street drives me nuts. I have to be careful not to mess up. I'd hate to have my career cut short by being stupid. But of course, if I do mess up and only get a ticket, I can plead that I'm new to the country. Works for the Old Boys with New Wealth. Even those who have been here thirty years. It's always nice to have an excuse ready.

The address Sweet gave me was a new building, twenty-two stories high. Made of glass so it reflected into the eyes of drivers and pilots. I'm not a big fan of modern architecture, which puts me at odds with Prince Philip. He's into buildings. They say that makes him dull, but I think everyone ought to have a hobby.

There was no Mystic Seer on the "You Are Here" in the lobby. I felt like Ziggy. That left me with the option of knocking on every door or using my wits. I opted for the latter. Who wouldn't?

Picking up the phone, I called the operator. I explained I was the Xerox repair man and had gotten an emergency call from the Mystic Seer. Could she please tell me which floor he occupied? If I said I was Prince Philip, I couldn't have gotten the information faster.

"Third floor," she informed me without the slightest hesitation. Everyone has a copier that's broken. It's a given.

Third floor. That was pause for contemplation. I wondered if Mr. Seer knew something those folks on the upper floors didn't. It gave me the creeps. I hate to cover high-rise disasters. So messy. Hard to get a usable quote from anyone, if they're all dead. The ones which survive don't say anything more elucidative than "Thank God." Especially the ones who wouldn't know the inside of a church from a nuclear reactor. Makes them wonder why they were spared.

Doesn't say anything for regular attendance at church, either.

If God really works in mysterious ways, why bother tithing ten percent?

I'm not an atheist, don't make that mistake. I'm a sometimes agnostic. Other times, I'm just as grateful to be alive as the next man. If God does you a good turn, it's only polite to thank Him. It's called covering your bets.

One last thought. Most people don't capitalize "Him" any more when referring to God. I think it has something to do with George Orwell. He hated punctuation.

I got in the lift and punched two buttons: three and four. I wanted to see what three looked like before I got off on it. If there was a guard standing at the entrance, I'd be forewarned.

The elevator went right past three, stopping at four. I got goose bumps. Well, I had my answer. I exited and took the Emergency, "Use in Case of

Fire" Exit down one flight. The fire door on Three was locked. Something to remember if I needed an excuse to call the authorities. It was illegal in every country but Texas to lock a fire door. Oil barons are exempt. They know how to capitalize all the proper "hims."

I proceeded on down to One and came out by the main lobby. People stared at me. No one ever takes the stairs. I know, for a fact, that in St. Louis you can lose your job for taking the stairs down one flight, rather than waiting for an elevator. I don't know if that Rule ever made it to an employee manual, but believe me, it's true. Just visit any hospital and you'll see for yourself.

I got back in my automobile and drove around. When no inspiration came to me, I headed back to the office. A liter of gas shot. It would be hard to justify on my expense account.

I ate at the deli on the first floor of our building before going back up. Fish and chips. I wanted to look like a native. Everyone knows Arthur Treacher was a Brit. He was the guy with the funny accent in all those Shirley Temple movies. When in Rome and all that. The locals ate French cuisine but that wasn't covered by my expense account, either.

I was walking up the back stairs when I heard a commotion, so I stopped and poked my head through a door. Several people were clustered in the hallway shouting at one another. Assuming is wasn't a mass protest against socialized medicine and the unavailability of hearing-aid batteries, I paused to listen.

Normally, this would be called eavesdropping. But when a reporter does it, it's called work. Snoops make the best news hounds. They hear everything and justify it with a byline.

"Shares are up five points," one man in a three-piece suit said. My ears were immediately tuned to his wave length. He must have some smarts, I reasoned, to be wearing that getup. If I tried walking into the newsroom dressed like that, they'd call the men in white coats.

"What about Cross Electronics? That was stable an hour ago."

"Up seven and climbing."

"And Fabrico? They were selling at fourteen this morning and are at twenty-seven now."

There was a loud groan by someone who either missed his chance at some easy money or sold a thousand shares of Fabrico yesterday for thirteen-nine.

"What's happening?"

No one said, "It's the end of the world," proving, once again, that real life is not depicted accurately in the movies.

"Who's buying?"

"Morell; Tyler; Breaksmyth; Gerhusen, Young."

"Good God."

Which, I thought reluctantly, was as close to, "It's the end of the world" as anyone had a right to expect. My esteem for LaLa Land rose one point.

"If they're buying, I'm buying," said a man, rushing away.

It was at that moment I was eyeballed. The gentleman in the three-piece suit gave me a dark look. You know the kind. That which expresses the fact he has just spotted something which crawls along the ceiling and you call an exterminator to get rid of.

The group moved inside their office, slamming the door behind them. Bamb! I sniffed under my arms, just to be sure. Nothing there. My deodorant was still working. It must have been my face. I look Irish. At least, that's what people tell me. Irish and Slav. Could be. I sure didn't come with a pedigree.

I hurried to the office and read the news as it came spilling across the tape. Stock market volatile. Huge gains by Cross Electronics, Fabrico, Hammerstone Communications.

This was my cup of tea, all right. Just what I had been assigned to find out. And right on cue.

Sweet grabbed me by the lapels as soon as he saw me. His face was flushed with excitement.

"Write whatever you've got, Andy, and put it on the wire. The story is hot. The Old Man's called twice while you were out."

"What Old Man?" I just couldn't believe Sweet would refer to Mr. Poxie as the *Old Man.*

"Poxie. You know," he growled. "Never mind that. Just write something fast and get it on the wire. They're clambering for anything right now. And don't forget," he added, looking at his watch. "We're five hours ahead of New York. What happens in London will affect the New York Exchange."

"I don't have anything," I protested. It was no good. His ears had gone bad and he had never even seen *The Guns of Navarone.*

I went to my desk and re-skimmed the info Sweet had given me. Nothing. Which was exactly what I had to write. Nothing. I started typing, just to see words on the page. For inspiration. Like running water in the bathroom.

All I had was a bunch of words. "A. Words-Smith Kimbo." That's me. I liked the hyphen. It made me sound British. Europeans love everything American as long as Americans stay in their own back yard.
They'll watch American movies, eat American food, emulate American politics. But just watch out if they run across an American tourist, eat something genetically altered by Monsanto, or discover one of our diplomats has conferred at 10 Downing Street about NATO bases. Then all hell breaks loose.

I don't really blame them. Well, maybe just a little. But I wouldn't eat corn that kills butterflies, either.

I know, I know. It's not the corn itself that kills the Monarchs. I'm off the boat from St. Louis, home of biotechnology. I read all the pros and cons. The propaganda-spewers and the doomsayers. They both made convincing arguments.

I decided the butterflies didn't die. They just never existed.

I mean, how many spotted owls do we need, anyway?

But, I'm getting ahead of myself.

I ended up writing a story about the economy and how people were attracted to the stock market like loan sharks to bankruptcy courts. I threw in lots of data. Pronounced with a long "a," by the way. Day-ta. Accent on the first syllable. Not datta. The word should have vim and vigor. "I'm going to the *Day*tona 500," not "This is my son and this is my *datta."* I'm a bug about pronunciation. While we're at it, it's Eee-cology, not ugh-cology and it's most certainly Mizouree, not Mah-zouraa.

I don't have a dialect, myself, although some people guess I'm from Los Angeles or Pennsylvania. Once, when I was feeling particularly alien, I special-ordered a birth certificate from a guy in Lauderdale. One can buy anything in Florida as long as it's illegal. Like dope and elections.

I had no particular reason for making myself a Floridian, except that it makes people think I have an "in" with the Cubans. They occasionally ask me how Castro is doing and then offer me money to purchase them some imported cigars or arrange a hit on their father-in-law. I keep the money and conveniently forget their phone number.

Sweet was born in Queens which is a borough of New York City. He sounds like he was born in Queens. He looks like he was born in Queens.

He has the complexion of an Italian and the dialect of Christopher Walken. I try real hard not to insult him when we're in close confinement together. Just in case they're cousins.

I had to have an angle for a quick follow-up article. And then the conversation in the hall came back to me. Those blokes may not have been inside traders but they knew something I didn't. Five last names. I scribbled them down from memory, guessing on the correct spellings.

These five were in on the stock market rise. It made me wonder what else they had in common. Like a mystic seer, maybe?

There wasn't any way I could get a list of the Mystic Seer's clientele, but I could do a search to see if these men invested in the same stocks – and what their track records were. If I found a similarity in their portfolios and could document an unprecedented run of good luck, I'd be onto something.

It took me a few phone calls, some bribe money and the cashing in of several debts, but in the end, it was worth it. I was right on the money. Each one of those men: Morell, Tyler, Breaksmyth, Gerhusen and Young were high-rise investors. They had lots of money to spend and they were spending it on many of the same stocks. And they had all recently tripled their wealth.

I didn't have the opportunity to trace them back to their roots, but it gave me a beginning.

The story I wrote had nothing to do with mystics, or the manipulation of the stock market. It had to do with investors hitting it big. I threw in a few veiled hints, without naming names. I would have liked to, but I didn't have the *day*ta to back it up. Luckily, Sweet didn't read it. He just initialed my copy and put it on the wire.

So, I had about a twenty minute reprieve before Mr. Poxie read the articles and called to find out why Mr. McGraw's name wasn't on the byline. He'd have to admit he gave the story to his best writer. That wouldn't go down well. Mr. Poxie did not like me. We had a history.

I'd be gone in a flash. *Flashgun Casey.* That's me.

Out of the office, that is.

Ironically, I was beginning to like this story a lot better. It had possibilities. If I could wrangle interviews with these five investors, maybe one of them would confess to using the stars as a guide to the market. Remembering these men had just made a killing, at least on paper, I reasoned one or more might be in a good mood. Good enough to talk to a reporter.

A quick investigation ruled two out, right off the bat. Gerhusen was German and Young was Japanese. Neither were known to be in the U.K. Both used intermediaries to run their operations. I called Morell's office. An unemotional sounding, gender-neutral secretary informed me Mr. Morell was "not entertaining." I said I was sure he was dull, but I'd still like an interview. He/she hung up on me.

I should have kept my mouth shut. The secretary would remember my name. I should have opted for Smith or Jones. Kimbo reminds educated people of "akimbo." It's a mystery to me.

One I'm stuck with. Anyone who changes their name past the age of seventeen or after graduation from high school is totally deranged. You have to notify the Social Security Office, the Department of Motor Vehicles, the Selective Service if you're a boy, and all sorts of other people. Women who marry later in life and change their names risk raised eyebrows, frustrations and potential embarrassment when the diplomas on the wall don't match the name on the door.

"Excuse me, Doctor Wilson, but why do you have Doctor Hagger's degrees hanging in your office?"

On the other hand, if she doesn't change her name, her kids, who will inevitably have the father's name, will sound illegitimate.

I hit pay dirt with Mr. Tyler. He would be pleased to see me, if I could come immediately.

He must have been reading my mind. Which was a disconcerting thought, come to think of it. Here I was, investigating a mystic seer, and one of his client's was picking up on my brain waves. Perhaps the ability was contagious.

It was, and I should have listened to myself. But reporters are notoriously lax when it comes to heeding good advice. Even when that good advice comes from within their own skull.

Mr. Tyler's office was the penthouse suite. His secretary was informed of my imminent arrival, for she had a cup of coffee waiting. After allowing me to slip the handle of the mug between my fingers, she ushered me into meet the Great Man.

"How do you do!" Tyler boomed. He was so big and so loud, I would have bet real money he was from Texas. All he lacked was the cowboy hat.

The color of it, however, I had yet to determine.

It was like the comic strips. They arrive at the newspapers in black and white. If the paper wants to print that particular strip in color, one of its artists fills in the hues along pre-established guidelines. Once in a while they make a mistake and the Little Redheaded Girl turns into a brunette. It's very disconcerting.

I hoped I wasn't about to make a mistake with Mr. Tyler.

"You want to know about why I've been so successful in the stock market," he began, settling himself down in a comfortable leather chair. I nodded, while seating myself opposite in a smaller version of his own. Looking beyond him, I could see the city, innumerable flights below. Since the window faced opposite the sunset, Tyler's head was outlined in darkness, making a queer effect of shadow.

"Yes, sir," I agreed.

"And you work for CANS?"

I always cringe when anyone articulates that particular acronym. And I didn't remember telling him who I worked for.

"Yes, sir."

He nodded and I had the sneaking suspicion he had either traced my original call or had me investigated while I drove over. In either scenario, it indicated a vast, complicated network at his disposal.

"You have an interesting portfolio, Mr. Kimbo."

"I do?"

That was news to me. I didn't own any stock and the only "Bond" I was familiar with came with a "Ward" or a "James" affixed to the front.

"Yes. Quite a number of byline-stories, spanning two decades. You're primarily a crime reporter, but you manage to get your nose into a lot of –"

"Trouble?" I filled in for him.

He laughed and shook his head.

"No. That's not the word I would have chosen. You're hard-nosed – some would say hard-headed – but you have a good instinct for news, especially on stories no one else is interested in, or where others have tried and failed. You're pretty generally disliked by local authorities." He knit his hands together. "You have worked in New York City, Albany, Utica, Los Angles, San Diego, Chicago and St. Louis."

Somehow, he had turned the tables on me. *I* was the one being interviewed. And his background check was good. Too good. I felt like an actor who's just been told his photo was going to run in the *Star* without a toupee.

"I have information that when word of your imminent departure to London was announced at Police Headquarters in St. Louis, there was great rejoicing. In fact, one 'Lieutenant Chandler' had your apartment – what was it – quarantined? So that you had to leave without collecting your belongings. Wasn't that it?"

His sources weren't just good, they were phenomenal. I couldn't imagine how he had managed to glean that tidbit in the half an hour since my phone call.

He was correct, right down to the official rational behind my lockout: quarantined.

I tried to laugh it off. Me, the bad actor. What else could I do? Lie and say I shaved my head for a juicy part?

"You called St. Louis?" It was the only defense I could think of and it was a poor one. I could see my fans dropping dead by the score.

He gave me a blank stare, which was even more disconcerting than his information. For a moment I wondered if I were really talking to a robot which had not been programmed to answer illogical questions.

"I am afraid, Mr. Kimbo, that I really have very little information you can use. I am an economist by trade. I graduated from McGill, then took my doctorate at Cambridge."

"Oh," I said stupidly. "Where's your Old School tie?"

He laughed as though that were the funniest thing he had heard this year. On second thought, perhaps it was. Wealthy men are not generally known for their wit, and the company they keep are either as dull as dishwater, or come 36-26-36. Or both.

"Actually, a lot of hard work goes into every move I make. I'm sure you did your homework. Trends. Assets. Management. The state of the economy." He mispronounced it. I cringed. "The products being sold; future, long-range plans. It all makes for very dull reading."

He pronounced each word as though it were written with a capital letter. Very Dull Reading.

Which means, in any language, in any country, "back off."

I understood warnings as well as the next man. Unfortunately, I ignored them better than most.

At least I was good at something. If "good" was the right word.

"I appreciate that, Mr. Tyler, but –" He tried to speak over me but I kept on going, like a Timex. "There is a persistent rumor circulating the news rooms that you get a lot of hot tips from a psychic."

He burst out into loud, raucous laughter, then paused to wipe his eyes. I hadn't seen any tears.

"I thought you were going to say, '*psych*iatrist.'"

"Yes," I agreed. "They do have the first five letters in common. But one, I imagine, is more expensive than the other."

"I wouldn't know," he said. Good comeback. Someone punched the right key that time.

"You were quoted as saying," I tried, but he cut me off with a chop of his hand. It went along with my previous thought: takes a licking but keeps on ticking. I hoped he didn't hear my gulp.

I may have the values of the Lone Ranger, but I didn't have his courage. If it came to it, there I'd be in the crowd, waving him good-bye as he and Tonto rode off in a cloud of dust.

Yet, I heard myself saying, "You were quoted last year in the *Guardian* as saying you were utilizing the talents of a very – unusual individual. For that, I substituted 'Mystic Seer.'"

"The *Guardian*? You know what they print."

I ought to. They subscribed to CANS.

"My editor –"

"I liked the piece you did on how Cross and Hammerstone and Fabrico were jumping in price. Very good."

"How did you know about that? That story can't be out yet."

"Can't it?"

He removed a piece of paper from a portfolio on the floor by the chair. I had not seen it before.

Now I was imagining things.

"Isn't this it?"

I took the paper and scanned it. That was my work, all right. I handed it back. He replaced it.

"That's it," I agreed.

"Keep at it," came the booming endorsement.

"It was flat; boring," I protested. "Just copy to meet a deadline."

"I liked it. It was incise, terse, to the point."

"It said nothing."

Again that blank state. I wondered if that portfolio indicated I liked compliments, and he had not been programmed for my rejection of his praise.

"Well, thank you for coming by." Mr. Tyler stood and beamed down at me. "I have prepared some autobiographical information for you to use in your next story. Always like to see my name in print, as long as you spell it right."

He paused. I laughed. That was as funny as it was going to get.

"But about –"

"Thought of that, too. There are several photographs included in the material."

I found myself saying, "Thank you."

"Think nothing of it." Which is exactly what I was thinking of it. Nothing. "Good-bye."

"Good-bye. And thank you."

It never hurts to be polite. Well, almost never.

I walked to the door and was out on my ear so fast I broke a land speed record.

There was no point looking at the material he gave me, but I stopped in front of the elevator and opened it anyway. I just had the odd feeling all the pages would be blank.

I was wrong. There were several sheets of boring data and three or four pictures, "suitable for framing." Professionally touched up. Well, I supposed he wouldn't want to be seen without a toupee, either.

CHAPTER 3

What to do, what to do, what to do? If I repeated that often enough, I might think of something. It was on the order of getting a tune or a snatch of lyrics caught in your head. It was never a song you liked. It was always "Georgie Girl," or "Maggie Mae," or something like that. Worse than Chinese water torture. They say that happens to prevent your mind from working on something disturbing.

Sort of a safety valve.

My safety valve was ready to pop the cork.

There were probably any number of investors going to the Mystic Seer. If I committed myself to the task, I might be able to nail a dozen on the strength of their track record. But what was to say any one of them would talk to me?

I had no key, no opening, no leverage to use against them. I didn't even have my thoughts together. There was something odd prickling at the back of my brain and then I remembered. Mr. Tyler had done research on me; knew me to be a crime reporter. So why wasn't he surprised to have someone, better known for sticking his nose into a murder on the South Side than sipping tea with the Boardroom boys, asking him questions?

Like the joker who calls the police to report a burglary and doesn't question when a homicide cop shows up. That's because the joker knows he just committed a murder and is only using burglary as a cover. Guilty knowledge is a career-maker for cops – and reporters.

I lectured Lieutenant Chandler of the St. Louis Police Department about that very idea no more than six months ago. I was working on a case the lieutenant was covering and thought I had some pretty good ideas. Fashioned them into a series of articles, too. For my good citizenship efforts, I found myself locked out of all future police briefings. When I refused to "cease and desist" my efforts, the lieutenant quarantined my apartment and confiscated my car.

Quarantined it! When I complained about that antiquated word – and totally incorrect application of the Public Safety Rules – I was informed "disease-bearing cockroaches" had been discovered in my kitchen. The place required fumigating and a "period of adjustment."

Yeah, I saw that play, too. In summer stock. Wasn't one of my favorites. I only went to see the actor. He was an "A" list television star, which is higher on the alphabet than an "A" list movie star, at least to me. It didn't make the play any more interesting.

In accordance with police orders, the lock on my apartment was changed. I couldn't even get in to pack my belongings before being shipped overseas by CANS. That forced me to buy a change of wardrobe. That's the commonly accepted euphemism for underwear shorts and socks, and I had to borrow the money from Sweet, at that. He was a good sport about it, but I had to stand through one of his lectures about "antagonizing the police," and how he hoped "I would have better relations with the London authorities."

I tried to protest, in my best, red-faced sincerity, that I had never had "relations" with Lieutenant Helen Chandler, good, bad or otherwise, but he wasn't listening. I think that's a qualification they put on job application for editors and kindergarten teachers: must be able to block out spurious noise.

If you score well on that one, you're in.

If you fail, you either become a reporter or a zoo keeper.

We both work with and around animals. Noisy, dangerous creatures which belong behind bars.

Unless you're in San Diego, at the Wild Animal Park. They let theirs run around without cages. I don't guess they'll ever have a theme park like that for murderers and death row denizens.

But, then, they're not as cute as lions and tigers and pandas. Not nearly as rare, either.

I paid Sweet back for the loan but I was still mad at Lieutenant Chandler. She had no right shutting me out of my apartment. I didn't care so much about the clothes or the pitifully small amount of cooking utensils I left behind. There wasn't much of value in either the wardrobe or the culinary items. It was my notes I wanted back.

Notes on all the cases I had ever covered. Some were jotted down, some typed, others dictated on a cassette. It was my plan to write a book. (This is it, by the way.) I hadn't yet decided whether I would write a biography, or turn my adventures into a novel. Neither was likely to sell. The important thing to me was feeling comfortable when I was writing it.

If I came off better as a real, true-to-life, gritty, snot-nosed crime reporter, that's the way I'd go. If I thought the cases I worked on needed a little tweaking here and there, I'd turn the whole mass into a fictionalized account of how a talented reporter breaks all the rules to get his story.

I was a bug for the truth. It was either tell it like it was, straight up, or turn the thing into make-believe. I never mess with Truth. I guess if there's one thing sacred to me, that's it. I don't respect much in this life, but Truth is one thing I look at as Universal to Mankind. Without truth, we have nothing.

Without truth, governments rule our lives, pseudo-scientists turn us from the paths of knowledge and the arts are so censored, Marshal Matt Dillon can't be seen opening *Gunsmoke* with a showdown on Front Street because it's too violent.

Ever look into James Arness' eyes? Ever see the deep emotion registered there? The guilt? The onerous duty? The dedication to keeping the peace, and thus saving innocent lives at the risk of his own?

That isn't violence, it's sentience. When we confuse the two, then we've lost Truth, Justice *and* the American Way.

Perhaps it was the "ence" at the end of both "violence" and "sentience" which confused CBS.

But what do you expect from a TV network, when the entire State of Kansas refused to have evolution taught as a science? Those worthies want Creationism crammed down kids' throats. Now, that's *really* scary.

Maybe they can hire "Moses" to promote their point of view. He did wonders for the NRA.

I want my notes back. I feel naked without them. I've been keeping those notes since I was a kid, a wet-nose reporter who didn't know enough to duck when someone was shooting at him. It's the story of growing up in a hurry; of learning the hard way. No one gave me anything. I worked for what I got. That's what I want to say. Not exactly Horatio Alger, but I'm pretty damned proud of my accomplishments. I started with less than nothing. God knows what I'll end up with, but whatever I have, it will be honest.

I can't even afford to give up the lease on the apartment, for fear the landlord will go in there, think all my stuff is junk, and chuck the whole in the dust bin – English for "round file." If I keep the payments up, he'll keep his nose out. That's all I can hope for.

It's all *her* doing.

She's got my car, too. A white Chevy Monza, four-cylinder, specially made in Canada. 1976. Drives like a bat out of hell. I've replaced the engine once and the transmission twice. Has over 300,000 miles on it. Not one rust spot. I don't care if my suit is wrinkled or if my socks don't match, but I have this thing about cars. Not any old cars. *My* cars.

I usually take three or four days off a year. When I do, it's invariably because the car needs paste waxing.

If my Monza gets rusty sitting out in the police impound lot, Lieutenant Chandler will have a lot of explaining to do.

None of which brought me any closer to solving my current problem.

What does a good reporter do when he's stumped? He goes to an expert. Now, who was an expert on mystic seers? When in doubt, consult the phone book.

There were no entries under "Mystic" or "Seers." Looking under "Astrologers," I discovered sixteen names listed. One had taken out an ad. With a photograph. The women depicted thereon looked like a Halloween witch. I called her for the Heck(ity) of it.

She calculated her fees like the IRS and promised to tell me "whether my girlfriend really loved me." I didn't have a girlfriend. I've only been close to two women. One of them was Helen Chandler. That was when she was slapping handcuffs on me.

The other one is none of your business.

I was innocent – of the charge – and Sweet had to come in the middle of the night and post bond for me. He didn't like it very much, but then, I wasn't dancing on my toes, either. I wouldn't be surprised to know Ms. Chandler got a bonus over the whole deal.

Cops hate me. It's a genetic thing.

I could either toss a coin, or close my eyes and run my finger down the column in the directory. The name I stopped at would be the next one I called for background information. I figured they were all phonies, anyway, so it didn't make much difference.

Have you ever had the experience that once you've written something off as phony, you get all cold and tingly for no reason? I looked at the list again. The names were all made-up. Madame Delilah. Master of the Universe, who sounded more like an escapee from the World Wide Wrestling Federation. Hazel-Eyes Sees All. It was the acronym which stopped me. With punctuation and spacing, it turned out to be HE'S A. He's a what? He's a ass? Like the law?

The others were of the same ilk. Only one was different. There was no name at all. Just "Gypsy." No gender indicated. The "Gypsy" could be a man or a woman. The peculiar thing was, there was no phone number, either. Why would somebody be listed in a phone book when they didn't provide their number? Just a street address.

Gypsy.

That was the one. As I repeated it out loud, my left wrist got cold and felt like it was dripping wet. When I touched it, it was clammy.

"Gypsy."

Whatever.

Joe Gypsy. Like Joe College. Since I couldn't call him, I jotted down the address and drove there.

I expected to see half-moons with bright yellow stars dangling from the windows. Sprigs of wolfsbane (actors never enunciate the "s") "bat thorn"; aconite, for the literate, well-educated werewolf; or monkshood blooming in flowerpots by the door. I prepared myself for the overwhelming power of incense, the Eastern atmosphere of bead curtains, and the familiar Tarot cards and Zodiac symbols placed at strategic locations.

I expected to be seated opposite the "Gypsy" at a round table, placing my palms up. Or holding hands. Once we started concentrating, the table would shake and voices of long lost editors from my past would chastise me by stating in words on one syllable why I was no longer working for them – in generalities, of course.

The address was easy enough to locate but the establishment wasn't. There were no half-moons, no astrological symbols leading the way. When I finally found the door, I had to climb up three flights of stairs to gain the entrance.

There was no nameplate, no sign announcing this as the residence of "The Gypsy." Nothing but a number. Four. I was born May the 4th. For some reason, the coincidence stuck in my mind.

There was no buzzer, either, so I tried the old fashioned approach. I knocked. I had almost convinced myself there wasn't going to be an answer when the door opened. By itself. That is to say, when I peered in, no one was standing behind it. I had not turned the knob.

I felt four years old. My suit jacket seemed to slip off my shoulders and my breathing came in irregular gasps. I was sweating profusely.

I wanted to run.

"Hello."

I jumped a foot, landing awkwardly. I was so embarrassed I could have cried. I looked around for the source of the voice. Definitely female. That answered one question but increased my embarrassment tenfold.

"Hello," I called. "I was hoping you could help me."

Which sounded pretty foolish.

"Come in, Andy."

It was then that I tripped over my feet and fell, headlong across the threshold.

"Oh, I am so sorry. Let me help you," the Gypsy said. I knew it must be she – must be *The Gypsy.* How, I don't know. Because she looked like a Gypsy, I guess. The genuine article.

Which was the last thing I ever expected.

I tried to get up, but she was all over me. Not literally speaking, but I mean, she was holding my hand and giving me a boost up before I could refuse. The flesh of her hand was smooth, warm. The strength in her arm was unexpectedly powerful. I gave her a closer examination as I rose, my face kissing-close to hers.

She was the most extraordinarily beautiful woman I had ever seen. It wasn't just the facial features, or the shapeliness of her legs. Nor was it her dark eyes which crackled with humor and mystery.

There was about her an aura, a visual/sensual glow of otherworldliness. I don't know how else to describe it. She seemed half human, half alien, yet there was not a bit of standoffishness about her. Quite the contrary. As I stood beside her, I felt as though we were old friends.

Had we actually been, that would explain why she knew my first name. As it was, there was no reason she could have known.

Short of being a mystic seer, herself.

Which was preposterous.

"Come in. Please sit down," she invited. "I have been waiting for you."

"What do you mean, you've been waiting for me? And how do you know my name?"

I felt like Wally Ford in a Monogram "Poverty Row" production.

"Sit down," she repeated. I looked for the round table. The one where we held hands and voices came out of nowhere. She saw, or sensed my suspicions, and laughed. Her voice tinkled like well-tuned wind chimes. "What are you looking for?" The question was rhetorical.

Caught red-handed.

"The table. You know. Where we sit and you call upon the services of your Control."

"Oh." She sounded disappointed. "I have no Control. I hope that will not spoil things for you?"

I blushed. My freckles stood out like a road map to the stars.

"No," I heard myself saying.

"Good!" She sounded genuinely relieved. "But I do have a table. Would you like to sit at it?"

I nodded dumbly and she led me into an inner room. There it was. The Round Table. Even King Arthur could not fail to be satisfied.

"I've come for some background information," I began. "Not to get my fortune told. I'm a reporter." I flashed my Press I.D. Her eyes grew as round as flying saucers. (Reference: *The Thing from Another World.*)

"A reporter," she repeated.

"Yes. May I ask you some questions about a competitor – and how much will the answers cost me?"

"Oh," she softly cooed. "You do not wish to hear the disembodied voices of long lost editors reminding you why you no longer work for them?"

I stopped dead in my tracks.

"How could you have known that's what I was thinking?" I demanded.

"You wear your thoughts on your sleeve."

So help me, God, I looked. There was no printing on my jacket. I shook my head.

"You knew my name, and you know what's in my thoughts. How?"

"How now, brown cow."

She said it in so innocent a way, and with the traces of a Hungarian accent, that I burst out laughing. She laughed with me and that made me feel comfortable.

Too comfortable, if you know what I mean. My heart hadn't beat this hard since Lieutenant Chandler threatened to turn me over to her "goons" for a little loosening of the tongue.

And there had been the threat of ice cubes inserted where the sun don't shine, if I didn't come clean.

Chandler called me "Mr. Clean" for a few months after that incident.

If I found a genie in a bottle and were granted three wishes, I would use one to have her busted down to traffic duty.

We got along like fire and ice. And you know which one of us was the ice.

"Come on," I said, easing up. "Level with me. Did someone tip you off I was coming?"

She stared at me with childlike eyes. They were the kind of eyes a man could get lost in. And be glad he was genetically incapable of asking directions.

"You tipped me off."

"Me?" Incredulity.

"Did you not look up the address in the telephone directory?"

"Yes. But there was no phone number. Just a street number."

"Oh." She dismissed that with a wave of her hand. Her fingers were long and shapely. The nails were relatively short and unadorned.

In fact, there wasn't much of glitter about her at all. She wore a colorful, pattern-less, flowing silk kimono, tied at the waist. She had sandals or slippers on her feet. I couldn't be sure which in the dim light. Her hair was jet black and wound around her head, turban-style. There was one large jewel in her hair which caught the light and sparkled. By the size of it, I deduced it was fake.

The woman's complexion was two shades darker than mine, but I'm a pale-skinned man if ever there was one. It comes with the red hair and freckles. I'm not sure whether my coloration originates from the Scottish-Irish or the Czech. Could be either. Since I never saw my parents, I don't know.

Well, that's not exactly true. I have a photo but it's old, wrinkled, cracked and in black and white. I was told she was "Orange Irish," and he was "Bohemian stock." The woman in the photo looked old-fashioned and the man looked grim. Someone at the orphanage told me they were my parents. I've looked at that picture five thousand, three-hundred and ninety-eight times and never saw a resemblance.

Since I was dropped off on the church steps with no one the wiser, it stood against reason they were my people. I always suspected one of the staff found the photo in an antiquarian book store, either stuck between pages as a bookmark, or, more likely in a bin filled with the photographs of film stars no one remembered anymore, and this couple were a pair of silent actors; extras by the looks of them. Posed together as a means of highlighting the costumes rather than the no-names. Ordered by the clothing designer to see how well they held up under bright lights. Or the continuity department for matching. No names were inscribed on the back. If there had been, for sure they wouldn't have been Mr. and Mrs. Kimbo.

I don't know why my mind went to that. It must be the atmosphere of this place. The spirits were aroused. Something like that.

"No," Gypsy quietly informed me. "They were not your parents. You assumed correctly. It was a 'trick,' although I am not certain whether it was meant to be mean."

I swallowed my heart.

"Oh." I never thought to ask how she knew.

"But, I am sure if they had been, they would have loved you."

My heart hardened and I accepted that statement with as much sincerity as, "The check's in the mail." Although, perhaps, I did her a disservice. But, it did prompt me to take a closer examination of her. She sounded and looked like an authentic Hungarian Gypsy. She continued speaking. I forgot what I had asked.

"... I do not like to bother with the phone. Too many people soliciting."

She meant it one way and I took it another.

"I don't blame them."

The Gypsy blinked then smiled.

"You want voices from your past?" She sounded hopeful. I shook my head. "A long-lost puppy?"

"I never had a puppy."

"I am so sorry."

There was no questioning her sincerity, now. Her concern almost brought tears to my eyes.

"It's all right," I found myself saying. "I've learned how to live without a lot of things."

"You need a puppy. I will get you one."

"No!"

"A kitten?"

"No."

"Oh. You live for your work, then?" Her question was neither accusatory, nor was it smug. I wanted to tell her. I wanted to explain what Life meant to me. And why.

When you don't know who you are or where you came from, there's a hole in your heart that is never filled. Every child born deserves one thing: the love of his parents. Not money, not a chance at an education, not brothers and sisters. Just love: by the two people in the world who owe you that basic need.

The unloved child is the classic Outsider, the solitary human being abandoned by the herd to the wolves and the elements. He can never become a social animal. Those which survive may make a good stab at it, but ultimately, most fail. A child, unloved, un-nurtured, unnamed, becomes a loner, always seeking approval, never getting enough praise.

If Outsiders do succeed, they are hard, tough, self-achievers. They don't make excuses. They know not to bother. No one is listening.

That's what I wanted to say; what crossed my mind. What my lips pronounced passed the modern-day paperback editor's seal of approval.

"Yes. I live for my work."

The world won't be satisfied until *The Brothers Karamazov* is reduced to under 80,000 words. Words have become the enemy.

If I wanted to live well, I could get a job doing things like reducing all 1,034 *pages* of *Gone With the Wind* to six words.

"Frankly, I don't give a damn."

I even cut out the "my dear," which the scriptwriters added to the dialogue. Every *aficionado* knows Margaret Mitchell (who wrote under her maiden name, by the way), never penned "my dear," in that fateful sentence.

The rest of the world thinks Clark Gable originated it.

Yes. I live for my work.

Six words. We live in a world of *Reader's Digest* Abridged versions of everything.

"Is it enough?" she kindly inquired.

Is it enough? I always thought so. I'm not exactly the *Father Knows Best* type. A home, hearth, wife, kids never held any fascination for me. There wasn't enough Truth in that kind of Life.

"Yes."

"Then you are a dedicated man."

That was not the response I expected.

"I need your help."

Not, "I would like your help," or "I require some background information." What was wrong with me?

"I will help you."

Her words were so serious, so reassuring, I believed her. The next thing you know, I'd be investing my 401K in the stock market.

On the advice of a mystic seer.

Or a Gypsy.

"What is your name?" I inquired. "You didn't list it in the directory and there's nothing on your door."

"Oh," she mischievously laughed. "You could not pronounce it."

I wasn't falling for that one.

"Mister Spock used that line first. You're not a Vulcan."

She sadly shook her head.

"No. I do not have pointed ears. But I wish I did. I like pointed ears. All elves and faeries have pointed ears. You would look good in pointed ears."

"Me?"

"Yes. You. If I say so, then it is true, for I always speak truth. Truth is important to you, also?"

"Very."

"Then between us, we will make a pact to always speak truth. To seek truth. I like you."

"You don't even know me!" Which, of course, implied familiarity bred contempt.

"I knew you were coming." She held her head back in a show of childlike pride. Not childish – childlike.

"How?"

"Oh, I cannot tell you that." I pouted. She responded to my childish grimace. "I divined it. Do you like that better?"

I scowled.

"I thought we agreed to always tell the truth."

Her eyebrows arched upward in a show of surprise.

"I did tell truth."

"You divined my coming?"

"I have been waiting."

I started to ask her for how long, then bit my tongue. Too hard. A small groan of surprise escaped. I felt foolish. She immediately put a hand to my face.

"You have hurt yourself."

"Doing something stupid," I agreed. There was no point denying it. And I had promised to speak truth.

"Do you wish to put some ice on it?"

"If you wrap some bourbon around it."

It was bravado because I never drank on duty. Point of honor.

"I do not have any." She sounded regretful. "Shall I go out and get some?"

"No! Please don't bother. I – don't want any. But I do want your help."

"I am ready to give it." She indicated the Round Table. "Would you like to sit there, or would you be more comfortable elsewhere?"

"The table is fine."

I sat down, mindful not to trip over wires, or pull the tablecloth for fear of disrupting the spirits.

"No wires," she said.

This time, my mouth fell open and I left it that way.

"Are you reading my mind?"

"Reading is, perhaps, not the correct word. Sensing your thoughts is better."

"How do you do it?" As though I expected a rational answer.

"I was born with the ability," she explained with a soft, almost apologetic smile. "I am what you might call... gifted? Among my people, I am..." She faltered, but not from unfamiliarity with the language, with which she was well versed.

"Among your people..." I encouraged. Her smile turned rueful.

"I am special. I was born with the Gift. Not many are. Perhaps one a century. I... see things. I have the ability to foresee the future... or the past. Not completely. It is sometimes unclear. If I require more specific information... I have other means."

For once in my life I was afraid to pursue a dangling sentence.

Afraid.

Not physically scared. Just didn't want to hear more than I was ready to accept.

"Why are you in London? The pickings better?" It was a cheap shot. Yet she did not seem offended.

"Oh, no! I am not here to make money. I do not need money. My people have given me money, gold, jewelry of great value."

"Then why, if you'll excuse the expression, are you nickel and dime-ing it as a fortune teller?" She fooled me with her expression and I quickly rephrased my sentence. "Why are you pencing and shilling it as a fortune teller?"

That sounded so ridiculous we both laughed.

"I understood your reference," she said as she caught her breath. Again, I couldn't help but note how beautiful her laughter was. It seemed to strike some chord deep within me.

"So? What's the answer?"

"I am here for some great purpose."

"Could you be more specific?"

I didn't know if I was going to get anywhere with the mystic seer story but I was working up a heck of a Sunday supplement on Gypsies, psychic ability and Roma gifts.

She shook her head.

"Not at this time."

I was more disappointed than I cared to be and wondered why.

I drummed the middle three fingers of my right hand on the table, looking down as thoughts swirled through my head.

"Miss – excuse me, but what *is* your name?" I asked with some consternation.

"I do not go by any name."

"Then what am I to call you?"

She shrugged.

"Call me what you like."

"All right, Miss Gypsy –"

She interrupted me by giggling. I felt my face flush.

"Go on," she waved, her eyes twinkling with amusement. "So, I am to be Miss Gypsy, now."

I tried again.

"All right, *Gypsy*. I'm investigation the success several men are having in the stock market. It's rumored that they're getting information – psychic advice – from someone known as the Mystic Seer."

"Yes," Gypsy thoughtfully mused. "I have heard that."

"You have?" I asked in astonishment.

"Yes. I like to keep in touch with my fellow Tarot-card-readers." She pronounced the last three words syllable-by-syllable, in an, "I-am-making-fun-of-this-but it-is-not-funny" statement. "The man's name is Holloway. Jason Holloway. I do not believe that is his real name, but it is the one he has been going by for many years. That is, of course, when he is not referred to as 'The Mystic Seer.'"

I grabbed my pad and pencil from the pocket of my jacket and wrote down the name. Looking up, I asked, "Do you mind if I record this?"

"No."

I had a small recorder the size of a hand calculator. CANS had issued it to me and I was required to sign my life away before walking out of the office with it. You would think it was valuable. I priced it at Radio Shack right before we were transferred and it was going for about fifty bucks.

I'd like to think my life was worth slightly more than that.

"Do you know him?" I asked.

"We have never met. But he is a dangerous man."

"Because he's a fake? How does he do it?" I was speaking at my usual clip, and merged my words into one long sentence. A New Yorker's common end. To people in other parts of the country, it's a character flaw. To those born or raised in the Empire State, it's no more or less than a necessity. If others don't understand us, that's too bad. They had better kick themselves into hyperspace where we are, or they won't make it past the rim of the galaxy.

"He is not a fake."

I paused from my writing to look up.

"What do you mean, he's not a fake?"

"Exactly what I said. And if you are going to investigate him, you must be very careful. You have already been to his London office once. If you go back, he will become suspicious."

"How do you know?" I began, then gave up and let my shoulders sag. "OK, I won't ask you how you know anything. You know it. But how does *he* know it?"

"He has psychic power. He has a very strong mind."

"Stronger than yours?" I was setting her up for an easy answer, but she didn't take the bait.

"I do not think so. But I have never pitted myself against him. Not in the way you are proposing to go against him."

"I didn't say I was going to go against him. I don't even know if he's done anything illegal. Or, immoral."

"Tell me what you do know. Then I will tell you what I know, and perhaps we can put together a whole."

I settled back in my chair. From somewhere overhead an old woman's high-pitched voice cackled.

So you thought you could get away with murdering me, did you, Bill? Well, just because I'm dead doesn't mean I don't have any power.

It was just my overworked imagination. But that didn't prevent me from tipping over backwards in my chair.

Overhead, the spirits were laughing.

CHAPTER 4

"Oh, Kimbo!" the Gypsy cried, rushing to me. "Are you all right?"

What could I say? That my derriere hurt? I opted for the more truthful, albeit less socially acceptable answer.

"I'm fine. It's my pride that stings."

She grinned and offered me a hand.

"Would it hurt your pride if I helped you?"

Ordinarily, I would have been suspicious of a woman giving me a hand up. I could easily imagine Lieutenant Chandler assisting me – then tossing me over her head with a judo move.

"Please do. Otherwise I might have to conduct our interview from the floor."

She laughed again and I marveled at the frequency and the innocent way in which she expressed delight. I was more prone to a grimace, or a pursed-lip sort of grin. I suppose that's because I've seen so many dark sides of life; lived them, covered them. Yet, I didn't suppose she was uninitiated in the evils of the world.

"There!" she cried, well pleased to see me on my feet. "Now: will you sit at the table again, or shall I talk to you while you pace?"

"Do you have any trap doors in the floor?" She looked puzzled then burst out into a huge grin. "Oh! You mean for Grandfather to come out and give the secret password to Grandmother?"

"Something like that." I was beginning to feel foolish.

"No trap doors." She had the knack of sounding so sad, as though the information she had to impart was destined to disappoint.

I put my hands on my hips – akimbo – and stared at her.

"All right. I like a good scam as much as the next. If I promise not to betray any trade secrets, tell me how you operate."

"I cannot do that."

"You don't trust me. I don't blame you –"

She interrupted me with an imperative shout.

"I do trust you!"

The Gypsy was so sincere, so obviously earnest I was put in the awkward position of trying to live up to her expectations.

"I shouldn't have asked that, in the first place. Just say it's none of my business, that's all. I'm used to people shouting 'No comment' in my face."

"I would never do that."

I was dumbfounded. I do not trust easily and expect the same, cynical lack of faith from others.

I also lived for years in the Empire State and if I am anything, I suppose I'm an adopted New Yorker. New Yorkers know rudeness. It is not that they are rude themselves. It is other people, foreigners, people from Pennsylvania, or Los Angeles who are rude. And slow. So, when someone displays kindness, patience, expresses a concern for my feelings, I'm left bewildered.

Why expend the energy when it's not necessary? You'll need it when the guy ahead of you in a Kansas-beige Volkswagen cuts you off. Or, when some jerk getting on an elevator doesn't stand back to let you off, first.

When I worked in St. Louis, I continually mumbled to myself, "If you try this in New York, you'll be flattened in three seconds." People thought I was odd. But it got me through the day.

Whenever anyone asked for my opinion on where to vacation, I always suggested the Big Apple. And wished them good-bye.

"I would be glad to tell you the 'tricks of the trade,' as you say, but I do not use them myself."

"Then how do you make a living?"

She shrugged.

"I give... help. I see things. Although I do not always tell what I see."

"When I was going through the phone book, I called one of your competitors. She offered to tell me if my girlfriend loved me. You do that sort of thing?"

"You want me to tell you if your girlfriend loves you?"

It was my turn to shrug.

"Why not? You know how insecure men are."

I had not meant to challenge her, but when the opportunity fell in my lap, I jumped on it. Call it an occupational hazard.

The Gypsy gave me a studious look, then smiled wistfully.

"I do not see a girl in your life, Kimbo. Although I can see there was one, once.... Her name was... Kim?"

I stared, then shook my head. People do that. They look like dogs coming out from a dousing by the neighbor's hose. It's a manner of shaking away disbelief.

"How could you possibly have known that?"

"I see it in your mind."

I was going to ask the Gypsy to describe what Kim looked like but then didn't bother. If her research was this good, she would have gotten a photo, too.

No way I could believe she was actually picking up such thoughts from my mind.

Besides, I hadn't thought of Kim in years.

Honest.

"You were engaged to marry Kim?"

"Yes," I answered before remembering I shouldn't. Never tip your hand, never give away anything.

"And then there is... another. Let me see. She has been in your mind more recently. This other woman is a – I have it! A police officer! Yes. I see her face very clearly, Kimbo. You have a vivid memory. She was wagging her finger at you."

Gypsy held out her hand in perfect imitation of Lieutenant Chandler. I grabbed her hand. The memory was just too vivid.

"You were a very bad boy, Kimbo. You broke up a stake-out she was on and the criminal got away."

"Alleged criminal," I corrected.

"That is not what Lieutenant Chandler said. She was very angry with you."

"The feeling was mutual. But," I argued, "she is not my 'girlfriend.' In fact, I doubt if that cobra ever was a girl. I think she was born with a badge and an attitude. She hates reporters. The feeling is mutual."

I was getting a little hot under the collar. The Gypsy did not seem to notice.

"She is very beautiful."

"Is she?" That was one on me. Gypsy didn't make that interpretation from anything gathered in my mind.

"Tall, slender, with a fine, strong face. She is younger than you are... by several years."

"How would I know? I don't want to talk about Lieutenant Chandler."

"Helen," the mind-reader supplied with a helpful grin.

"Whatever. I want to talk about mystic seer."

"Talk," she invited.

"I mean, I want *you* to talk about mystic seer." For some reason, my tongue was tied, my thoughts unclear. I wondered if I was getting incense poisoning.

"I will open a window."

"Stop reading my mind!"

Gypsy winked and wrote down an address. I took it.

"That is where the Mystic Seer lives in London. He may be there now. I do not think he will receive you but you can try."

"What about a phone number?"

She frowned, then took the paper and added the requested information. Before handing it back, she looked up.

"Something else?"

"If he's really setting these big boys up for a fall, is there a timetable? Will it happen soon?"

No way I believed a mystic seer was making other men rich out of the goodness of his heart. I was a crime reporter, after all. My business was to suspect the worst until proven otherwise.

She tried. If she had been a cartoon character, steam would have come out of her ears. When she finally gave up, she looked disappointed.

"I cannot read that from his mind. I may have better luck when he is preoccupied, or asleep. Right now, I have probably put him on the alert. He can sense someone is probing his thoughts. He may not be sure how much information I obtained, or who 'I' am but he has blocked me for the time being.

"Kimbo," she continued, putting out a hand out to me. "Be careful. Do not go to his penthouse today. If you do, there will be trouble."

"All right," I agreed. "And thank you. How much do I owe you for the information?"

"Free," she spontaneously replied.

"I'm serious. You gave me –" I checked my watch. "A half hour of your time. How much is that worth?"

"But you did not ask me any really important questions."

She suckered me into that one.

"Like what?" I frowned.

"Like which horse will come in first at – Fairmount. Or the winning lottery numbers."

"Do you give out that kind of information?"

"No." That was blunt. "But it does not stop people from asking."

"So, what's the winning lottery number?"

"2, 4, 5, 27, 33. And the Powerball is 1."

"Really?"

It didn't occur to me she was also listing the designations of the Stonewall Brigade, plus "1," which is my favorite number. Did I mention I was a Civil War buff?

"Those were the first numbers which came into my head."

"I'll gamble twenty on them, if you play the same amount."

"I do not bet."

"Everyone likes money."

"I am like you," she replied. "I work too hard for my money to waste it on a fool's pastime. I would have better luck standing in a field waiting to be struck by lightning."

I had said that only last week to Sweet when he was soliciting numbers for some shady gambling operation or other he was being let in on. Then I told him he looked Italian and ought to be careful, or someone would accuse him of being in the Mafia. After dodging a right fist, I gave him a number. Just to keep him quiet.

He didn't win and scowled the rest of the day.

Also, he does look Italian.

"So – how much do I owe you?"

"Nothing."

"I won't leave here until you tell me."

"Good. That way, I can be certain you do not go to the Mystic Seer's penthouse today."

My face fell. Of course I was going there. It was my job. And if I had to break up a stake-out along the way, I'd do that, too. Some hard-nosed police officers just didn't understand that a guy has to make a living.

"I'll be on my way, then. And thank you."

"You are welcome."

She saw me to the door. I waved, then took a few steps down the stairs. She closed the door. I hurried back and slid twenty pounds underneath it.

Feeling more satisfied than I had in a long time, I made good my escape.

Somewhere in the back of my mind I could hear her say, "I will not take your money, Kimbo. You must come back for it."

I wouldn't mind going back, but not for the money. She had earned it. And if any of the information I got from her panned out, she had earned a bonus. A big one.

I'm a firm believer in paying my own way; and paying those who tip me off. A man who pays well is remembered when there are other juicy tidbits to pass along. He who stiffs his stringers lives to work for the *Star*.

All right. I admit it. I was thinking about the Gypsy and my mind was not on my driving. Most people drive by instinct. Make that by habit. One part of your mind is on the grocery list, another on that job you didn't get finished, a third part on the electric bill. You're reviewing all the brilliant rejoinders you didn't think of in time to tell your boss off, the ending to the movie you saw last week, and trying to remember the name of an actor you saw on a TV program from 1955.

When the guy in front of you slams on his breaks, it's only by the grace of God you don't rear-end him. When the dog leaps out in front of you, you swerve without thinking. If you're lucky, there's no one in the right lane and you keep on going with nothing more serious that a bad case of the shakes. If you're unlucky, there's a red Toyota on your fender and both of you end up needing a tow.

And probably dental work.

So I was thinking about the Gypsy and the way she moved and listening to the sound of her voice and wondering how she phrased certain questions, like, "Want to come over to my place tonight so I can give you a more intimate palm reading?" when I noticed this truck coming toward me, head on.

I swear I was in my own lane. I swear I hadn't swerved, from habit, to the right, the American side.

I swear I would have wet my pants, had it not been so reinforced from childhood not to commit so heinous an act.

I took a class once in remedial driving. I forget why I had been sent there – too many speeding tickets, maybe. The instructor was droning on about all the horrible things which happen to the body when struck at high impact. One of them was a burst bladder. Not from the seat belt pressing into your abdomen, but from holding in urine until the ambulance comes and makes your sacrifice moot.

The point being, it's better to empty your bladder than have it explode because all sorts of really nasty things happen to you after that.

I heard one kid behind me whisper that his mother warned him about that phenomenon every time he went out to drive. I didn't have a mother, so I had to hear it from a driving instructor.

From what I gathered, my way was no more effectual than his.

I didn't wet my pants, and my bladder didn't burst, either, but, if you'll excuse the expression, I sure had the piss scared out of me. Clasping both hands on the wheel, I looked to the left and swerved. The son-of-a-bitch truck driver must have the same instincts I did, only in reverse, for he swerved to the right, bringing us both back into position for a head-on collision.

I slammed on the breaks. The car jumped, then went into a terminal ring-around-the-rosie. I've done enough driving on ice to know how to handle a car in a tailspin. You drive into it, not out of it. My compact skidded across another lane, then mercifully reached the side of the road. I heard the tire blow before I felt the effects, probably because my body was numb from fear. My ears were still working OK.

I cursed, held on as the car spun again, then made a valiant attempt to right her. Failing in that, I let go of the wheel and brought my arms up to protect my face as the vehicle jumped over the six inch curb and rolled down an incline.

All the way down I listened for the crash of the big lorry rig that I had barely escaped being struck by. Either he was a better driver than I was, which I doubt, or his truck was easier to handle. I doubted that, too. In any case, I didn't hear anything but a few mad drivers sitting on their horns, so I assumed he got away pretty much unscathed.

Good for him.

I know truck drivers. I've driven a few big rigs myself when one would stop and pick me up while I was traveling across country. Contrary to popular belief, they don't give you a lift for the pleasure of your company. They let you in only after they ascertain you can drive awhile while they sleep. It's a convenient working relationship and I honed my skills pretty fast.

Of course, that sort of thing is totally illegal. But then, this was years ago. Got it?

It took me a few minutes to start breathing again and when I did, I cursed a blue streak. I was not only mad, I was furious. I was not only angry to the point of boiling over, I was pretty damned shook and ashamed. Cursing always makes a man sound in control. At least, that's what we tell ourselves.

Women don't curse. They adjust the rear view mirror and fix their hair so that when they get out, they'll look like nothing happened, and they don't have the slightest idea how they ended up in a canal. Unless, of course, they are police lieutenants. Then they leap out and blame the sergeant in the back seat.

Men curse, send a lot of threats heavenward, none of which they expect to be held accountable for, then turn on the radio to get the latest ball game score. That way, when they're carted away in the ambulance with a burst bladder, they'll have something to talk about with the attendants.

I didn't turn on the radio but I did finally get out of the car. One tire was shot, for sure, and the rim was bent. Oh, joy. The front fender was damaged and there were a few major dents but nothing fatal. Not unless it would kill you to spend your entire next paycheck on automobile repairs.

That sort of sentiment I could sympathize with.

I couldn't drive the car with a bent rim so I scrambled up the slope and started walking. I was too jumpy to hitch a ride and didn't suppose anyone would stop. I didn't look like a respectable type; not with my suit rumpled and my shoulders drooping.

My mind didn't stop working, however, and as I walked, I replayed the accident in my mind. Reconstructed the crime. It was part of my make-up. And no matter how I replayed the scene, it didn't come out right. Seeing the near-tragedy in stop-action frames, going from one camera shot to another, I just couldn't reconcile the situation as being my fault.

Yes, my mind was wandering. And yes, I may have meandered across the line, but I couldn't have been all the way over onto the other lane. No way. Which left only one explanation. The truck driver was aiming for me.

Now, why, I asked myself, would some trucker aim for me? I hadn't been in London long enough to make any enemies.

And then I remembered. But it didn't make any sense.

The Gypsy had warned the Mystic Seer was onto me and he was someone who played hardball. If he didn't want any snot-nosed reporter fooling around with his scheme, he wasn't above a little accidental murder.

It was then I wet my pants.

Sweet came to get me. I called him from the garage and told him I had been in an accident. He was all concern and tenderness until he found I wasn't hurt but the car was. After that, it was bellyache and complain all the way home.

He drove with two hands on the wheel and maintained the speed limit. That was worse than the lecture.

"I've told you and I've told you and I've told you to be careful," he said. I nodded wearily. "Didn't I tell you to be careful?"

"Yes, sir," I acknowledged.

"I send you out to do a nice, simple story on the stock market and you fall asleep at the wheel and don't even have one paragraph written for deadline."

I had been too close to "deadline" to be comfortable with that word. I wished he had chosen another but didn't say so.

"I've been doing background," I tried. He perked up a little.

With Sweet, it's always work. I appreciate that. I really do. It's what makes us friends. We have nothing in common but work, and we don't do the same jobs.

"Well, how shook up are you? I can take you home while you change clothes and then bring you back to the office."

Every bone in my body ached. I wanted to take a steaming hot shower, grab a bite to eat and go to bed. But if I told him that, he would be disappointed. I don't know why, but I hate to disappoint the man.

"All right," I agreed with less than enthusiasm. He stared at me from the corner of his eyes. I wished he would turn them back to the road. I was feeling a little squeamish. Also, I didn't look my best.

Men never worry about their appearance except when it doesn't matter.

"Well, I don't know," he changed horses in mid-race. "Maybe you better lie down. Get some rest."

"No," I protested. "And don't bother taking me back to my flat. Just drive me to the office."

"You're going home and that's it!"

And so we argued all the way to the CANS building.

He let me off at the front door while he went to park the car in a garage just left of Antares.

I waved good-bye, then went in the building. I think it was condemned in the Big One and that's why we got it so cheap. The lift was reputed to be "in order," so I took the stairs. No sense taking chances. Not after the day I'd had.

It was late and I was the only one there, a fact for which I was grateful. I wasn't in any mood to explain what happened to me, or why I looked better than normal. Usual office stuff. I should have told Sweet to go on home, himself. When he never showed up, I figured he used the same reasoning I did, or got killed in the elevator.

I didn't have my camera with me, or I'd have gone to investigate.

There really wasn't any story for me to write, which was just as well, for I fell asleep at the typewriter. When I woke, it was a little after 2 A.M. I was cold and had the shakes. I picked the lock to Sweet's office and made some coffee. There was a communal office pot but I didn't contribute to the coffee fund. If I got caught filching coffee when I was too cheap to put anything in, there'd be a row. Sweet never noticed when any of his coffee was missing and besides, he always locked his door.

Picking locks is a talent most reporters cultivate early in life. I learned the fine art as a kid. I was always hungry and the ice box in the orphanage where I grew up was locked. It didn't take much to learn how to open it. It wasn't fair to the rest of the boys, but it kept me from starving. Every kid for himself. You learn that early in life, too.

I was loaned out one summer to work in the service department of a community hospital. Like Oliver Twist picking oakum, they wanted to teach us useful trades so we wouldn't be a burden to society when we got out. The supervisor was a big, burly old farmer who lost his land in the Depression. He was the kind of guy everyone hated, so in order to get rid of him, they kept promoting him up the chain of command until he finally became supervisor of the Supply Depot.

Anyway, he kept a diary, jotting down a lot of gossip and daily observations on the comings and goings of his staff, including his "orphan boys." A lot depended on his good opinion of us. Having access to that diary always gave a kid fair warning when he was about to be canned.

The diary was kept in a locker. One of those prison-grey things you find in gyms and airport terminals. I didn't open the lock – it was the huge kind you see gangsters and super heroes firing guns point blank at to open. I didn't have a gun and tried picking it all ways to tomorrow but couldn't manage it. Then I got smart.

With a little finagling I discovered I could work the locker door up on the hinges, then slip it off. Wala! I'd remove the door, we'd take a gander at the diary, have a good snicker or two about who was doing what to whom and then I'd put the door back on.

That whole summer I was the favorite among the boys. It didn't get me out of any work, but some evenings when everything was closed up, I'd get a "gratuitous" ice cream cone, or soda from the coffee shop. The kid who cleaned it out was one us "us." He'd occasionally take the risk of rewarding me for a job well done by pilfering out of the stores.

I've gotten a fair share of bonuses in my life, but nothing was ever sweeter than that ice cream, or went down smoother than that soda.

I drank my coffee, typed my story, put it on Sweet's desk where he'd find it first thing, then called it a night. Avoiding the lift with the faith of a convert, I came outside into the early morning air. It took me awhile to adjust my breathing pattern. There isn't a lot of oxygen in the air over any European city.

I could have walked home and gotten there eventually, but opted for a cab. They don't have Russian drivers in London, like they do on the eastern seaboard. Somehow, it comes as a shock each time I get in one. The drivers speak English, too. Or, some reasonable facsimile.

The cabbies in London, like cabbies everywhere, know everything. They drive with one ear to the ground. Ask them the best place to lay a bet, they know twenty joints. Inquire about pubs and they steer you right. Need the lowdown on Elizabeth I? Their history is better than a salt water college professor's.

Ask one to take you for a drive around the block and it'll cost you seventy-five pounds.

"What do you know about this stockbroker-adviser who calls himself the Mystic Seer?" I asked to pass the time. The guy looked into his rear view mirror and shrugged.

"'e's gone, Pulled out this evening."

I felt a tingle run from the top of my head to the tips of my toes.

"Is that so?" I was casual. About as uninterested as a bull run amok in a barn full of cows.

"Yup. 'e's gone."

"Where to?"

I should have known better than to think I could get that kind of information free. I offered him a twenty but he wouldn't take it.

"I dunno. To 'eathrow. 'e owns a private plane."

"Did you take him there?" He shook his head. "Do you know who did?" For that he took the bill. "Can you take me to this driver?"

"'e's off duty."

"Then tell me all he knows."

"You some sort of investigator?"

"Do I sound like Scotland Yard?"

He stared at me a long beat.

"What are you?"

I could have lied but he picked me up in front of the CANS building, for Cripe's sake.

"I'm a reporter."

"What's your name?"

Instead of telling him, I produced my press card. He read it like he was doing an audit for the IRS.

"'e was in a big hurry," my informant of second-hand-as-good-as-first-hand-knowledge spat out. He seemed nervous. Or maybe he just wanted to earn his twenty and dump me off. "Carried a suitcase 'is self. 'e usually has a driver take him 'round the city, but 'e called a cab at 5:07 P.M. Driver arrived at 5:30 P.M."

"Why so prompt?"

Babies have been known to be conceived and delivered while waiting for a cab in London.

"The address, guv. You get called to that address, you'd dump Queen Bess 'erself."

"OK. So then what?"

"'e's waitin' outside. Opens the door an' gets in. Gives 'is destination and off 'e goes. Doesn't say nuthin' durin' the ride. But orders the radio turned on. Listens to the news."

"Anything in particular interest him?"

"No."

"He make any conversation?"

"'e says, 'hear about any accidents on the road today?'"

I was feeling all right until that point.

"Well?"

"The driver says no. The passenger looks... disappointed."

"What did you – what did he – the driver – infer from that?"

"No unusual holdups on the route."

An unusual choice of words. Holdup. Not a "holdup," exactly. More like an assassination.

"So he was disappointed. Then what?"

"They get to the airport an' race on through to 'is private 'anger. 'e gets out. 'is stretch limo was already there. Unloading baggage. 'e pays the cabby an' waves the motor away."

"How much tip?"

"Nothing." My cabby was contemptuous. I knew the reason why. Mr. Seer figured the driver – or one of his coworkers – would get their tip from *me*. My mouth went dry.

"Thanks."

"Don't mention it." Which meant exactly that. I glanced up at his driver's I.D. He didn't appreciate it. I gave him a faint smile as I got out, two blocks from my destination. Suddenly, I didn't want him to know where I lived. Accent on *lived.*

Just in case someone was reading his mind.

"G'night, luv," I called. He growled something about my ancestry I don't care to repeat.

I entered my two-room flat and slumped into a chair. There was no couch, or I would have fallen onto that. I could afford better but why waste money? I'm never home.

I glanced over at the telephone, expecting it to ring. It didn't. If it had, my laundry bill would have skyrocketed.

I wished I had the Gypsy's number. I thought I ought to warn her. Thank her. Something. But it was unlisted. She didn't like solicitors. I had half a mind to send her my number by telepathy then felt foolish.

I didn't believe in this mystic stuff. It was all bunk. The guy had set up some fat pigeons and was about to pull the string. What was I supposed to do about it? Call the London Stock Exchange?

But then I remembered. I didn't have their number, either.

CHAPTER 5

I slept late and woke up with a stiff neck. Every chronic chair-sleeper knows that's the price you pay for being too lazy to make it to bed. Unless the chair *is* your bed. In that case, it's the penalty you pay for being broke.

In this world, it's the "haves" versus the "have nots." The lines may blur but they only cross one way. Which explains why the ranks of the "have nots" swell every day, while those of the "haves" continue to dwindle.

Economics, distilled.

Distillery, by the way, has a lot to do with how the world goes 'round. Not booze, but getting down to basics. Mankind has always sought the path to success. Forget the Fountain of Youth. While that's a nice thought, it's not practical. But the Fountain of Dreams, now. Then you're onto something. Men have been selling other men dreams since the dawn of time.

God sold Eve the dream of knowledge from the Tree of Life. That started it all, if you believe in that stuff. Me, I don't talk religion. Don't practice it, either, but that's a personal choice. When you get religion crammed down your throat as a kid, it's hard to believe in a loving, merciful God.

Lapsed Catholics slink back to Mother Church when they get old. That's because their past sins start weighing heavily on their conscience. Redemption is a dream the Roman Catholic church sells. Proclaim your faith and you get Life everlasting. They're not the only ones, of course. Existence after death is preached as a major tenet by all the great religions of the world. It keeps people in line. Makes them scared. As any Bible thumper can tell you, fear is the name of the game.

And as any branch water-hawking confidence man will say – if he's being honest – selling salvation by dispensing fear is his greatest weapon.

Everyone is afraid. Pain, suffering, lack of money, frustrations, broken hearts – they all drive our pitiful species into dreaming. What good is courage, if not for the dream of ticker-tape parades? What author scribbles in a garret and doesn't believe he's written the Great American novel? What painter dabs reds and blues on canvas and doesn't fantasize about private showings and a wing of the Metropolitan Museum of Art to himself?

Praise is their dream. Tell the soldier no one will see his heroics and you turn him into a cautious man. Let the writer understand no one will ever read his tome and he takes a handful of pills. Critique the artist's work and his hand goes numb.

Fear of hell, fear of obscurity, fear of poverty, fear of loneliness. Put them in any order you wish. Then imagine yourself without a dream to cast your fears back into the shadows where they live and breed. Do that, and you'll never get up to go to work in the morning.

Guaranteed.

Me? I rise and shine because I'm a perpetual dreamer. What dream keeps me alive? That's tougher to answer. Maybe the cynicism I've woven around myself. It's the armor I wear to protect my heart. I like to imagine it deflects the slings and arrows.

Drink helps most people along the way. It's cheap, legal and reasonably effective. Street drugs are the ticket for kids and musicians. Romance novels and soap operas keep housewives trudging through their daily tasks.

I don't drink – much – and I've never seen the fascination with the so-called mind-expanding mushrooms or snorts of white powder. They're a cheat and a cop-out. If creativity ain't in you, pal, no artificial stimulus will bring it out.

I must be some kind of plaster saint.

Right?

Like I said, I slept late and woke up with a stiff neck. I switched on the radio as I stumbled blindly into the kitchenette – what a stupid word – and opened the cold water tap. I always let it run a full minute before daring to stick my coffee pot under it. Wouldn't matter if I was in Rio, at a Burma railroad station, or in Los Angeles. I know what settles in pipes overnight.

If you knew, you'd let the water run, too. It doesn't do any good, of course, because the germs and the chlorine and the fluoride and whatever else they're putting into it these days will still be there. But it's a ritual. Not exciting enough to call it a dream. Let's say it's a hope.

I don't usually make my own coffee. It's easier to shower, shave, throw on the same suit of clothes I wore the day before and stumble out to a diner, or a fast food place. I was edgy this morning, however, and I didn't want to be seen in public. You know what I mean. Call it a bad hair day, or a, "Oh, my God, there's a zit on my chin" day. Never fails. Big interview and your hair looks like shit. Getting your picture taken for the yearbook, or for the big scene you're filming and your face breaks out.

I didn't have my photograph published in my college yearbook, by the way. I don't know why. I've never broken any mirrors. Call it a latent criminal complex. In case I grew up to be a famous Brinks robber, or a Watergate burglar, I didn't want the authorities going back to when I was twenty-five years old and publishing that photo on a wanted poster. Of course, they'd have the boys in the crime lab touch it to make me look older, and so more recognizable.

Maybe I've seen too many dead eyes stare back at me from the sides of milk cartons. "Have You Seen Me?" It breaks my heart. Not because some father has run off with the kids he lost in a divorce settlement. Because if I dropped off the face of the earth, no one would put together a search.

Not when I was a kid. Not now. It's depressing. When you're friendless dreams are all you have.

I'm a loner. I was born that way. Some children are born bald, others pop out with a full head of hair. A few come into this world old and wise. The rest are just as stupid the day they're born as they day they're planted. I came into existence as a solitary being knowing more than I should have. It marked me in more ways that I care to speculate on.

Sure, I've roomed with fellas, sharing expenses. I've slept with bums on railroad cars, shacked up with girls, sharing other things. I even thought I was in love once. That was a joke. I couldn't handle it. She was a street-wise, smart-alack woman, didn't take any crap from anybody. We might have made it as a couple. But I doubt it.

We both worked nights.

Which reminded me of Gypsy. Damn her, anyway. How the hell did she get the name Kim from my memory? That wasn't fair. When I had the time, I'd have to do some research on her. Find the Prince Charming in her life and smack her across the face with his name. See how she liked it.

And that image of Lieutenant Helen Chandler. She's a cold cat. She makes the blood freeze in my veins. I never thought of her as beautiful. Who ever heard of a good-looking cop?

I turned on the radio while I was standing around in my rumpled clothes, stupidly watching the glass carafe fill with coffee. I prefer audio to faces. Watching a wooden martinet babble in sound bites, distilling the most gruesome news story into two minutes, then introducing the pretty boy who is going to tell me what the News Channel 8 weather map predicts, gets on my nerves.

Besides, I find I can never take my eyes off the announcer's three-thousand dollar hair piece and his well-tailored suit jacket. How is anyone supposed to take a made-up, overly coiffured, Gucci-suited man seriously? The news on TV has turned into another installment of *How the World Turns.*

I remember Kim asked me once why I listen to the news, when news is my business. "Don't you get enough of it at work?" she asked. I retorted by asking her why she liked sex at home when she sure got enough of that at work. She only laughed at me and said one was pleasure, the other business. Which made it easy for me to answer her about why I listened to the news.

Her income was better than mine, by the way. And she had health benefits.

Guys don't like to live with women who make more money than they do and it's embarrassing to be carried on a hooker's health policy. Maybe that's why we didn't make it. Make a go of it, that is.

It's too early to be making bad jokes. They're stale, anyway. And there's nobody here to laugh at them. Put a comic in an empty room and see how funny he is.

I was only listening with half an ear because I was mumbling to myself about dreams and dreamers. We're all Don Quixote's in one way or another. Not the character from the book, by the way. I was referring to the play. Dreamers dreaming impossible dreams. Richard Kiley made you believe. That's because he believed. Sir Richard the Original.

"...in total chaos."

My attention was grabbed. I perked faster than the java, and jerked up the volume.

"More news at the top of the hour."

I sent the blackest curse I knew into the atmosphere, then spun the dial. It used to be radios had buttons you could preset to whatever station you wanted, like those in your car. They don't make them like that now. I think it's a conspiracy. The managers know what a pain in the ass it is to get up and roll a knob, scrolling through three dozen sound-alikes before you find another station playing what you want to hear, so you just leave the dial where it is.

I fooled them this time. News. I needed a full news report. What the hell was in "chaos"?

But I already knew.

I found what I was looking for and drew up a chair. Where were you when John F. Kennedy was shot? What were you doing when you heard Martin Luther King, Junior was assassinated? Where were you sitting when the European stock market crashed?

I knew it last night when the cabby told me the Mystic Seer had absconded with the goods. I should have stayed up and waited for the ball to drop. Just like on New Year's Eve, Times Square. Everyone around the world knows the New Year doesn't start until 12:00 AM, Eastern time, U.S. of A.

Stock in Fabrico, Cross Electronics and Hammerstone Communications had risen well over market value recently, the report said, "in wake of interest shown by several major investors, and rumors of much higher-than-average returns for the 2nd Quarter."

At the opening bell, trading in those stocks was unexpectedly heavy on overnight speculation of corporate buy-backs at 15% over last night's close.

After nearly one-third of all shares had changed hands, it became apparent there was not a major "buy" taking place, but rather a sell-out. Company officials reached for comment at 10:30 AM expressed concern that earnings would come in at, or below market expectations. They were at a loss to explain why their stocks had risen so high in the first place. Analysts at the major brokerage firms downgraded the ratings of Fabrico, Cross and Hammerstone, belatedly indicating such shares were grossly overvalued.

Within half an hour, prices had plummeted nearly 70% in all three companies, igniting a sharp downturn in the market.

The mad frenzy to sell wiped out sharp market gains over the past three months. With the failure of Fabrico, Cross and Hammerstone, the drop in other high-tech stock had literally wiped out hundreds of thousands of pounds in valuation, and prices continue to tank.

"News of the European collapse has already adversely affected the Tokyo Market and will undoubtedly send Wall Street into a tailspin. The American stock exchange, which has not yet opened, is expected to follow suit and send stock prices plummeting. This trend is expected to continue throughout the day.

Next update in ten minutes."

So. There it was. The Mystic Seer had advised his syndicate of speculators to invest in tech companies, making them appear as growth stocks. That influx of capital increased their market value well above actual worth. The moment before the authorities called a trading suspension for investigation, Holloway, aka the Mystic Seer, unexpectedly sold his own holdings, reaping the unnaturally high profit. Those who didn't get out at the same time were ruined.

Neat. Very neat.

And scary as hell.

I heard the news of Breaksmyth's suicide on the car radio as I drove to Gypsy's. There would be others following, I didn't wonder. There were five big investors – five clients of the Mystic Seer. Breaksmyth must have had the most to lose. That left Morell, Tyler, Gerhusen and Young.

If they, too, were ruined, the fallout from Mr. Holloway's coup would be great, indeed.

The question was, had the Mystic Seer done anything illegal?

"Yes," I explained to Gypsy as she let me in. "What he did was against the law if his entire intent was to advise these men to buy stock in a company to falsely inflate its value, then cash in himself while leaving them to hang."

She grimly nodded.

"It is only just beginning." I didn't like the sound of that.

"Go on," I encouraged.

"He had other clients besides the five you mentioned. Many others. With smaller investments. But added up, losses will be staggering."

"Maybe he won't be able to collect. Maybe the banks will withhold payment. If somebody makes a fuss – if somebody suggests the probability of collusion and dishonesty –"

"That somebody being you?"

"Of course."

I sounded more matter-of-fact than I felt.

"You must be careful."

"It's my story. I sent one article out on the wire very early this morning. Or was it last night? I have to wait until the American market closes, then I'm going to put another out. This is big."

"Bigger than you think."

"The guy's a crook."

"You are not a financial writer."

"No. I'm a crime reporter. And this may be the crime of the century. The new century," I added for emphasis.

"Why did you come here?" she suddenly demanded. I started to answer then left my mouth hanging open.

"For coffee?" I tried. It was all I could think of to say.

"Did you bring your portable typewriter?"

The word sounded odd coming from her. One thought of Gypsies casting spells with herbs, goat blood and bat's wings. Tucked into the last century. That is, two centuries ago. Or three. Someone out of the Dark Ages. Not asking if I had brought my typewriter.

"No. Why?"

"I thought you could work on your story here, while I made coffee."

"I was just kidding." I foolishly grinned. "Actually, I don't know why I showed up at your doorstep. Because you gave me some insight on this Mystic Seer. I thought..." But again, I didn't know what I thought.

"I shall make coffee, anyway. You can write on the table."

The round table. I nearly grinned with delight.

"Will it give me divine inspiration?" I asked to her back as she left for the coffee pot.

"Divine, as in godly?" she called. I could almost hear the laughter in her voice. "Most people think of Gypsies as being godless; allied more closely with Satan than the Higher Powers."

"All right," I cheerfully agreed. Once simply could not be depressed around this woman. She was too full of life. "Any kind of inspiration, then?"

"I do not know. You will have to tell me after you start. But," she added over the sound of running water, "If Uncle Ralph tells you where he hid his deathbed will and testament, jot the location down on the tablet. I have a client who is most eager for that information."

"Your client's name was left out of the copy filed in the lawyer's office, was it?"

"I did not ask."

Droll.

"Didn't you wonder?"

"No."

I couldn't tell if she was having me on, or not. Nor, did I inquire why she simply hadn't asked Uncle Ralph's spirit. It made me question whether her powers were limited or if she already knew he hadn't made a will in favor of his nephew.

A yellow tablet and two #1 pencils, sharpened, were set out for me on the table.

"How did you know I liked #1 pencils?"

In fact, I had a regular love affair with #1 pencils. The lead was soft, wrote with a firm, dark line and required less effort than the conventional #2 pencil. They also required sharpening far more often. I noticed a hand sharpener on the desk next to the table.

"I thought all reporters liked #1 pencils."

That sounded like a lie. All right, a fib.

"Tell me the truth."

"You told me to stop reading your mind," Gypsy said, entering the room with a pot full of steaming hot, deliciously-smelling java. Obviously, her machine worked faster than mine. My mouth watered. Salivated. It was embarrassing.

"Well, have you?" I demanded.

Her eyes twinkled with unexpected merriment.

"No. I just stopped telling you I was reading your mind."

"And made up a fib to fool me?"

"Oh, I never intended to fool you. I was just giving you the option to believe what you needed to believe."

"I see. Thank you."

"You are welcome."

I started writing. To speak truth, it had been a long time since I had written with a #1 pencil. So much of my work is hacked – excuse me – pecked on a typewriter, I had forgotten the pure, simple joy of cursive writing. Or even of the smell of a freshly sharpened pencil. Or, the taste of the lead (graphite) in my mouth as I sucked on the point from an old, long overlooked habit.

"Come on," I said, writing fast. "Give me the names of the other companies our Mystic Seer had an interest in. The small ones, which are going to collapse right along with the big ones. If we hurry, we may prevent that stock from being sold. Or at least having a run on them."

She gave me the names of six companies, none of which I had ever heard of before. My fingers flew over the page, pausing only for a sip of coffee, or to put a new point on the pencil.

"Ticonderoga is your favorite?" she asked once. I answered without questioning how she came by that odd-sounding, northern Indian (native American) name.

"Used to be. But the last several boxes I bought all have broken lead in them, so I gave up and switched brands."

"You should have returned them."

"Who remembers where I bought them, or in what city?" I shrugged. "I move around a lot. I don't have many belongings, but I can always fit a pencil in the glove compartment." I envisioned the glove box filled with maps, flashlight, pens, pencils, tablets curling at the edges, parking tickets, salt packets, loose change. "It's easier, I guess, to use a mechanical pencil. Do you know, those contrivances have been around since Civil War days?"

I should have said, "American Civil War," as England had its own civil wars, but it was a habit. I still wasn't used to being across the Puddle.

"And the fountain pen was invented not long after."

"Correct."

I patted my breast pocket. One thing an author has, no matter who he is, or what he writes, is one really expensive pen. It's a status symbol. He seldom, if ever uses it, but he carries it with him like a exact chance badge.

I have a Waterman pen. It cost me $150 and I never regretted spending that kind of money on it. I mean, for that price, I could have bought an old junker to drive around in, or put a down payment on a house. I bought it for myself many years ago. Before that, my best writing instrument was a Cross pen. They make expensive Cross pens, too, these days, as everyone wants to cash in on the trend, but who wants to say their best pen is a Cross? That's like bragging you drive a Chevy, when Big Shots drive a Cadillac.

I don't know that the Waterman writes any better than a Cross pen. Maybe it does. Mine is a fountain pen with a gold nib. About three years ago I bought a matching ballpoint. Now I have two.

I may not have a Pulitzer but I have two Waterman pens. It's a step in the right direction.

I mean, if I were no more than a hack, I wouldn't be able to afford a Waterman. And I'd be writing with a click pen with the words "Mercantile Bank" printed on the side in day-glow red letters.

I know, because I have one of those, too. For everyday use. If you loan it to a cop making out a report, you don't care. If he – or she – asks to borrow a pen and you give up your Waterman, its history.

I finished three cups of coffee and my story at the same time. I felt of warm glow of inner satisfaction surround me.

"It is good," Gypsy said. "You like it. You have done good work."

"How can you tell?" I asked, although I knew the reason.

Gypsy smiled. She had a beautiful smile.

"There is a glow around you."

"You can see it?"

She nodded.

"Yes. It is a good thing to see. It makes me proud of you."

If I had been a boy and not a man, I think tears would have come to my eyes. It had been a long, long time since anyone gave me a compliment that meant anything to me.

"I have to go to the office," I said. "And get this out." She nodded. I thought she would say something, make a comment, suggestion, anything, but she didn't. "Want to come along?" I asked on the spur of the moment.

She did not hesitate, yet I saw a slight wavering behind her eyes.

"I think not."

"Why not? Come on," I urged. What had started as a casual invitation suddenly became very important to me. "It's not far. Leave a note on your door: "Back in five." If anyone comes, they'll wait. Besides," I prompted. "You haven't found out where Uncle Ralph left his will. The real copy he meant to file, but died before he had a chance to. Maybe we'll think of a place as we drive."

"We?" Her eyebrows arched ever so slightly. I had a mad impulse to kiss them.

Damn. I hadn't even kissed her lips and I was thinking of eyebrows.

Where the hell was "Go" with this woman, and what was the matter with me, anyway? Don Juan I ain't. The World's Greatest Lover I ain't. Hot and horny over eyebrows I ain't. At least, I never have been, before.

And what was I thinking? I sure couldn't invite her back to my place after I filed my story. The rug hadn't been vacuumed in a dog's age. Come to think of it, I couldn't even remember if there *was* a rug on the floor. Well, for sure, the sheets hadn't been washed in an elephant's age.

That'd make a good impression.

Why was I such a sloppy housekeeper?

Because I never invited anyone over and I didn't care.

That excuse didn't hold water, any more.

"No," she said. My heart fell through the floorboards. While I was down there, I looked for Uncle Ralph's will. Didn't find it.

"Well, can I come back?"

What a way to make a date. You'd think I was fifteen years old.

"Of course."

"How late are you open?"

I almost tripped over my tongue. That innocent question, coming out of my fervent brain, sounded obscene.

"Oh, I shall be here. Working late."

She knew. I almost died of shame.

It's a good thing people don't die of shame, or there would be a lot of us pushing up daisies.

"Good," I mumbled. My lips felt numb. "Well, good-bye." I stopped myself from blowing a kiss.

"Good-bye, Kimbo," she said. She held out her hand. I took it and like the fool I am, brought it to my lips and kissed it. She did not seem surprised by my adolescent behavior.

If she were reading my mind now, I'd be a dead man for sure.

And forget the daisies.

As I went to the door, she patted me lightly on the side. Just a simple, innocent gesture of parting, I told myself.

With red cheeks and a wildly thumping heart, I hurried off, wishing she were coming with me. It was not until I was at the car, fumbling for my keys, that I realized she had slipped me the fee I had given her the day before. Innocent pat, hell. I was thinking one thing and she was performing another.

I would have to return, now. If for no other reason than to insist she take the money. I would tell her Sweet had already reimbursed me for my out-of-pocket expenses. Stringers and informants were a legitimate part of my work. I had an expense account. She couldn't question that.

Unless she were reading my mind, again.

What I really needed was Love Potion #9. And a Gypsy to take her own medicine.

CHAPTER 6

There were two more suicides the following day: Morell and Young. I talked to Sweet and he agreed it might make interesting reading if I were to do a piece on the men who died. Compare their lives, education, their meteoric rise as major players in the stock market. The obscene amounts of money they had made within the last five years.

I also thought it would be a nice touch to add a few paragraphs on the personality quirks which had driven these men to a mystic seer in the first place.

There weren't your rash entrepreneurs. They were Wall Street types. They were the Tried and True. Everyone likes to read about their fall.

Out the window.

Gruesome details.

That last, I failed to mention to Sweet. I was afraid he would be a little soft on the idea.

"Just the facts, Kimbo. You're not a psychiatrist. Don't try to sound like one."

If I attempted to even suggest I might use a bona fide shrink as background, he'd flip a gasket. That would sound too much like I would need *real* expense money.

Of course, there are some MD's who would talk to me for free; just to see their name in the paper. It's not a bad trade. I get the background I need and they look respectable. Hospitals *beg* reporters to interview their docs. Don't forget: if you read it in the paper, it's legit.

If you see a name in the paper, he/she/it is the genuine article.

"It" in this case being the hospital/medical center/doctor's group.

St. Louis is a one-horse newspaper town. I pity the media people who work for the hospitals. Most reporters have their favorite doctors/hospitals go to when they need a quick quote. It's not as political as you might think. One reporter had his gall bladder removed by someone at one of the local hospitals and they treated him OK. Since he survived, he thinks he owes that particular hospital free press. So whenever a big-wig faints, or a hockey player has black-out spells, he always calls an expert from that hospital.

Fries the rest of the healthcare providers big time but they can't let on. Sound pissed and they'll see their hospital in the headlines. "Nurses Vote To Unionize" or something like that. Sure, it's news. Maybe even front page stuff. But not what any administrator wants to see. And maybe – and I say maybe – if it was that other hospital – the one with the gall bladder surgeon – the picketing RNs would have been on page twelve.

Remember, I said "maybe." There's always the chance CANS will flop in Europe and we'll get sent back. I don't want burn any bridges.

Not even with Lieutenant Chandler.

Did I mention the reporter with the gall (stones) was also married to a nurse who worked at the hospital with all the quotable doctors?

That ain't political. That's family.

St. Louis is a very family-oriented city. You can read that line on any tourist brochure. You can visit the Arch. There's a zoo that doesn't charge admission, a science center and a world-class botanical garden. There's the symphony. (They really do have a first-class orchestra, by the way.) You can take in a hockey game or watch the Cardinals. Baseball is America's pastime and the Redbirds rule the Midwest. They're broadcast on KMOX radio, by the way. Its signal reaches nearly to the moon. If basketball is your thing, you'll have to watch college hoops.

Did I mention the Arch?

I got a free calendar from a loan company, once. A year of the Arch. The Arch from the Missouri side. The Arch from the Illinois side. The Arch at night. The Arch during the day. The Arch in summer. The Arch in winter. The Arch in fall. The Arch in spring.

Let's see. That's eight totally different views of the Arch. The Arch from Busch (Memorial) Stadium. The Arch shot by some photographer standing on a river barge on the Mississippi River. The Arch as seen from a bird's eye view. The Arch photographed by someone lying on his back looking up.

And then, of course, there's the view of the Arch as seen from the point-of-view of a motorist stuck in traffic in the parking lot, referred to locally as Highway 40. Looking east/west, of course, depending whether you're coming to work or driving home. It's referred to on maps as Highway 64. If that's the name you know it by, that means you're probably on your way out of Dodge. Dodge City, of course is in Kansas. You have to go through Kansas City to get there. Kansas City is in Missouri.

That's thirteen views of the Arch. I gave you a baker's dozen, which means one for free.

I can't resist one more potshot: The Arch as seen through the sticky fingers of someone who has Ted Drew's Frozen Custard dripping down his fingers.

I missed my calling. I should have been a photographer. Or a calendar designer.

I was two entire days and nights working on the follow-up story. It was a good one and I was hot. I never went back to Gypsy's flat. It wasn't that I had forgotten her – it was just that I was on the scent.

The three who had taken their own lives – Morell, Breaksmyth and Young – were all ruined when Fabrico, Cross and Hammerstone went belly up. It was a sad story, really. They didn't seem like bad guys, once I started researching their backgrounds. Just greedy. Well, if greed was a disqualification for getting into heaven, we'd all be in trouble.

They did all the usual things. Gave money to charity, sponsored cricket teams, patted babies on the head. All three were well educated, married and apparently happy with their millions. None, as far as I could determine, were wacky. Not the type you would ordinarily associate with palm reading, crystal balls or fortune tellers.

So what had driven these three men and the others associated with the Mystic Seer to use "divine inspiration" as a guide for stock market investments?

That took some back-tracking. A good reporter loves to research. Nothing moves him like the smell of musty old newspapers, printing press ink, and deep, dark, cobwebbed morgues where the past is as alive and current as the 1940s newspaper you hold reverently in your hands.

In the States, I'm sorry to say, a lot of those old treasure troves have gone away, the newspapers transferred to microfilm. It's sad. Reading about President McKinley's assassination just isn't the same when perused from the monitor of a microfilm reader. It loses the temper of the times. It makes you feel dissociated.

There aren't any smudged fingerprints or yellowed, curling paper. No smells to waft back cosmic memories of high-buttoned shoes and shirts with detachable cuffs and collars.

In Europe, things are a little bit different. You can still find original newspapers discussing the latest Jack the Ripper case. Or read some Joe's story of how life was affected when England was cut off from American cotton during the Civil War. Written in good ol' Victorian English. Replete with proper grammar. The kind you learned in school. Before they took away all the punctuation and spacing between sentences in the interest of saving space.

Saving it for what, I ask you?

A good news hound remembers dates. He has a good eye for something just slightly off kilter. He recognizes patterns, senses when he's being fed pap.

What I was looking for and didn't realize, was the bait. The original, titillating, unable-to-be-resisted teaser which brought these men to the door of the Mystic Seer.

I mean, even Jason Holloway had to start somewhere. He wasn't born with a reputation as a gifted stock market advisor. Where did he come from? How did he get his start? Was he always crooked?

Of course, like any good reporter, I already had my mind made up about that. Damn right, he was always crooked. So when did he make his first killing – literally? You see, I hold him responsible for those three suicides. Maybe those men were greedy and maybe they didn't sponsor clinics in South Africa, but they didn't deserve to be set up for a fall, either.

Not for a plunge out a twenty-story window.

Who came after them? They weren't the last. Not by a long shot.

Reading financial pages can be dull, especially when you're a writer and never had a penny of your own to invest. I thought my eyes would fall out, or my brain would turn spastic. It was a toss-up. Just when I was about to fall victim to both fatal diseases and give it up for the night, I saw it.

A small advertisement in the lower right hand corner of a page. "Stock Market advice given by appointment ONLY. Results guaranteed." There was no name. Just a phone number and a rider. "The Stars Can be on YOUR Side."

Destiny.

Fate.

Kismet.

Guaranteed.

There were no guarantees in this life. Certainly not for stock market information. But some men had obviously been intrigued. Compelled, even. They had gone and tried it for themselves. And found the guarantee ironclad.

Until the stars fell from the heavens.

With renewed energy, I began looking for more ads. I found one in a newspaper dated a year later. A year, as past history went, that is.

"Stock Market advice, based upon Cosmic interpretation. Proven 100% successful. References given to qualified investors."

This one was an eighth of a page, with a border. It jumped up at me as large as life.

The third time I found the ad, my heart was really pounding.

"Mystic Seer Offers No-Risk Investment Opportunities for those wishing High-Risk gains. Appointment by Referral, only."

The Stars. Cosmic Interpretation. No risk. High gain.

The time span covered five years. Mr. Holloway was a patient man.

Considering the capital he made in the past few days, I'd say the wait was worth it.

In five years, he went from reading the stars to mystic seer.

From an open door policy, references supplied, to appointment by reference only.

From Charlie Tuna to Moby Dick.

I called the phone number given in the last ad. After three rings, a woman answered the phone.

"I'd like to make an appointment with the Mystic Seer," I said. "I have a referral from a satisfied client."

"What is his name, sir?"

"I'm afraid I can't give that information over the phone."

There was a pause. Not a very long one.

"I am sorry, Mr. Kimbo, but I am afraid there are no appointments available at this time. Please call back."

"When?"

The phone went dead.

And then it hit me. How did the operator, or secretary, or whoever she was know my name? I hadn't given it. And even if she had the call traced, I wasn't at home, wasn't even in the office. I was in the...

... morgue.

My heart sank.

Anyone who tells you hearts don't really sink, don't physically shrivel up and send you into a cold sweat have never really faced danger before.

Have never really been in love.

I've felt my heart sink before, but never like this.

It took all the energy I could muster to hang up the receiver.

Maybe Sweet was right. Maybe playing shrink wasn't such a hot idea after all.

But it was too late. I knew it. Sweet knew it. Or he would, as soon as he got my story.

I got photostats of the advertisements and added them to the hand-written notes I had taken on Morell, Breaksmyth and Young. I needed to write this fast, right now. The sooner the better.

Before I lost my nerve.

My car, motor, automobile, whatever they call it over here was waiting for me, just out of the repair shop. Invitingly familiar, safe, secure. But all I could see was me, sitting on the front seat, turning the key.

Being blown to smithereens.

I hailed a cab. Not the first one which came along. The third. Three was a holy number and I was in need of all the protection I could muster.

Three was exactly the number of men who had leapt from windows in the latest stock market crash.

I wish I hadn't thought that.

I meant to go home and write my story there, but before I could give the address, I heard myself giving directions to the Gypsy's place of business. It was absurd. Why go there? It was three o'clock in the morning. She didn't live at her place of work. She was at home, wherever that was, fast asleep.

I got out of the cab, feeling juvenile. And considerably poorer. Taking a cab was not an inexpensive little jaunt.

Good thing I was so well paid.

With the aid of some convenient moonlight I caught sight of myself in the window of a shop. The rueful smile I imagined to be decorating my face more closely resembled a grimace. The realization did nothing to improve my mood.

I clumped up the stairs to the Gypsy's shop and knocked on the door. Just like it was three o'clock in the afternoon and I expected an answer.

By appointment only.

I snorted, blowing air through my nostrils. For my bravado, I was rewarded by a drop of mucus forming at the tip of my nose. I was hungry, tired, scared, cold and now my damned nose was dripping. What next? Tears?

"Come in, Kimbo. The door is unlocked."

It was the Gypsy's voice. At least, I fancied it was. But as I replayed the sound in my mind, I convinced myself it was not her voice at all, but rather that of the operator's I had so recently spoken to.

I froze to the spot. Rooted. Paralyzed. My heart sped at three hundred and sixty times normal.

Anyone who says a heart can't beat at 360 times normal has never felt fear.

Forget about being in love.

The door opened and the Gypsy stood there, a quizzical expression in her eyes. No. Not quizzical. Worried.

"You found out something," she said. I dumbly nodded. I think the correct word is "mutely," but I was feeling dumb, so let the statement stand.

She stepped aside and I entered. The room smelled of incense. I found my tongue.

"You were having a séance. I interrupted you."

She laughed. It was a tinkling, merry laugh. The innocence of it brought tears to my eyes. Which completed the cycle.

"I am alone," she said.

"Yeah. Just you and the dead." I tried to laugh. My laugh was even worse than my rueful smile.

She was going to think I was a lunatic. Certifiably insane.

"Come in and tell me what you unearthed."

The word went with "morgue," but elicited thoughts of vampires.

I went in and she shut the door behind me. I was shaking like a leaf.

Instead of thanking her for admitting me, I asked the Number One dumb question of all time.

"What are you doing here? It's late. I thought you'd be in bed."

"I was waiting for you."

"Why?"

"I knew you would need help. I did not give you my home address. So, you had to come here."

Simple. Precise. Truthful. I could have kissed her.

Which really did things to my heart.

Another kind of fear.

"I need to talk."

"I will listen."

"It may take a while."

She nodded. She had a wise nod.

"We shall go to my flat. It is not far. We will have a drink and you will tell me."

"You don't even know me," I stammered.

She laughed again. There was a youthful quality to her laugh. Not a girlish sound, but young. Ageless.

"What can you do to me?"

I almost dropped my notes.

Without bothering for an answer, she indicated with her hand. Her left hand. I had forgotten she was left-handed. I noted it when she poured coffee. The hand of... my savior.

We went out into the night air. She led, I followed. We crossed a sidewalk, went into an alley. There were all sorts of twists and turns. I tried to memorize the way, but was lost within a minute. The route made the Chicago cloverleaf look like child's play.

"Up these stairs," she pointed. I nodded. She went up, I behind her, taking them one at a time, which was just as well for if she had taken them two or three at a time, I would have fallen on my face.

She paused at the landing, I presumed to get a key. I was wrong. She was waiting for me. Her door was unlocked. I recoiled in civilized shock.

"I never lock the door," she explained, correctly interpreting my look.

"Why not?" I gasped. Remember, I grew up in NYC.

I guess I expected her to say because she had gargoyles protecting her possessions. Wrong again.

"The flat is hidden from the street. It is not easy to find. No one would even suspect there were living quarters here. It cannot be seen from any angle."

She was right, but that didn't excuse her negligence. It ran contrary to the rules of Paranoia. And Common Sense. To say nothing of Civilization.

"Didn't your parents ever teach you it's better to be safe than sorry?" I asked as we entered her home. She let the interrogative go. I fleetingly deduced she had no parents. Like me. Another link in the chain that was beginning to bind us.

The immediate impression of the interior of her flat was striking; so startling in fact, I found myself holding my breath for fear of disturbing anything.

It was not that she had an apartment full of tiny objects or breakables; it was just that every object appeared in harmony with its surrounds and with her. The room was decorated in soft reds, browns and golds, highlighting some areas, gently tucking others away into shadows.

The carpets were luxuriant and deep, the drapes full and drawn, the ceilings high and airy, giving the impression of a small, yet perfectly self-contained world. I expected to see toadstools growing on the windowsills, with minuscule elves and faeries popping out from behind the sofa and chairs.

"Toadstools do not grow on windowsills," she reminded me. She was so casual, in fact, she was apologizing before I realized she had read my mind again.

"What is it with you?" I demanded in a hushed voice. It did not seem proper to yell in such sacred and comfortable surroundings. "Can't you turn that off for a while?"

"But why would I want to?"

"OK," I agreed. "You wouldn't want to, but I would. I'd like to keep some secrets, you know."

"Is it a secret that you want to kiss me?"

I was too embarrassed to deny it. I blushed, swallowed, then put my hands on my hips – akimbo – and attempted to make up for my mistake.

"Yes, damn it!"

"It is one not very well kept. Perhaps you did not want to keep it," Gypsy suggested. For stating the obvious, I flew into a rage.

"If I wanted to kiss you, I'd kiss you! And if I don't want to kiss you, I won't!"

"I am glad to hear it," she wisely responded.

Before I knew what I was doing, I had my arms around her and was pressing my lips to hers. She responded with an immediacy I had not expected. Passion rose in me, fast and furious.

Inanely, I thought, "The old gear box is still working."

I paid for my sin of minor self-congratulations by having her break away and giggle.

"Gear box? I have never heard 'it' referred to in such a manner before."

"It's... old fashioned," I explained, shame-faced. "I don't use it very often. I don't know why I thought it just now. I hadn't expected... to feel aroused," I lamely concluded. "It's been a long time since anyone made me feel like that; since I cared about responding."

The taste of her lips was still on my mind. I could feel the pressure, sense the warmth. Everything about that abbreviated kiss was unique.

"Come in," she said. "We will kiss more later. Right now, I think we had better discuss what you discovered and what you plan to write."

All business. I clung to the "later," part of her sentence. Like a dying man wraps his arms around a life-preserver.

"Yeah. Sure."

She walked through the tiny threshold into the living room. At closer range, the effect of the colors was even more apparent. This *was* another world, hidden away in the heart of London. Everything was comfortable, nothing out of place. She turned on some music. It played in the background like a waterfall cascading into a lily pond. It was a classical piece I couldn't identify.

There was a rich commingling of odors, spices, incense – not the same incense she used at her place of business – flowers, and earthiness. The closest I can come to describing would be long grass and earth warmed by the sun, waving lazily in a slight, nearly imperceptible breeze.

"So, where are the elves?" I asked, looking around. "Aren't you going to introduce me?"

"I have never seen an elf," Gypsy sadly confessed. "But they are welcome here. I leave tidbits of food for them and I have elf-doors, so they can go from room to room as they please. An elf does not like to feel confined."

If an ordinary woman had said that to me, I would have snorted in disbelief, or run for the exit. But when the Gypsy said it, I smiled in pure, boyish delight. I didn't have to look hard to see the tiny doors set into the bottom of the larger, people-sized room dividers.

"What do they eat?"

"Elves are vegetarians. But they like sweets, so I always leave some fruit and candy."

"I never realized Gypsies were into elves."

"No," she agreed, stepping further into the elf world and consequently drawing me further into her little realm. "We are not known for that. Mysticism, palm reading, stealing babies. That can be very time consuming."

She almost lulled me into that one.

"I know. Gypsies never stole babies."

She smiled. It made me want to kiss her again. Remembering her admonition, I took a step away from her. In this room, it was going to take a lot of distance to keep my mind on the work ahead of us.

"Let us say, I never knew any who stole babies. I will fix us a drink, now."

I didn't say what I wanted and she didn't inquire. I mean, why bother? She surprised me, therefore, by offering a glass of ruby-red wine. I had expected something else. Something hard and crass.

"It is Rumanian wine," she said as we sipped. She had taken it from a decanter, I noted, which she brought in with the two glasses.

"I didn't even know Rumania made wine; or grew grapes, for that matter. This is very good."

"Do you really think so?" She had an approving quality in her voice which went to my head faster than any alcohol.

"Yes."

"It is a heavy wine, and sweet. I find it quite acceptable."

"Did you drink a lot of wine as a child?" I asked, suddenly curious. It occurred to me I knew nothing about her.

"Oh, yes. But not as good as this. The best wine is saved for export. What we drank was – the euphemism is table wine, is it not?"

I nodded agreement.

Her accent was delicate, yet pronounced. In it I could hear Eastern European, British and what I presumed to be French.

"What language were you taught to speak as a child?"

She suggestively raised an eyebrow.

"Oh, all the Romance languages, Andy." I started at her use of my first name. "Or is it always Kimbo? What do you prefer? Tell me."

I shrugged and tried my patented half smile.

"Andy is fine. Mostly I'm called 'Kimbo.' Usually at the top of someone's voice."

"But what do you prefer?"

I preferred to know what my real name was. Failing in that, I didn't usually care.

"Whatever."

It came out sounding flat, not casual and uninterested.

"You have some other name? A nickname, perhaps, you are more comfortable with?"

"No."

She took my hand, squeezed it and guided me to the living room. We sat on the couch and I set my notes down on the table.

"So: tell me what you discovered. In the morgue."

"That's a newspaper term," I started to explain, then stopped, realizing she knew perfectly well to what it referred. "All right. I didn't have time to do as much digging as I planned, but I found the earliest appearance of our friend."

I showed the photostats to her, which she viewed with a great deal of curiosity and gravity.

"How very interesting. I did not know. How... pedantic." I guffawed at her expression. She looked up sharply. "I misused the word?"

"No. No," I assured her. It's just that vocabulary has gone out of common usage. I don't expect people to use words out of a dictionary."

"I have made a great effort to educate myself. I like languages; I enjoy using words. But if I use them incorrectly, mispronounce them, you must correct me."

"I will," I said and meant it. She sounded a lot like me.

"He was building up his own confidence," Gypsy continued. "I see from these that even he was uncertain how far he would, or could, go."

"I imagine he has no cause for complaint. Not after the haul he's made."

"A man like him is never satisfied. There is not enough money in the world to sate him. Not enough power," she underscored.

"Then he's a megalomaniac."

"He was not when he started. Now, however, I would have to agree with you. He is also very, very dangerous."

"What can he do? He's fled the country for parts unknown. I had the course of his flight charted," I added, suddenly remembering. "He went to France. To a small airport off the coast."

"He will not stay there. He will have made any number of shorter, or longer, flights by now. To obscure his trail. We have lost him, but you can be certain he has not lost sight of you. Tell me more."

I told her about the call I had made and how the operator knew my name without been told. That carved worry lines into her brow.

"That is bad."

"Well, it didn't make me too happy," I agreed.

"You took a cab here?" I nodded. "It was as well. We will get your car back in the morning. I will search it."

"You're a bomb expert, too?" I asked, too flippantly. She put a hand to her head.

"I shall examine in psychically. If it has been tampered with, I will know. Anyone touching it will have left an impression. The glow will still be around it."

"Oh."

"And the rest?" She was eager to have it all.

"The five men whose names we have: Morell, Tyler, Breaksmyth, Gerhusen and Young, have been going to him for years. I determined that by the sudden, successful jump in their investment portfolios. That, at least, is a matter of record, easily traced. They either bought in their own names, or in the names of their registered companies. Nothing below board, from what I gathered, although I haven't finished my investigation.

"At first, they were guided into small companies with proven track records. All five seem to have joined the private circle between 1975 and 1980. For the most part, they invested in the same companies. When they diverted from that pattern – from the names the Mystic Seer gave them, I presume – they lost money."

She gravely nodded.

"Yes. That they did on their own. It would not surprise me if our Mystic Seer saw to it those investments failed, to make these men more and more dependent upon his advice."

"Exactly what I was thinking. Over the past two years, they have been putting money in obscure companies that shot up like rockets. Our boys made their money and got out before the companies either went belly-up, or their stock fell from over-valuation. None were ever hurt in any fall. In fact, it was their sudden, unexpected divestment which sent the stocks plummeting."

"The same game the Mystic Seer eventually played on them."

"They knew the strategy. They had just become inured to fearing for themselves."

"Whom the gods destroy, they first make careless."

"Exactly."

I liked her train of thought, her expressions, the way her mind worked. We were kindred spirits. There was a comfort with her I had never experienced before, as though she were my twin sister, separated at birth, rather than a complete stranger I had met for the first time only days ago.

On second thought, she could have been my twin sister, for all I knew. That idea would not have upset me, save for one very important factor: I was falling in love with her. It was the kind of romantic feeling a man does not entertain for his sister.

The gods could not be that cruel.

I reminded myself she had black hair, blue eyes and no freckles.

I repeated to myself, "Gypsies do not steal babies." And even if they did snatch an occasional infant, I doubted it would have been from a hospital in New York.

CHAPTER 7

The room was getting stuffy. Closing in on me. I needed to get up, to pace, to work off my nervous energy.

This was no time to think about romance.

At least, not when there was a story to be written.

The world is full of pitiful priorities and this was one of them.

"All right," I said, already sick of hearing myself talk. "What do we know?" I ticked the items off on my fingers. "We know some guy named Jason Holloway, calling himself the Mystic Seer, set himself up in the stock advisement business. At least five men went to him: Morell, Tyler, Breaksmyth, Gerhusen and Young." I could name the list by rote. "Beginning in 1975, individuals in this group began taking our seer's suggestions.

"They started small. As far as we know, all the tips were hot. Our boys made money. They began investing more and more heavily in whatever our little hocus pocus man suggested." I saw Gypsy cringe at the expression, but was too wound up to stop and apologize.

"Holloway picked a handful of companies with potential, then he and his clients bought up whatever stock they could get their hands on. Others saw the trend and did the same. Result: artificially inflated prices. Just before the regulators became suspicious and suspended trading, Holloway and his clients sold out.

"OK," I continued, reasoning as I went. "In the past, the Mystic Seer advised his clients to dump stock at the same time he did, so they all made out like bandits. But not this time. This time, no one got any forewarning. He cashed in by himself, taking sole advantage of the opportunity.

"Now, let us suppose his clients had a standing 'buy' order on these stocks. As soon as Holloway lists his holdings, Morell, Tyler, Breaksmyth, Young and Gerhusen's brokers snatch them up. The brokers then inform their clients. This time, however, our bright boys wonder why such a large amount of stock has suddenly appeared on the market. They look into it. Imagine their surprise at discovering they just bought out the Mystic Seer."

"They probably try to contact him," Gypsy continued, as excited as I. "Inexplicably, they cannot reach him. Perhaps they are even told he has – packed his bags – I believe is the expression?"

I nodded confirmation.

"They panic, assuming at first they missed the 'sell' order," she continued. "They put their stock up for sale. Unfortunately for them, this gives the appearance of a run. Prices fall dramatically as everyone begins divesting. In no time, the stock is selling for pennies on the pound."

"And in less time than it takes to tell the tale, the investors are ruined. If I can prove the whole thing was a set-up from the beginning, then Mr. Mystic Seer is a wanted man. He has to stay in hiding; change his name, create a new racket somewhere else, with a new gimmick. How's that?" I concluded.

She slowly dropped her head.

"It is true, as far as it goes. But you are overlooking certain pertinent facts."

"Such as?"

"Proof." I bristled at the word. "You have to prove he set-up his clients. It is not necessarily proof to say he advised his clients to purchase stock in certain companies so he could sell his own shares at an over-valued price."

"What about calling himself a mystic seer? Promising guarantees?"

"Men have been saying they can read the mysteries contained in the stars for thousands of years."

"It looks suspicious," I said.

"I am not saying you are wrong. On the contrary, I believe you are exactly correct in your supposition. But again, you must have proof."

The back of my wrists started sweating again.

"How do I get it? I tried contacting Tyler and Gerhusen. Neither would talk to me."

"Nor do I suppose they will."

"So? Where does the proof come in?" She hesitated. "I'm all for writing a story saying the Mystic Seer lured these rich investors up to his office, sold them a bill of goods about how he can read the stars, led them on for a number of years then pulled the rug out from under them – to his sole advantage."

"Will your Mr. McGraw go with such a story?"

I only hesitated a second.

"He has to."

"Then write it. But write it as a supposition, only. State what you know. Follow the paper trail." I groaned inwardly. It wasn't her fault. I was thinking of Deep Throat and its various connotations, when my mind should have been on my work. "There is one more thing."

"Yes?" I gulped, trying not to sound like a schoolboy with a crush on his teacher.

"The Mystic Seer had a perfect track record up until last week."

"So?" I didn't see it.

"He *can* read the stars."

"Come on. Don't feed me any of that kid stuff. No one can read the stars."

"But you are wrong, Kimbo."

She didn't say it, but I head the tag line, "dead wrong," in her voice.

We had touched on this earlier and I hadn't wanted to hear it then, either.

"If he can read the stars, as you say, then he had no need to set these bozos up. Or to set himself up in business, for that matter. He checks his astrological charts, divines that XYZ Company is going to come out with a new drug which cures baldness and he buys stock the week before they announce their new discovery. The drug sells off every shelf and he's a rich man. It's legal insider trading."

"That is very true. But it overlooks two factors." I raised an eyebrow. "First, I believe he is power hungry. He likes to manipulate. He likes to hold life and death in his hand. Over the course of the nine years he worked with those five men, they have certainly come to – lick his hand? To worship him, in fact. Not in a divine sense," she hurriedly amended, "but in a worldly sense. To obtain the information they did, they must have flattered him, played up to him, bought him presents.

"That kind of admiration, from those wealthy, worldly men is irresistible to a man like Holloway. He thrives off it; it stimulates him."

"That makes sense," I agreed. I had been so set on the money aspect I had failed to look beyond it. That bothered me, because I flatter myself that I am pretty good at seeing the whole picture.

"Second," Gypsy continued, her voice assuming a harsher tone, "I do not believe he is through."

"Explain."

"It is all very well and good for the Mystic Seer to make a killing in the stock market on selected stock. It shuddered the world but it did not shatter it. Wall Street, London, Tokyo will recover. The markets will lick their wounds and go on. Investors die, others take their places.

"I believe our Seer wants to manipulate others – possibly men in different lines of work. Exciting, dynamic, powerful men. This was a test. A successful test, to be sure, but just that, no more. He has proven himself. Now, he will go further."

I pouted. No, that sounds petulant. I frowned.

"If he is a true psychic as you say he is, then why doesn't he look into the future and see the result of his actions? I mean, surely he can't succeed." She did not answer. "Can he?" I inquired in a less assured voice.

"I did not say he was perfect. I perhaps should have said he is gifted. Gifted as I am, although our powers are not exactly the same. We have different... tools. Different abilities. He may be able to look into the future at some things – to see which stocks will rise in value, to give you an example – but I doubt he can see the entire picture. No one, on their own, as far as I am aware, can do that."

"As far as you're aware?"

She hesitated, then raised an eyebrow, Kimbo-fashion.

"It would be foolish of me to state with any certainty there is no person living today who can see God's divine plan."

"Jesus," I swore. She took me at face value, although that was not my intent.

"No. Not a Second Coming. There may be persons who have vast psychic ability. Persons who do not care to share their knowledge with the world. Persons who will live and die with few, if any, knowing of their gift."

"Why?"

"They may be Tibetan monks. Or merely ordinary people who do not want to be held up to ridicule. There are many things, Andy, you do not know. And are better off for not knowing."

"That sounds like protectionism," I scoffed.

"Oh, it is," she blithely agreed.

"I don't wish to be protected."

There went that eyebrow again. If she did it once more I was either going to kiss her, or check her ears to see if they were pointed.

"If I told you now, right this minute, that you would die on a certain day, that information would necessarily change the course of your life. Do not interrupt," she warned as my mouth opened to protest. "If I said you were to win a Pulitzer prize, you would go crazy, looking for that special story to write. So crazy, in fact, there would be every probability you would overlook it in your rush."

"But if I'm to win it, then I would have to find it eventually."

"Perhaps. Perhaps not. But what would it mean to you? Would it hold the same significance? I do not think it would. It is the not knowing which enriches our lives."

"Or tortures us," I added.

"That, too."

"So, tell me my future," I demanded.

"No."

"Why not?"

"I do not know it."

"Then look in your crystal ball."

"If I could – if I told you the date – how would you confirm it? You could not. But it would prey on your mind. If you believed me, it would tempt you to do foolish things – walk out in front of a train, to prove or disprove what I predicted. If you were killed, then I would be proven wrong.

"If you survived, you might only be horribly mutilated. Remember: a date is no more than the expiration of your earthly body."

I groaned. From the heart. I saw her point, yet it annoyed me.

"Tell me something else. Something easier, less catastrophic."

"Such as?"

I hesitated. Gypsy stared into my eyes, then sighed. From the heart.

"You were going to ask me who you had your life insurance made out to. Yet, that is no more than reading your mind. That, I have already proven to some small degree, have I not?"

She was correct and I was embarrassed.

"Can you read all my thoughts?" I lamely inquired to fill in the silence.

"No. Not all. I would not care to. That would be an invasion of privacy. I do not enjoy that type of mind reading. I, too, like my surprises."

Bless her, she smiled. I colored as red as a lobster.

There were other questions on my mind but I decided that, like her, I would rather be surprised.

"All right. You win. For now," I added. "So, what should we do?"

"You should write your article. The one you came here to tell me about."

I had forgotten about that. I nodded.

"Yes. I have to do that. But it'll be incomplete."

"Then you must do a series of articles. You will know what to do as we go along. Write about the Mystic Seer – his rise to power. That much is on the record. Tie him to the five large investors. Note their past history: the stocks held in common. Establish the pattern. No one can sue CANS for putting out that story. Conclude it by stating what you know: that Jason Holloway sold all his holdings in three companies, starting a run. Detail what the losses meant to other investors. That is fact. Stop short of saying the entire episode was contrived for just that end."

Her reasoning was sound. "And then?"

"We must put our heads together. We must track our Mystic Seer. Try to discover what he will do next."

"We," I said with a smile. I liked the sound of that. "I've never had a partner before."

"Nor I," she said. I had a sneaking suspicion there was a double meaning behind those words but it escaped me. I went to work.

It was morning before I knew it, but the story was done. It was good. I mean, really good. I knew because when I reread it, a muscle in my arm began to twitch. Gypsy nodded in satisfaction.

"Get it to the office and have Mr. McGraw read it." I started to protest but she stopped me. "He must be informed of everything you do and everything you plan on doing."

That, I put my foot down on. Hard.

"You don't understand the way it is between writers and editors. A natural animosity exists between the two. If I told him I was going downstairs to buy a hamburger, for Cripe's sake, he'd have an objection!"

She gave me a long, inscrutable Gypsy look. Those of you who think Asians are the only ones who can look mysteriously passive have never met a Gypsy.

"Andy, I tell you again, what you are doing is dangerous. And you do not believe me."

I shook my head in mild protest.

"I do believe you."

"Then, it is as well for you to have someone know what you are about."

"Sweet?" I asked in some surprise. "You think Sweet would bail me out of anything? Not if he can help it," I snorted. "I think he'd prefer I was stuck in jail on a jaywalking charge than loose on the streets. Something about, 'I'm safer behind bars.'"

"You have said it and not heard yourself," she pointed out. "You are safer behind bars."

"I didn't mean 'safer' as in safer for *me.* I meant 'safer' as in safer for *him.* If I'm locked away somewhere he..." I left the "doesn't have to worry about me" part out. I was talking in circles. "Just exactly what do you want me to tell him?"

"That you have obtained information that the Mystic Seer is dangerous and that your life is in jeopardy."

"OK," I agreed. Too readily. She saw right through me.

"That you are going to follow up on several leads but you thought he should be aware this man has been the instrument of several deaths and probably will be again."

"That's my job, babe," I replied, using a crude familiarity and regretting it almost instantly. "I'm a crime reporter. People who commit crimes are often violent. It's a violent society we live in. I'm not afraid."

"The man who is not afraid gets himself killed." She said it with point blank accuracy.

"All right. I'm bragging. I've been afraid in my life. Shit ass-scared." I hesitated, debating my options. With a sigh of resignation, I nodded my head. "I'll tell him."

Good. She believed me. I had a sneaking suspicion I believed it myself. Or perhaps it was just her faith making a truthful man out of me. In either case, it was disconcerting.

I left with the story safely tucked away in my pocket, got to the office, printed it and marched into Sweet's office. He read it without bothering to audibly breathe, which, in itself, was something of a miracle. When he looked up there was a queer expression in his eyes.

Queer as in odd. I have to remember not to use that word.

"This is good, Andy. Really good. I like it." I had almost relaxed to bask in his praise. You'd think I knew better. "It almost doesn't sound like your writing at all. As though you've found God or something."

"What the hell does that mean?"

He hesitated then shrugged.

"I don't know. It's inspired. Almost poetic."

Them's fightin' words to a newspaper reporter.

"All right," I demanded. "What don't you like about it? What's wrong? Did I use too many ten dollar words? Sentences too long? Grammar incorrect? Come on. I'm a big boy. I can take it."

He rose from his chair and stared at me. I mean, he made eye contact. That was it. I was fired.

"It's wonderful. The best work you've ever done."

"Who is it who wants my hide this time? Who have I offended? How long do I have to clean out my desk?"

"I mean it, Andy. It's great stuff."

He was a sadist at heart. I always suspected it.

With a name like Sweet McGraw, how could he be otherwise? Of course, Sweet wasn't his real first name. He never used it. I knew the feeling. As long as I've known him, no one has ever called him anything else. To his face, that is.

"What's wrong with it? Has the story been killed? Is that it? Has the Mystic Seer bought CANS? He's got enough money. Lay it on me. I can take it."

Famous last words.

"I want you to start carrying this around." He handed me something which looked suspiciously like a pager. I recoiled in horror.

"What is it?"

"A pager."

I knew it.

I shook my head. I took a step back. Not because I was afraid he was going to shove the thing at me. Because I was afraid I was going to hit him with it.

"No."

"Andy, this case is getting dangerous."

My eyes slanted. Now, I got it.

"Getting dangerous, is it? So, who told you that? You sure didn't figure it out all by yourself. She called you, didn't she?"

He gave me a blank stare. Had his complexion been any darker, I could have run my fingernails down it and made a screeching sound.

"She?" he innocently inquired. He was bucking for an Academy award nomination.

"She. The Gypsy. You know. Crystal balls. Palm reading. She called you, didn't she?"

"I don't know what you're talking about."

He was another Columbo. In a different line of work. Playing dumb.

"Look, Sweet, I wasn't born yesterday." Another expression I'll have to ditch from my vocabulary. It's fine when you *were* born yesterday, but it gets stale as the years roll on. Which doesn't mean I'm long in the tooth. Not by a long shot. "She called you because she was afraid I wouldn't say anything. Fine. I get it. You're in cahoots."

"Cahoots? Andy, you sound like you're ninety years old."

If he were reading my mind, it was the end of the world as I knew it.

"I'm not wearing a pager."

"You are. New company rules."

"What company?" I knew CANS was too cheap to buy pagers for all its employees, so that had to be a lie.

"CANS. The company you work for. Remember? The company, the name of which is on top of the paycheck you receive every month?"

"CANS is issuing pagers? Why? What's the deal? Make me believe it, I dare you." The last I actually thought, rather than said. I just included it in the quotes to make me sound braver.

"Mr. Poxie's brother-in-law bought a paging company. He gave Mr. Poxie a deal. There's some incentive thing. It wasn't fully explained to me. All right. Does that satisfy you?"

It did, but the timing was suspicious.

"I'll take it." I held out my hand. Sweet placed the damned thing inside my palm. I inspected it briefly. I'm a whiz with mechanical toys. If they have an ON/OFF button, I can handle it. It was ON. I turned it OFF. "There."

Sweet's face grew red, then purple by degrees. Actually, he looks better in purple. More natural.

"Remember your blood pressure," I warned. There was nothing wrong with his blood pressure. It was a standard line. I heard it from a medical reporter. He tried to explain to me what the hell blood pressure was, and how it came to be the Silent Killer. It made John Gotti look like Little Bo Peep.

"Turn it on and leave it on. I mean it. I want you to be available if I need you."

"I thought you were giving it to me because you were worried. Now, I see you only want me to carry it so I can be at your beck and call."

He glowered at me from beneath bushy eyebrows.

His eyebrows aren't really bushy, either, but it sounds dramatic. Actually, few men can get away with bushy eyebrows these days. It makes them look out of touch. I mean, would you buy a Frigidaire from a man with hair growing over his nose? No. Would you let someone whose eyebrows meet in the middle, teach your kid math? No; you'd be too worried he'd turn into a werewolf and bay at the moon.

Personal grooming has become a science. We all have to look the same; like we just came out of makeup and were getting ready to shoot a film. Everything we wear is a costume. Hospital workers, dressed in sea-green scrubs, wander around long, empty corridors with stethoscopes slung over their shoulders because they saw an actor doing that on *Ben Casey.*

Remember Dr. Casey? He always wore his stethoscope around his neck, with the ear pieces biting into his flesh. That style chokes off blood flow to the brain but it looked manly. You never saw a nurse wearing a stethoscope around her neck like that. They were too smart. It took a neurosurgeon with eyebrows knitted in the middle to pull that off.

Richard Kimble was on the lam four years and he had a manicure to die for.

Bad choice of words. Sorry. But he got off in the end. All's well that ends well. Except for the wife, of course. She was still dead. And the One-Armed Man. He was dead, too. And Lieutenant Phillip Gerard. His life was in shatters. Then there was Gerard's kid, Kurt Russell. He graduated to science fiction movies and went on to destroy New York City, or something.

He wore an eye patch. And stubble. Imagine cute little, Walt Disneyish Kurt Russell with a stubble? That's like seeing Lassie doing his/her business in the bushes. Shatters illusions.

So Sweet didn't have hypertension and he shaved his eyebrows. That still didn't mean I was going to wear a beeper.

"What if you page me when I'm in the car? Do I get a car phone?"

Despite my disclaimer, Sweet's eyebrows did a good imitation of knitting in the middle.

"No."

"I see. The Old Man didn't get a deal on car phones. What about a walkie-talkie? Do I get one of those?"

"No."

"Then how am I supposed to respond? Attach a tin can and string to the antennae?"

"You stop and use a pay phone."

"In the middle of the highway?"

"At a petrol station."

"Who's gonna pay for the call? Can I list it on my expense account?"

He had had enough.

"When are you going to wake up and realize you're not working for the New York *Times?* You don't have an expense account. You are paid over and above what any other reporter for this wire service makes so you can deduct reasonable expenses from your salary."

"Then why do I fill out vouchers and beg you to sign them?"

"Have you ever been reimbursed for any?"

There was just a touch of curiosity in his voice.

"I'm going. I have work to do."

I slipped the beeper over my belt and stomped away. Rita waved at me as I passed. I noticed she was wearing her beeper around her neck, like a pair of reading glasses.

That made me feel a whole lot better.

Loads, even.

I went back to the Gypsy's. She wasn't at her place of business so I tried her at home. I was afraid I'd get lost in all the twists and turns but I found it, first try. Who said reporters weren't like homing pigeons?

Check that. They're extinct, aren't they? Or is that carrier pigeons?

How many Spotted Pigeons do we need, anyway?

Don't get me started.

I'd give up Ticonderoga pencils to save a tree. How many Republicans can say that?

I knocked on her door and she answered it. Seeing her took my breath away. She was wearing a sort of pants suit, of the same brown and yellow and muted blue as her flat. Earthy colors. She smiled. I smiled. We must have looked like a bunch of yellow circles with dots for eyes.

"Come in."

She saw the beeper right away.

"It's off," I explained. It was the Travis McGee thing to say. I listen to his adventures on audio tapes. Darren McGavin does all the voices. He's awesome. I paid real money for those cassettes, on the hope he'd get a few cents from the sale.

And, of course, making pirated copies is against copyright laws.

"Turn it on."

I turned it on.

"Come," she said. "I want to show you something."

I tripped over my own two feet and went sprawling into a chair. This testosterone thing has got to stop.

She led me through the living room, stopping at what, to a practiced eye, looked like a blank wall. I had a fleeting thought we were going to do isometrics together. She waved her hand, or made some quick gesture. A concealed door slid open. It must have been on rollers because I didn't hear a thing. We went inside.

I expected voodoo dolls, shrunken heads, eyes of newt and hair of toads. I was, therefore, disappointed to see nothing of the sort. Actually, the room was pretty empty, save for a small round table with a black table cloth spread over it. There were two identical chairs placed on opposite ends. If you can say that about a circle.

"Sit down," Gypsy directed. I knew instinctively which chair was hers and took the opposite. She joined me at the table, setting upon it what appeared to be a softball, covered by a black felt washcloth.

I never said I was the romantic type.

Removing the washcloth, she revealed a crystal ball. I felt my cheeks grow hot. Not from too much hormone, this time.

"Come on," I said. "Not a crystal ball. I was just kidding you before, when I accused you of consulting one."

She was nonplused. "It is very old. Timeless. It has been entrusted to me for as long as I need it. It is not actually a 'crystal ball,'" she added. "But you may refer to it that way if you wish. You will not offend it's feelings."

"Offend it's feelings?"

"It is alive."

"Oh."

God, why do I always fall for the odd ones? A living crystal ball. (Which explains, of course, why I put an apostrophe in "it's.") It figures. To confess, I was ready to get up and leave.

Bite the bullet.

You get the picture.

"I know you do not believe." A good bit of clairvoyance there. I was feeling bitter and vindictive. "I would not show you this, but I believe we can obtain information we need about the Mystic Seer."

"You mean your ball talks to his ball?"

I didn't care how that sounded, although in the expression of it, I did feel a tinge of jealousy.

"Oh, no." Straight. "He does not have a crystal ball. At least not a real one."

"Oh, good. Are we going to hold hands and start chanting?" Here was where the dead Indian guide came in.

Without bothering to reply, Gypsy ran her left hand over the glass softball d/b/a a crystal ball. Immediately images appeared. She peered into it. I peered into it. It seemed the right thing to do. I'd take her to the best shrink I could find.

Even if she wasn't covered on my medical plan.

I had it bad.

"Do you recognize what you are seeing?"

I played along. Looked. Then looked again.

"That's the Mystic Seer's London office."

"Yes. Look closer."

If I got any nearer, I'd kiss her and forget the Pulitzer Prize.

"That's inside the office?"

"Yes. Just as he left it. But he did not have time to take everything with him. Perhaps because he did not see the need. Perhaps because he thought he would come back. He may," she added. "We must be alert for that possibility."

"I hope he does."

"I hope he does not." She talked to the crystal ball. "Can you show us if there are any papers; anything incriminating?"

The scene changed. Not like watching a film. Just dissolved into another room.

Gypsy nodded and looked up. The crystal softball went dark.

"What did it say?" I asked. Not exactly convinced.

"There are papers; some sort of a small book. They will help you." She closed her eyes as if replaying what she had seen in her mind. I looked from her face to the softball, then back. Whatever she was reading, I wasn't getting it.

The price you pay for being an Infidel.

"If you go now, you may be able to get in. There is a numbered lock on the door. 22-12-22." I never liked the number twenty-two. I'm not the only one who feels that way. That number pops up in all the oddest places. Like *The Twilight Zone* on the door to the morgue. It always portends bad luck.

"All right."

"Go past the reception area, into the third office on the left. There is another combination. 12-22-12."

"Original."

She ignored me. I clamped my teeth together.

"In the desk. There is a hidden compartment. I cannot see it clearly but I know it is there. Find it. Remove the papers."

"What'll I do with them?"

She hesitated, clearly torn.

"You had better bring them back here. Not to my place of work. That is not well guarded." Apparently she didn't have enough trolls to go around.

"Not trolls," she said. Me and my big mind. "Sprites. They are very rare."

"Oh."

I thought Sprite was a soft drink. I didn't say so.

"Bring the papers here."

"What will they tell us?" As if I believed all this.

"I cannot see them clearly."

She had said that.

"I'm sorry."

"Kimbo, you must believe. You must not take this lightly."

"What if his place is guarded by sprites?"

My joke, if joke it was, fell flat.

"Then you will not get in."

I stifled a yawn. Heroes never yawn in the cinema. I was embarrassed.

"I'll go."

"You will come directly back here?"

With rings on my fingers and bells on my toes.

"Yes."

"Then go. Now."

"Why couldn't I have gotten them before?"

"The time was not right."

The stars were out of alignment.

"Is it safe to take my car?" I asked before remembering I had driven it this morning.

"Yes. Do not tarry. You are tired. Being tired makes a man careless."

"Will you come with me?"

At this point, I would let her drive. What greater privilege can a man give a woman?

"The next time. By then, he will know I am working with you."

"How?"

"It will be in your mind. By your actions."

"But how will he know?"

She opted for a three-dimensional answer. One I could relate to.

"Because you will write another news article. With proof of his complicity."

My pupils went to pinpoints. I had never really given upon the Pulitzer.

"I'll be back."

"I would rather have you be Kimbo."

She was making a funny. Jesus, I was in love with this woman. Even if she did keep sprites and talk to softballs.

Love can make a man believe anything.

More poetry.

Sweet was right.

Now, there was a galling thought. Enough to keep me awake all the way to "Mystic Towers."

CHAPTER 8

I managed to bypass morning rush hour, which had its pros and cons. The traffic was one degree lighter than it would have been, had I been out and about an hour earlier, but there wasn't an affordable parking space within two light years of the business complex in which I had an interest.

The truth be told, what Europe really needs is a deal between nations. Something like borders without passports because so many Europeans have to park in other countries, then walk to the office. It's such a waste of time to keep getting that little book stamped.

I was on a high, so I dug into my expense account (at least, I *thought* I had an expense account), opting to park in the underground lot beneath Mystic Towers.

Did I say underground? Subterranean is more like it. I started looking around for Dante as I descended, level after level. It was almost worth it, though. There was the Queen's Level, the Duke's Level, the Prince of Wales Level (someone had spray-painted an "h" in the word. I'll leave it to you to figure out where it goes.)

There was a King George VI level and a King Edward VIII level beneath. That designation was painted over, but still legible. It had been renamed in graffiti the Wallis Level.

By the time I was down into the Marquis and Earl Levels, I had lost "count."

I parked in a space marked "Commoner."

I got a nose bleed going up on the lift.

I finally arrived in the main lobby, waited until the vertigo passed, then pushed number three. This time, the elevator door opened. I found myself facing the locked and shuttered doors of the Mystic Seer's office. His name wasn't on the door; just a pentagram. Using the combination with which Gypsy supplied me, I was admitted. A silly smile spread across my face.

As a reporter, I always knew I had a natural affinity for the cat burglar trade.

Call it an upgrade.

The room was empty. None of the overhead lights were lit. That made me figure the management of the office building paid the utilities. I couldn't see Joe Mystic putting the cat out and unplugging the night lights.

That was not only plebeian, it was penny-pinching. A guy who had just made a kabillion pounds on the stock market didn't have to worry about ounces.

It would also make it look as though he weren't coming back. As though he were afraid. The palm reading/astrological-chart set wouldn't appreciate knowing the Big Bang was scared.

I switched on the lights then held my breath, waiting for alarms to sound. They didn't. The room was washed with incandescent lighting. The yellowish kind which makes everyone look as though they have jaundice and you have to hold your copy of *National Geographic* close to be able to read the captions.

The front room was obviously the secretary's domain. A small antechamber to the left was a waiting room. I peered over – no magazines. No newspapers. I glared up, half expecting to see a depiction of the zodiac chart painted on the ceiling. Nothing doing.

I don't know whether I was disappointed or relieved.

I repeat. I-am-not-a-believer. What I do hold to be self-evident is that no one can foretell the future. No one. The future hasn't been written yet. If it ain't in the can, no one knows how the film ends. Not even the Great Director in the Sky.

They call that free will.

Figuring the Mystic Seer wouldn't put anything of significance in his secretary's *desk,* I bypassed it and went into the hall. Following Gypsy's instructions, I walked down the corridor, entered the second combination on the third door to the left and let myself in. This was the Think Tank, where it all happened. There was a whiff of Chateau Latour in the air. Don't ask me the year; I think I picked up the name of the vineyard from John Steed. He was talking to Mrs. Peel and she already knew the proper vintage.

Secret agents make more money than schmos. They are also extremely sophisticated.

I'll let you make your own judgments about "talented amateurs."

Before I came to England, my entire working knowledge about the country came from *The Avengers.* Imagine my surprise.

I would have had it otherwise.

The Mystic Seer's office was leather and brass. Just kidding. It was decorated in what I suppose would be referred to as "psychic chic." Very modern, clean, almost austere. Not comfortable; functional would be a better word. But very, very expensive looking.

I bet the executive washroom had gold taps on the flush handle.

I didn't stick my head in to look. In fact, I didn't see one.

Don't drink the wine.

Crossing to the desk, which occupied fully one half of the room, I pulled back the master's chair to have access to the drawers. Gypsy said what I wanted would be hidden here. I didn't doubt it. Just looking at the thing gave me the willies.

I tried the top center drawer. Locked. I tried the drawers on the right, just to be contrary. They all opened at a touch. There was nothing in them but a tin of Altoids in the middle one. I think if a cobra's head had leapt out at me, I couldn't have been more surprised.

The Mystic Seer had halitosis? Dry mouth? A taste for peppermint?

Maybe it was the "unusually strong" which appealed to him. I bet he sucked on two at a time.

God bless Madison Avenue.

The mints may be two hundred years old, but some bright boy put it on a billboard in Times Square and made it a household phrase.

Now, even cinema stars were demanding them as part of their perks package.

I'm a butter rum Lifesavers man, myself.

That's because when I was a kid, that's the one flavor no one else picked. I always had last choice.

No problem. At least no one ever steals them out of your pocket. It also lets me get away with calling myself a rummy when I'm down in the dumps, or trying to impress my date.

The top drawer on the left was locked but those below it were accessible and empty. That drew my attention back to the top one. I jiggled the knob. My hand was trembling so badly, I left sweat marks on it. On impulse I pulled out my handkerchief and wiped it clean. It was only then I realized I had left my fingerprints all over the place. I tried to console myself by remembering it wasn't the cops I was worried about, it was leaving *psychic imprints* around the place.

I pulled harder in case it was just stuck. Same result. I muttered an unkind expression about the Mystic Seer's ancestry.

I pulled the chair back further, finally giving it a vicious shove to get it out of my way. The springs groaned. It was not used to such unkind treatment.

I hoped it would go to Sotheby's and be auctioned off to a dentist.

Squatting under the desk, I felt around for a hidden panel, a trip switch, an indentation anywhere which might indicate a hidden compartment. Failing in that, I removed my trusty Eveready pocket torch (penlight, to you) and directed it around the metal casing. Nothing obvious.

I stood back, took in the dimensions of the desk, make some mental calculations and got back down on my haunches. I started tapping.

"Say 'ah'," I quipped.

The desk was obviously unused to obeying orders.

Unable to detect any unnatural or unexpected hollow sounds, I resorted to the tried and true. I balled up my fist and pounded. Last resort would be to kick it.

Nothing.

I stood back up, looked around the room and tried to put myself in Mr. Holloway's place. He was a man, like any other. No more clever than most of us, I flattered myself. Asking how *I* would conceal a drawer, an idea hit me. I replaced the chair into position, sat in it, then pulled up close to the desk. Stretched out my legs and felt around.

I wasn't wearing Italian leather, hand-stitched, custom-fit shoes, but I detected the button with my toe. It was concealed in the shag rug. Depressing it without excessive pressure, I had the satisfaction of hearing the gentle whir of a mechanical device. It was not that of a drawer opening, but the sliding back of a tiny panel.

The secret drawer held a tiny ledger and a hefty sum of cash neatly tucked inside.

My first thought, IRS forgive me, was that if I kept the money, it was all tax-free.

I knew I wouldn't keep it but it's the thought which counts. Reporters are all born thieves. The problem is, we're honest thieves.

The material was small enough to fit inside the pockets of my jacket. That was a relief, as I didn't want to be seen carrying notebooks out of an office I had no right to be in, in the first place.

After emptying the drawer, I tidied the room and replaced the chair exactly where I found it. Since early training tells and thus not insensitive to the fingerprint issue, I wiped all the places I remembered touching with my almost clean handkerchief.

The only reason I carry a handkerchief, by the way, is to swash my windscreen in case of wiper breakdown.

With a smugness I had not felt in a long time, I walked demurely to the door of the office, then turned to survey what had become, temporarily at least, my kingdom. It was a good feeling. I was master of all I saw. If the Mystic Seer himself had come through the door at that moment, I would have stared him in the eyes, decorated my face with a lucky Irish grin and asked if he had come for a palm reading, or a phrenology analysis.

I once offered to read the bumps on an editor's head, and was lucky to come away with my own intact. But, hope springs eternal.

"Not interested in the past or the present, Jason?" I inquired of the imaginary Mr. Holloway. "A pity. What about your future? I see numbers." I placed a hand to my forehead in melodramatic style and pretended to "see" a vision. "7-6-0-8-1-6-3." I did not have to explain where I conjured that sequence. Being a mystic himself, Jason could envision them below his face. He would be wearing prison stripes, and have his hair razored into a buzz cut.

"You've got me, Kimbo," he admitted. "Sheer downright determination and luck."

"Don't forget to add brilliant detective work and exemplary writing," I reminded him.

Just as I waited for Jason to 'fess up and admit I was a genius, a loud, ear-shattering noise exploded in my immediate vicinity. My head jerked back, muscles tense, heart doing a mad drumbeat in my chest.

"Son of a crap game!" I swore. If I hadn't been so cock-sure of myself, I would have been out of this damned office and safe. Now I was caught red-handed.

I closed my eyes and waited for the bullet to come crashing into my skull. Not even in the bloody country six months and already dead.

They don't bury commoners in England any more. No room. Not unless I was encased in cement and deposited under a high-rise. It's cremation for me. And I'll never have gotten my apartment in St. Louis out of quarantine.

No shot rang out; no demoniacal laughter ushered me on my way to the Great Typewriter in the Sky. Not even a "Whadda ya doin' in here, gov?"

The noise ceased. My pulse slowed. I began breathing again. I dared open my eyes a crack. Then a quarter inch, then half way. Nothing.

I swallowed my courage, which had risen to my mouth and tasted like bile. The room was as still as a tomb.

I was just convincing myself to try out my peripheral vision when a single BEEP sounded. Seeing as how my nerves were already jangled, I did not even flinch. I waited. There was a second BEEP.

Realization washed over me like Niagara Falls. With a shriek of anger and humiliation (not in that order), my hands regained their mobility. Dropping immediately to my belt, they tore off the pager Sweet had given me. Staring at it in stark disbelief, I realized what had happened. Someone, some evil genius, had beeped me. My three-alarm fright had been no more than a common, ordinary pager going off.

My shoulders sagged and I leaned against the door frame for support. Some hero. Imagine what would have happened if I had heard a toilet flush.

I stared numbly at the number. It took me a moment to place it. When I did – and there could be no great surprise, for only one person had the beeper number – I want into a paroxysm of cursing.

"Sweet" was the only distinguishable word. Mr. Sweet McGraw had paged me.

No doubt to see if the pager was working. In business, they call that a beeper check. What I called it would burn the sulphur off Satan's trident.

There was only one thing to do; the only option left me. I turned it off. I knew Sweet would understand. I was on assignment, deep within enemy territory. I dared not use the phone. It would leave fingerprints. Even he could fathom that excuse.

Replacing the pager on my belt, I scurried out of the room like a drowned rat. Gone was my smug attitude, my flippant interrogative with an imaginary Seer. I had too many real demons to worry about.

I did remember to shut the door, leaving everything the way I found it. Moving down the corridor in a semi-dignified trot, I passed the secretary's desk without a side glance. I paused at the front entrance only long enough to ascertain the Macy's Day Parade was not passing by outside, then made my exit. After a brief pit stop in the loo to rally the troops, I made it to the parking garage in one piece.

I tried laughing at myself as I trotted down the nine thousand, six hundred and thirty-nine steps to the Commoners Level. My chortles more closely resembled choking noises. By the time I had descended fourteen hundred steps, I was too winded to keep up the facade. Breathing was more important than humor, I reminded myself.

It had rained motor vehicles by the time I made it to the bottom. Not a parking space was left unfulfilled. I did not have the faintest idea where I parked my car. The thought occurred to me to sit and wait until quitting time, when hordes of office workers would come and claim their prizes, but I was too agitated. That left me the option of searching for it.

Nothing makes a man feel more helpless than having lost his "motor" in a "car park." I wandered aimlessly, probably passing it a dozen times before finally spotting it a half league off. Nothing could have looked more beautiful. I hopped, skipped, then ran toward it, arms extended for a lover's embrace. It was all I could do to forego a kiss before opening the unlocked door and sliding into its familiar seat.

I attempted to insert the key into the ignition. It did not fit. I tried again. No go. Squaring my shoulders, I tried force. The key went in a fraction, then stubbornly refused to budge. It was the Mystic Seer; he had hexed my car; changed the ignition. Or perhaps the key had really gone into the ignition and I was too flummoxed to realize it. I made myself listen. No sound. No roar of engine, no comforting tremble of inexpensive metal vibrating under the two-cylinder motor.

"What's going on here?" I demanded. No one answered. I looked around the interior of the car, then started a series of incoherent babblings. No wonder the key wouldn't fit. I was in the wrong car. This one was a look-alike, one of several thousand which had come off the assembly line as carbon copies. I got out and took another look. Rust spots in exactly the same places. Dents, dings and unpainted parts where the sprayer had missed, exactly as my car.

"I will never think bad thoughts about G.M. again," I promised. At least General Motors' vehicles rusted in different spots.

With a sigh of resignation, I trudged back out into the temporary interment ground for lost and displaced vehicles. I started again, walking up one aisle, then down the next. I lost count of all the identical Czech vehicles. I was so desperate for a separate identity, I almost decided on an

Arch decal for the back window or a bright orange ball for the tip of the antenna.

When I found my motor, I was too tired to sing any hallelujahs. I merely slipped inside, carefully shut the door (slamming often resulted in dislocation, like a jaw), and inserted the key. Second best to an obscene dream was implanting that key into the ignition, having it turn the engine over and listening to it roar with power. That was just about the greatest feeling in the world.

I meant to look at the papers lifted from the Mystic Seer's office but I was too wired to bother. Merging into the flow of traffic, I settled for a nice, easy, in-and-out drive back to the Gypsy's. She had warned me not to go to her place of business, so I didn't bother dropping by to see if she were working.

Instead, I parked as near her building as possible, then scampered over to her flat. Up the stairs with a song in my heart and titillation in my breast (that is how it goes, isn't it?), I rapped on the door. When she didn't answer immediately I nearly died of inflation.

I knocked again, then a third time. By then, I was really scared. "Shitless" is the street expression which, of course, being an educated man, I do not use.

I began pounding on the door, banging, kicking the bottom.

"Gypsy! Gypsy! Open up!" I corrected that hurriedly. "Gypsy, it's me. Kimbo."

The bastard had gotten her. While I was wandering through the murky levels of British aristocracy, the Mystic Seer had come and dragged her away. Or, murdered her. How could I have been so thoughtless, so careless? So crass?

Setting my jaw in a classic "I hate the world" pose (which, I am told, I do very well), I threw my shoulder against the door. Unfortunately for me, at that exact moment, the door opened. Doing a stand-in's imitation of Superman flying without the special effects, I hurtled through the opening and into the flat. Bouncing off some obscure piece of furniture I did not remember being there, I crumpled like an empty Coke can and fell flat on my face.

Other parts of my anatomy were not quite so fortunate. Those were screwed through the carpet and into the wooden floor beneath.

"Kimbo!" It was Gypsy's voice. Relief flooded over me like a White Rain commercial. She was alive and capable of speech. My gratitude knew no bounds. All was right with the world. No matter what fiend had come, I would save her. I was born for this moment.

Like a wild man I scrambled to my feet, eyes blazing, lips curled back in a defiant snarl, fists clenched. I located her, standing several feet away, restrained by powerful arms. Adrenaline surged through my frame.

"Step aside and face me like a man!" I screamed, totally oblivious to what the neighbors would think. At times like these, you are aware of all the blaring television sets, the walls rattling from Ghetto blasters and the arguments over what Aunt Matilda's husband's cousin is named, coming from neighboring flats. You are equally cognizant everyone, from the basement to the penthouse can hear every word you're saying.

I threw consideration to the wind. Let these toadies complain to the apartment manager. What could he do that hadn't already been done?

The monster did not release his grip on my Gypsy. Nor could I see his face, for she stood in front of him, blocking my view. It did not matter. I would slay him like the subhuman creature he was.

I didn't know how right I was. About his being a Neanderthal, that is.

As I surged forward, wishing for no more than the chance to wrap my fingers around his slimy throat, Gypsy moved. The arms fell away from her like butter melting over flapjacks. I met the stranger, eye to eye. And then he spoke. My whole world fell apart.

"Kimbo, where the hell have you been?"

It was Sweet.

"You!" I managed to articulate as my world grew dark. "What are you doing here?"

"Drinking coffee," Gypsy replied. There was a thoughtful timbre to her voice I did not appreciate.

"Drinking my coffee?" I sputtered.

"Oh, no," Gypsy perked up. "I did not make him your special blend."

"But it was very good, Andy," Sweet said. I hated him to the roots of my toenails.

"I'm going to kill you," I promised. "If you harmed her –"

"Harmed her?" he demanded with an incredulity I found highly offensive. "I came here looking for you."

"Looking for me?" Sunspots exploded behind my eyes.

"When you didn't answer your beep, I thought you might be in trouble. I went through your story notes. On your desk," he added, no doubt trying to reassure me he had not read my mind. I was immeasurably relieved.

"You went through my desk?" It was meant as a lion's roar, but came out as kitten's purr.

"To try and get a lead on where you might be. I found this address. There was no phone number," he darkly added, as though the omission were my fault, done on purpose. "I drove over here. And what did I find but a very charming young woman."

I turned to Gypsy. "Why did you let him in?" I demanded.

"He said he was your boss. I did not want to get you in trouble."

"Too late." I'm not sure which of us said it: Sweet or me. Didn't make any difference.

"I explained to him you were out doing... leg work." The ocean roared in my ears. "I told him you were all right, but he insisted on staying. I saw no harm."

"You-saw-no-harm?"

"No." She smiled. I closed my eyes. "I had read in your thoughts –"

I interrupted fast.

"I got the page, Sweet," I said, turning to him. I had never noticed how broad his shoulders were, or how handsome he was. Perhaps I have never seen him in the light before. Newsrooms are notoriously dark.

That's because we all work under cover.

It's a form of self-delusion. Also cheaper.

I wasn't jealous, mind you. Not a wit. Nary an iota. So, he had broad shoulders. I could make a pun here, but I won't. It's neither the time nor the place. It would also be off-color and I didn't want present company to read my mind.

She giggled. Too late. That's the story of my life.

I had to work quickly to repair the damage.

"I wasn't near a phone. How am I supposed to answer the page? Shout from the roof tops?"

"I waited," he explained. His words were silky smooth. Calm. Poised.

What a lie.

"I got nervous," he continued.

"He was nervous," Gypsy echoed. She had bitten his story, hook, line and sinker. "So he came here, looking for you. It was sweet of him."

"Yeah," I agreed. "That's how he got his name. Sweet McGraw. Ain't it swell." I nearly gagged on the word. This was hardly the scenario I envisioned. "Well, I'm here now, so you can leave," I pronounced, determined to be stalwart.

"I invited him for dinner," she supplied.

"Oh, no. He's not staying. He has an engagement elsewhere."

"No, I don't." He was smiling. I never noticed how white his teeth were. What right had he to white teeth? He drank as much coffee as I did and was known, on state occasions, like Garbage Day, to smoke a cigar or two. His teeth should be yellow, stained, like mine.

"What good news hound has white teeth?" I demanded before realizing I was thinking out loud.

He was nonplused.

"Andy, you know I always take good care of myself. Something I have urged you to do for years. Take some pride in your appearance. Take a shower now and then; go to a barber and get your hair trimmed instead of cutting it yourself. Buy a new suit of clothes."

I wanted to get *out* of my clothes, not *into* a new wardrobe. Why was he talking such gibberish?

"I was telling the Gypsy before you arrived –"

"I don't want to hear it!" I put my hands to my ears. "The Gypsy," was it? He was on such familiar terms he was allowed to call her "the Gypsy"?

"Get o-u-t," I spelled. Then clarified, "Get out." He was an editor, after all, and had forgotten all he learned in journalism school.

"He was telling me all about himself," Gypsy explained. Why was she being so damned helpful? "I promised to read his palm."

"Oh, good."

It came out as flat as I had become.

"She was very impressed with my life story," Sweet smirked.

"And then you reached puberty and changed the subject," I jeered.

He stiffened. I hated him with every fiber in my limp body.

"I paged you and you didn't answer. It's part of my responsibility to look after you."

"I'm not your son." That came out more bitter than I expected. He looked hurt. "I'm only an employee. Just a hack writer. A dime a dozen. Didn't you say that to me just last week?"

He sadly shook his head.

"No, Andy. I didn't. I haven't said that to you in at least six months. You're losing track."

Going, going, gone.

I reached out a shaking hand, patted him on the back in a fatherly sort of way and ushered him toward the door.

"Thank you. I'll remember you in my will. Now, I have work to do. You'll have to leave us alone."

"I can help," he said conspiratorially.

"No. You can't. This is something only I can do."

"Oh." He nodded wisely. "Well, Gypsy, if Andy needs to be alone, you and I can go out for dinner. I found this great little fish and chips place. All the locals go there. You can get seconds for free if you know the waiter."

"Really?"

I don't know whether it was I or Gypsy who spoke. It was a moot point. I was up Moot Creek without a paddle.

"I need her." Badly. "I need to work on her." I grinned foolishly. "Need to work with her. Understand?" I winked.

"Something in your eye, Andy?" she inquired with genuine concern.

"No. I was flirting with Sweet."

It was meant as a joke. I was the only one who laughed.

"If you two would like to be alone, I can –"

"He's leaving. He's double parked. The Old Man will never reimburse him for that out-of-pocket expense. It'll set his retirement back two years."

I grabbed Sweet by the lapels of his tailor-stitched suit and dragged him to the door.

"Be careful with that," he warned. "I paid two hundred pounds for this suit. It's made of Italian silk."

Which came close to plunging me into Italian ice.

"It needs pressing. Now. Right away. You know, Sweet. Silk is a living thing. Let a wrinkle set in and it grows crow's feet. Pretty soon, it's aged beyond recognition."

"The tailor didn't tell me that," he protested. There was a thread of doubt in his voice. It gave me new hope.

"Go right away. There's a tailor's right down the street. I saw it as I drove up. Specializes in wrinkle removing. He's cheap, too."

"Maybe I better go see him," Sweet debated with himself.

"God, yes. He has this new aloe vera spray. It does wonders. Try some on your face while you're at it. Amway makes it. I know the chemist. Very brilliant. Has six dozens patents to her name."

His hand went immediately to his cheek.

"I don't have any wrinkles."

"Go find a mirror. There aren't any in the flat. Gypsies hate mirrors. They can't see their reflections in the glass."

Gypsy laughed. "That's vampires," she corrected. Too late to save McGraw. I had him out the door.

"Hurry, Sweet. That tailor has a sale going on. It only lasts another half an hour."

He was in the landing. I shut the door and braced my shoulder against it. It was not until I heard him thumping away that I dared breathe again.

"There is no tailor down the street, you know, Andy."

"I know. And you know. But it will take Sweet an hour and a half to realize it. By that time, we won't hear him when he comes back and knocks on the door."

I held out my arms and she came to me, gliding across the floor like a pull toy. I embraced her, pressed my lips to hers and kissed her. I held her close, madly restraining my impulse to tear our clothes off right there in the middle of the floor.

"Gypsy," I mumbled, half delirious. "I never thought I'd get you alone."

I withdrew my face, stared into her eyes. They were heavy; fraught with significance.

"Here we are."

We kissed again, with rising passion. My hand played with her hair, looping a finger around one of her locks, then tugging on it. She responded by running her free hand down my back. My leg began to shake in anticipation. Locked in a tight embrace, my condition could not have been lost on her.

"Gypsy. Gypsy." I repeated her name over and over. My world had come down to her body next to mine. It was the best trade I had ever made.

Taking my hand, she led me into her bedroom. It was a small room, carefully decorated in the same earth tones as the rest of the flat. I had eyes only for her. I had no more than a psychic awareness of her bed. That it existed was good enough for me.

We sat down together, still locked in one other's arms. I kissed her neck, then brought my head lower, kissing her breasts through the blouse. I unfastened the top two buttons, revealing warm flesh.

Even I could predict the future now. I undid a third button, then inhaled deeply through my nose, implanting her scent in my soul. I was slipping the fabric over her shoulder when she whispered in my ear.

"There is something you should know, Andy."

"Tell me," I answered in a husky voice.

"It is, perhaps, of no importance."

"Anything." My lungs were working fast and hard.

"I am a virgin."

I swooned dead away.

CHAPTER 9

I woke up. The world, as I knew it, was apparently unchanged.

The Great Lie.

Gypsy was standing over me, a look of anguished concern on her face. I knew she was reading my mind.

"Andy!" she cried upon seeing my eyes flutter open. "Are you all right?"

I tried a weak smile, then a hearty laugh. It came off sounding rather ghoulish.

"Oh, fine, fine."

"Do you do this often?"

"I try not to."

"Good." She sounded relieved. She could *not* have been reading my mind. "Let me give you a hand up."

I took it. After all, I had already compromised myself by fainting. Let me rephrase that: I had already made a damned ass out of myself. What did I have to lose but my virginity?

Bad joke.

"You were kidding, right?" I asked as she helped me to my feet. I was unsteady.

"About what?"

"About your... you know." I was drowning.

"Oh!" She brightened. I smiled. "No." I frowned. "Does it matter?" Innocent. I felt death encroaching.

"Yes," I eked out. "Very much."

She took my hands and squeezed them gently. I could see she did not understand.

"I do not understand," she said.

Any more of this and I'd be the Mystic Seer.

"Gypsy –"

"Yes?"

"Gypsy –" She was not going to make this easy. I thought this act was a put on, that she was pulling my *leg,* but by analyzing the sickening feeling in the pit of my stomach, I knew she wasn't.

Why me?

"Andy," she tried as she saw my obvious predicament. My mental one, not my physical one. "You must not let it bother you. It does not bother me."

"That makes one of us."

"I mean it. I am perfectly willing to go to bed with you."

I broke out into a sweat. I was either extremely aroused or having a heart attack.

"You can't. I mean, you shouldn't." And then more forcefully, "Why are you still a virgin?"

"I have been waiting for the right man. You, Kimbo, are the right man."

That sounded a lot like a marriage proposal, albeit in reverse, to me. It was the male who was supposed to make those kinds of noises, not the female.

"No," I protested. "I don't think I am. I mean, how can I be? I'm nothing but a hack reporter, while you're... beautiful. A Gypsy with a Gift," I hastily added.

"And as such, I am free to pick and choose as I please. I pick you."

"For what?" I suspiciously demanded.

"For bed." Her smile widened. My stomach tightened. If my intestines grew any more knots they'd turn into a Chinese puzzle.

"Gypsy, I can't sleep with a virgin."

"Who said anything about sleep?" She did not mean the question to be taken humorously. I wanted to take it with two aspirin and lie down.

"Gypsy." I tried to be reasonable. Avuncular, even. I met her gaze. She was unflinching. Ready for the firing squad. "If you are a virgin, then there is a perfectly good reason why you are one. I'm sure your people have a gypsy king, or something all picked out for you. Surely he will be displeased to find out his bride has played the field before his wedding night."

She giggled.

"Gypsies have no kings."

"Call him what you will."

"You did not take my meaning, perhaps. I am not royalty by divine right or blood. I am set apart from others by my skills. As such, I am free from any rules. I am yours. I like you," she added, without a trace of feminine guile or shyness.

"I like you, too," I hastened to reassure her. "A lot." That sounded too forceful. "But... there are considerations."

"Oh," she replied wisely. I thought she was subscribing to the program.

Wrong.

"You are worried you might hurt me."

"That... and other things." She waited patiently.

"Like..." Like what?

My mind was frozen. And then I remembered. Perhaps it was the nearness of her body heat which thawed me. "Birth control!" I blurted.

"Do not worry about that."

"You're taking the pill?"

She looked at me as though I had just swallowed a frog in front of her eyes. A live, wiggling, green amphibian. With warts.

"No. But I am not concerned about having a baby."

"Why not?"

"We would make a beautiful child. A special child. One who would inherit my psychic talent and your writing ability. With red hair," she added. Perhaps she thought that would change the tide in her direction.

Two moons couldn't have done that.

On the other hand, my testosterone wasn't helping matters any.

"I don't want to be a father. I don't want to make a child out of wedlock." It sounded oddly old fashioned coming out of my lips. I had never been squeamish before. To be honest, I had never given the consideration much thought. Like most men, I always assumed the problem of fertility belonged to the woman. Remembering past dalliances now, I felt unclean.

"You do not want to go to bed with me?" She sounded hurt. My blood pressure rose faster than an Apollo spaceship. And just as dangerously.

"I do. But –" I helplessly threw up my hands. She waited. There was no help for it. "I'll have to wear a condom."

"All right."

"I don't have one."

It was not in my field kit. I carried pens, paper, a notebook with emergency numbers, assorted change, a pocketknife, handkerchief, identification, and a photo of Sweet's niece and nephew in my wallet. I had my press card, a ticket for a free oil change after paying for ten full-service visits to the Oil Slick Garage in San Luis Obispo, and my Social Security card, signed so long ago I couldn't duplicate the signature if I tried. I did not have any condoms. Nor had I ever carried condoms.

I had used a few for water balloons while in college, but had never actually enjoyed the full flower of a lady while wearing one.

You might say, I was a condom virgin.

The laughter in my throat almost choked me.

"Where can we get one?" she asked.

"Anywhere, I suppose," I lamely answered. I was wondering the same thing myself.

"Then I will go out any buy one."

"You might as well buy ten while you're at it."

"All right," she happily agreed. I knew, then, I was hallucinating. If I didn't get help soon, it would turn into a wet dream.

"You can't buy condoms for me."

"Why not?"

"You don't know what size to buy."

"I will buy extra-large, humungous. With polka dots. Daiquiri flavored."

"I'm afraid I couldn't live up to that billing." It was meant as a joke.

"Super, extra-large, stupendous."

"Well, I think large would do," I humbly demurred.

This time she guffawed. I was insulted.

"What's so funny?"

I may not have been "extra-large, stupendous," but I was hardly a peewee. At least I flattered myself I wasn't. I had never had any complaints in the size department before.

"Condoms are all the same size," she explained. I wondered why I was seeing polka dots before my eyes. "They come in different sizes," she explained, "but that is just vanity. In actuality, one size fits all."

"Like pantyhose," I gibberished.

"No," Gypsy corrected, as though I were a schoolboy. "Women's bodies come in different sizes, so pantyhose must be made to fit accordingly. But men come in one basic size."

"Super, extra-large, stupendous?"

"That is what men think," she happily agreed. "There is not a male born who would willingly buy a 'small, or a 'medium-size' condom, so why market any? All men like to think of themselves as large, super, Jolly Green Giant size, so that is what condom companies put on the package.

"If a man were to try on a condom marked 'small,' he would feel constricted. Blood cut off from his male organ would pool in his brain and he would not be able to function. But if that same condom were labeled 'XXXX Large, Super Stud,' he would do just fine."

"You're making this up," I protested. My world was growing smaller by the second. Pretty soon it would be the size of an unsalable condom.

She shook her head.

"I never make things up." Coming from a woman who made her living reading palms, that sounded fishy.

"Swear to God." Next I'd be asking her to cross her heart. Which had nothing whatsoever to do with bras.

"I swear."

"How do you know this? Did you divine it?" My eyes narrowed. It was a slim hope, at best.

"A man who sold condoms for a living told me. He worked for his father-in-law and filled vending machines. He gave up a very lucrative practice selling cardiology equipment to go into the condom business. We had a good laugh together."

"I just bet you did."

That guy, whoever he was, was a rat. I hoped all his vending machines spit out ten pound notes.

Some secrets were better off kept to oneself.

"Shall I go out and buy you some?"

"No," I miserably muttered. "I'll go."

"Will it make you feel any better to know the current market trend is to sell condoms without sizes?"

I thought that sort of stripped away the fun. Or, was that the self-delusion?

I went. Standing in the corner would have been preferable, but it was my manly duty and I dared not shirk it. I couldn't "bare" the thought of wearing a polka dot condom.

There was a chemist's open on the corner. I slipped inside. The clerk gave me a dark look. No doubt he suspected me of contemplating robbery. I suppose it was the guilty air which hung over my head, like a miasma. I went down the aisle where they sold shaving articles and deodorant. Manly items. No condoms.

I was beginning to feel giddy. I crisscrossed the store, reduced to searching the breakfast food aisle in vain, before finally succumbing to the shame of having to ask. I was pointed in the right direction. It was worse than I imagined.

I had to shield my face as I walked down the aisle stocked with feminine napkins, douches and baby powder. There, at the end, next to other unmentionables, were the condoms. Forcing my blurred vision to read the words, I made out the sizes. Large. Extra-Large. Extra-extra-large, promising a comfortable fit for the "big man."

Apparently this shoppe wasn't trendy enough to have "one size fits all."

My hands trembled as I selected "extra-large." Vanity knows no bounds. I paid for my purchase using exact change and slunk away as though I had used counterfeit money. It was humiliating. Especially after the pimply-faced boy at the register winked at me.

I returned to the Gypsy's flat using a circuitous route. I was afraid of being followed. Why, I have no idea. I was beyond reason.

I did not have to knock. She was waiting for me. She was just as beautiful as ever; more so. I rallied my waning courage.

"Let us go to bed," she announced. Her words were spoken in a normal tone of voice, yet they seemed loud to me, as though she were actually shouting. I don't know why I was worried. There was no one to hear but the neighbors. I followed her into the bedroom.

"Shall I undress?" she asked. I nodded dumbly. Now, I had another problem. Just how and where was I supposed to put this stupid thing on? Was I supposed to go to the bathroom and perform the ritual there, in private? Do it with my back turned while pretending my zipper was stuck so as not to be obvious? Or was I supposed to perform a show? *Hey, look at me struggle to get this on!*

While she was undressing, I took the evil latex thing out of the package and stared at it. The condoms were all individually wrapped. They looked like a gold coins. I peeled back the covering. The condom resembled a finger cot. It didn't look like it would fit around a pencil.

"Want me to help?" Gypsy offered. I was learning the meaning of Ultimate Humiliation.

"No!" Then softer, "No. I can do it." Be a big boy, Kimbo. Men performed this act all the time. Remember the bastard who gave up a lucrative job in cardiology to stuff vending machines full of these little items. I sent a curse heavenward. You would think I was in for a proctoscopy.

Worse. A vasectomy.

I kept telling myself, "This is supposed to be fun." I was learning the meaning of "choking on your own words."

I closed my eyes. I did not want to look at myself. I looked puny. I wondered what would happen if I got it on and it fell off. I felt death encroaching.

I bet they sold a lot of condoms in Hell.

I decided to delay things by taking my shirt off. My fingers wouldn't work the buttons. The button holes had all grown two sizes too small. Like the Grinch's heart. I could hear Boris Karloff's voice. He was talking about Whoville and little Cindy Lou Who. I didn't have to wonder where she came from.

A failed condom.

It cast Dr. Seuss in an entirely new light. I wondered if he had been a pediatrician when he wasn't composing nonsense words.

"Andy?"

"Ugh?"

"Have you fallen asleep?"

Sitting on the edge of a bed, holding my male anatomy around which was wrapped an ever-tightening rubber band?

"No," I groaned. She put a hand on my bare shoulder. My vision cleared instantly. The scent of wild flowers, I presume from her perfume, filled the air. I heard the tinkling of tiny silver bells. My hair stood on end.

I forgot all about latex nooses.

Dropping one triviality for something which really mattered, my hands found her breast. As Gypsy moved back, I moved forward, until we were lying, side-by-side on the bed. I kissed her. Our lips melded into each other's. We breathed through our pores.

After what seemed like a moment and must have been an age, we separated, only to seek new discoveries on one another's bodies. The expression "uncharted territories" slipped so easily into my fervid brain, I knew not where it originated. The thought made me groan with delight.

It was as perfect a pairing as though we were a combination of long separated lovers and rabid teenagers. As much in a hurry as I was, my somewhat questionable maturity allowed me to be gentle and supportive.

When Gypsy fondled me, then tugged with curious intensity, I returned the favor and we laughed like two innocents.

Her delight inspired me, made the act of intercourse new and entirely innovative, without depriving either of us of the intensity of the moment. I did not remember whatever it was I had been afraid of. (That hymen thing, for God's sake).

I whispered things in her ear. She responded by whispering in the Roma tongue, which, as I discovered, was the most romantic language in the universe. I did not understand a word of it, did not have to. It was the delicious, singsong cadence, the emphasis on certain vowels, the repetition of sound.

We communicated to each other in a lover's dialogue of soft moans, loud, excited exclamations of surprise and pleasure, bodily demands.

Applying myself with renewed vigor, I astonished us with a straining of loin, which lived up to the billing promised on the little gold "coin" as "the world's greatest aphrodisiac." In truth, it was, for it wiped away the fear of consequences, allowing us to spread that freedom throughout the night.

As I lay back, nearly plastered to the bed sheets, I discovered, with a whimper of protest, Gypsy was hardly satisfied. Laughing like a fiend well sure of her owner's rights, she slipped her fingers beneath the grossly inflated condom and tore it off. The action, by itself, did not hurt, but I shrieked from sheer animal delight.

Playing along – at least that's what I thought at the time – Gypsy held a hand dramatically to her face, staring at the limp, misshapen condom.

"I have pulled it off, Andy." "It" having an unfortunate dual connotation in my mind. As she registered my expression, her grin turned serious. "I shall put it back on."

Pretending – I *hope* pretending – she went to the root of the problem, surgically reattaching that which had become pretend separated. The condom she tossed glibly across the room. It landed against something solid and made a plump squashing sound, similar to that heard when you drop an overripe tomato on hard ground.

All my life I had been a selfish lover because I had never been in love. With Gypsy, I became another creature altogether. Vanished into thin air went the greed and anger of former sex acts, faceless partners. Our intimacy brought us together, melded us into one, rather than separated us into hard-cased strangers. Without the slightest knowledge I possessed the instincts to please, I strove to satisfy her, and in so doing, drove myself over the edge of mere physical delight.

As I lay, finally exhausted and satisfied by her side, she tapped me on the shoulder. Fearing I had hurt or otherwise disappointed her, I jerked spasmodically, lifting my head to hers in immediate concern.

"Yes, Gypsy, what is it? Are you all right?"

Rather than answer, she held out something to me.

"Cigarette?"

I don't know whether she meant to be humorous, but it was just too funny. I burst out laughing. She joined me. Where once out bodies had blended, so now did our voices.

"No," I thanked her, pushing it away. "I haven't smoked cigarettes in a long time. At least not unless I was stuck in the bathroom and needed some – inspiration?"

She put the pack aside, then turned back and began playing with my chest hair. I watched her with a fascination equal to that which she experienced.

"Thank you," she said finally, winding her pointer finger around some of the longer strands. I kissed her tenderly, an act I might have performed with a child. Yet Gypsy was no child. She was a woman. In one all too brief encounter, she had bestowed on me the right to employ tenderness to an adult. It was a sobering lesson. One I would not have thought possible; one I had not even considered.

Not that I was a rough or a brutal man. I was not. My early life had been both, so I took care, as an adult, not to abuse those who were blameless or helpless. The absence of violence, however, was not the same as the gift of affection.

Always after intercourse, I had felt strangely unfulfilled. My body was sated but not my mind. I attributed that to something lacking in myself, an inability to feel. I never blamed my partners, but rationalized the hollowness to an innate lack of soul on my part. I was correct, as far as it went, but I had never taken the time to analyze further.

Once I thought I had been in love. I was younger then, less adjusted to loneliness, not completely consigned to being an outsider. We were good together, our intimacy was pleasing and I anticipated it as a physical pleasure. What I had shared with Gypsy was as far removed from that as water from wine. One keeps the body alive; the other raises one to the clouds.

Before and after Kim, sex had been a convenience, rather more an accident, or a desperate attempt to ward off isolation. In that, it failed miserably. I read the condition was called post-coital depression but there was more to it than that. It was an acknowledgement I had not found intimacy; had failed to peel away the armor of self-protection I cloaked myself in.

The women I had been with knew no more of who and what Andy Kimbo was after intercourse than they had before. I knew no more of them. To be sure, we knew one another's sighs, groans of release, the physical movements which enacted gratification. But that was as much acting as truth, a social game every adult learns, like charades or twenty-questions.

I did not want to know any of them more thoroughly than I had; I did not want them to know me. We exchanged no dreams, shared no family history. We talked of where we would go to eat instead of envisioning plans for the future.

We smoked cigarettes, blowing easily dissolved rings into the unfamiliar, unmitigated darkness.

"Thank *you,"* I replied, pressing my lips to her ear so a whisper would suffice. Had I merely thought the sentiment, she would have heard. In that was the difference between hotel rooms and bedrooms.

"Will you sleep?"

I was half way to the Land of Nod when she asked.

"No," I demurred, more for the pleasure of seeing her frown than from any semblance of truth. "I will get up and show you what I found at Mystic Towers."

"That is not the name of the building." Which, of course, meant she knew I was fibbing.

I lifted my arm and she snuggled beneath it. Her flesh was warm and comforting, her hair silky against my cheek. Had she made a similar offer, I would have snuggled into her as though I were a kitten. That, I realized with surprise as I drifted off, was as close to admitting love as a man could come without getting on his knees.

When I awoke hours later, it was to the delicious scent of food being prepared. Rising weakly to one arm, I made a fair approximation of being alert.

"Gypsy?"

She floated into the room on faerie wings.

"Good morning."

"It is good," I admitted with a lopsided grin. "But is it morning?"

"It is."

"Is that breakfast I smell?"

"It is."

"Why aren't you still asleep?" I remembered from the recesses of my still numb mind that men should always be the first to rise.

"I was the hungrier of the two," she said with a slight shrug of her shoulder. "Are you not hungry, now?"

"Absolutely starved," I confessed with an honesty which was my first nature but which I had abandoned somewhere along the road of life. "But," I added as a warning, implying there was no true happiness in this world.

"Yes?" Her delivery was good but I knew she was not deceived.

"There is a question I must ask."

She pointed out the room.

"Down the hall. Second door on the right. The first is a closet. For clothes," she impishly detailed. "You may use it if you wish, but I think it would be easier on us both if you managed to reach the bathroom."

"Are you reading my mind?" I could feel my face grow red.

Her eyes opened to the size of saucers.

"No."

"Then how –?"

"I have been there myself. You are not so different than I, after all, are you, Mr. Kimbo?"

I grunted by way of asserting my masculinity. "Where are my clothes?"

She stared with ill-disguised amusement at the floor. "Where you left them."

"Hand them to me." I had not meant it as a test, but the demand stood before us as one.

"I think not."

"Why not?"

"Because it will give me pleasure to watch you struggle to wrap the sheet around your body before you reach for your underwear."

"I see."

Rather than provide her with such an anticipated spectacle, I threw the blanket off, stood naked in all my majesty, then trotted to my shorts. Feeling her eyes on me, I raised one leg, then the other, not without some muscle strain, and drew the boxers up. When I was safely ensconced, I squared my shoulders and turned to her.

"Thank you," she said.

"For what?"

"For doing exactly what I knew you would do. I wanted to see your body once more before you dressed. I did not wish to ask."

"Son of a gun!" My words were more carefully chosen than I gave myself credit for.

"Down the hall. Second door on the right."

"Don't listen," I groused. She made no reply but I felt her laughing. Once in the bathroom, I shut the door, then paused before the commode, frozen in place like a statue of David. "Make some noise" I called. She rattled pots in the kitchen. Utterly unappeased, I turned on the tap and ran cold water down the drain.

This time, I did more than feel her good humor. It did absolutely nothing to unfreeze my bladder. It was not until Gypsy turned the radio to a station playing loud music that I relaxed enough to begin my most necessary business.

This was not only a new relationship, it was an entirely bizarre and unlooked for existence. One I had never dreamed possible.

Emphasis on dreamed.

CHAPTER 10

She had prepared enough breakfast to feed me comfortably for a week. I stared at the fixin's with calorie-conscious guilt.

"If I ate even half of that, I'd look like an editor put out to pasture."

She laughed but not for the reason I supposed.

"I think Mr. McGraw is very nice."

"That's because you don't work for him."

Her lower lip protruded just a fraction, showing she was displeased with my harsh words.

"He is very fond of you."

"Yeah," I agreed, sitting down. "Like a glutton loves his supper."

"Andy!"

I looked up at her, eyes squinting in concentration. I signed inwardly.

"So, he gave you the hard sell, did he?"

"The hard sell?" she asked with a puzzled expression. "He did not try to sell me anything."

I hopelessly shook my head and placed my order.

"A couple of jelly doughnuts and a cup of coffee would do just fine." She mouthed the words with me in perfect synchronization. To cover my dismay, I pointed to a food product on the table. "What's that?"

"Lox."

I had meant it as a rhetorical question but she chose to answer it. What good was reading my mind when she didn't do it all the time? I shut down that thought so fast I bit my tongue.

"Lox?"

"I will have both bagels and cream cheese to go with it tomorrow. Just the way you like them."

I was so momentarily startled by her assumption I would be having breakfast with her again tomorrow, I nearly forgot my question.

"What makes you think I eat lox and bagels for breakfast?" I did, on occasion, but only if they were free and only then on Wednesdays.

"Why Wednesdays?" Gypsy inquired.

"I just made that up."

I hadn't eaten lox since Sweet held an early morning staff meeting many years ago. It had been in the middle of the week; Wednesday sounded about right. Those were always BYOD days, rakishly pronounced "bod" around the office. Sexist in the extreme, but that was the era before anyone thought to be offended by such a not-so-innocent acronym.

BYOD was short for Bring Your Own Doughnuts.

That morning, refreshments were served to impress the invited company, one of whom was Mr. Poxie. I suppose Sweet drew the obvious conclusion from the gentleman's name. At any rate, he paid for the eats himself, making a special trip to a Jewish deli to get the lox and bagels. The food for the staff was purchased from "Joe's Fried 'O's,'" which boasted "never a stale hole."

As I recall, the Old Man ate four cream-filled "donuts." We threw out the lox two weeks after it had fatally contaminated the office refrigerator.

"Mr. McGraw was joking, then?" Gypsy sounded disappointed. "He said you enjoyed lox." For the life of me, I could not guess why. I smiled thinly.

"Perhaps he was remembering his own enjoyment of them," I suggested, not so innocently. If Sweet ever wrangled his way into her good graces enough to be invited for breakfast (only), I didn't want him to have a good time.

You know the expression. Let them eat lox.

It was a reporter-editor thing.

I was ravenous. I expected Gypsy to peck at her food, but she matched me bite for bite, which inspired copious ingestion of breakfast. I was extremely pleased. Skinny women are cheap to feed (if you avoid the upscale rabbit food places), but makes a man feel like a pig for scarfing down his 16-ounce sirloin and baked potato.

(So help me God, I almost envisioned an "e" on the end of "potato." Chalk it up to the power of the press, and their coverage of a certain former elected official who failed third grade spelling.)

I waited until we were on our second pot of coffee before I went to my coat and brought back the spoils I filched from Mystic Towers. Before I opened the ledger, however, I gave Gypsy a raised eyebrow.

"No," she replied. "I am sure. The room is secure. If anyone tried to 'bug' it, I would know."

"What about Big Boy reading your thoughts? I don't want him to get a link on you. You said you weren't sure what he could do."

"I am safe here. *You* are safe here," she added with more emphasis.

"Yeah, well, I can take care of myself," I muttered. I only wished I believed it.

With the table cleared of everything but coffee cups, I displayed the contents of my heist. I wasn't very interested in the money, but Gypsy counted it.

"Five thousand pounds," she said.

"We'll have to turn it in to the police."

Rather than answer me, she clutched it to her breast as though pleading to keep it. She nearly broke my heart. If she needed cash that badly, I'd get some for her somehow. I didn't have a lot but I had some, and payday was at the end of the month.

That was my first thought. Or maybe I should say, it was a fleeting hope. The easy explanation. The sane rationale. An act for which I could make an appropriate reaction. But I knew in a second I was wrong. It discouraged me more than I can tell you.

"He is very fond of money, Andy," she slowly began. "There is more where this came from. Much more."

"Where?"

She hesitated then shook her head.

"I almost got it but it slipped away. We will keep this."

My mouth went dry.

"Keep it?" I squeaked. Visions of prison bars and Lieutenant Chandler walking past, running her night stick clickity-clack over them made my skin crawl. "They arrest people for withholding evidence."

This time, it was she who gave me an eyebrow.

"You have never withheld evidence?"

"OK," I agreed. "But not to the tune of five thousand. What I take isn't that significant. A button, an address book... nothing of value."

She grinned at me. I grinned back.

"Nothing the authorities would book you for?"

"Hey. Just doing my duty as a good citizen. Picking up litter. Just like the KKK." The Ku Klux Klan had signed up to pick trash along some deserted stretch of highway outside St. Louis to get their name on a sign. Concerned citizens kept taking the sign down. It might have turned into an issue of freedom of speech vs. the Evil Empire, but the KKK solved the problem themselves by failing in their civic duty.

I don't suppose they ever had any intention of stooping to trash collecting. They saved that for membership drives.

"We will give the authorities 5,000 pounds," she informed me in so calm a voice she might have been a gangster's moll. "But not *this* 5,000 pounds. Will that ease your conscience?"

"I don't have a conscience," I protested. "I just don't want to get bagged and sent up for the rest of my unnatural life."

"I want this money. He has touched it. He likes money," she repeated. If she meant to impress me, she succeeded.

Putting the money aside, we opened the ledger. In the world of printing presses, typewriters and pagers, Mr. Seer was a very old fashioned fellow. His penmanship made it appear as though he had been taught by 18th Century pettifogs, and while the writing was in code, it was obvious to even the most casual onlooker, of which we admittedly were not, this was Important Stuff.

When Sweet beeped me at 10:10 neither one of us heard it. When he beeped again at 11:01 we ignored it. When the third page came in at 11:30, I finally responded. Going to the phone (and incidentally memorizing the phone number listed thereon), I checked in. He started to yell until he heard the tone of my voice, then hushed as fast as if I had shoved a pillow down his throat.

"I've got it, Sweet. The story of a lifetime. It's all here. Well, not all of it, but a big chunk of it."

"Where's 'here'?" he asked.

"In the ledger I stole from his office."

"You stole a ledger from his office?"

"Yeah."

"Are you going to turn it over to Scotland Yard?"

Americans love to say the words "Scotland Yard." It conjures up images of Sherlock Holmes and Jack the Ripper.

"When I'm through."

He was placated. I could hear it in his breathing. It was times like this when I knew why I loved the man. When he remembered his roots and not his paymasters. When he shed that gross shape of editor-monster he habitually wore and transformed back into a reporter.

"It's big? Really big?"

"Honest to Edward R. Murrow it's big."

There was a long, sacred pause before he continued his respectful cross-examination.

"Well, what are you doing about it?"

"Writing it, you –." I calmed. It wasn't his fault. He could only stay human for so long. "Writing it, sir."

"Well... get to it. Do you need any help?"

Which was more innocent than it sounded. I trusted Sweet. He would never steal my story. Edit the crap out of it, but never steal it. That's why we were friends. Best friends, although I wouldn't admit that to him under torture. It would ruin everything.

"No."

"When are you coming into the office?"

"I don't know." My voice quavered with excitement. "Let me see how far I get with this. I may come in to do some research."

I thought the line had gone dead and then he asked, "You will let me see it, won't you, Andy?" My God, the man tugged at my heart strings.

"Yes, sir."

"I mean," he clarified, clearing his throat, "there might be points of grammar or something you've overlooked." Then, louder, "There might be political ramifications you don't understand."

He knew I could put it on the wire without his say-so because I had once been a Big Name Reporter for a major New York paper and because he trusted me. There's one born every minute. Not like him, though. He's one in – Oh, never mind. This is getting maudlin.

If it's one thing I hate, it's sentiment. I don't even jump up and down at football games.

"I'll show you the story," I promised Sweet. I owed him for trusting me, that was all. It was payback time. "I'll call you."

Again, that deadly dead line. I wondered if it had cholesterol in it.

"Are you safe? I mean, if this Mystic Seer is supposed to be able to read minds...."

"Gypsy says so." I looked over at her. She nodded. "Gypsy says so," I repeated with more emphasis.

"All right. When will I hear from you?"

I glanced at my watch. It was a habit. I was thinking in days, not hours.

"Give me until the end of the week."

He groaned from the heart. It sounded like angina pain.

"Saturday is the worst day of the week to break a story, Andy. No one reads the paper on Saturday. They're all too hung over from Friday night."

"Hold it until Sunday."

"That's even worse! You know most Sunday newspapers are printed with the Saturday papers so the grocery stores can sell them all weekend."

It had something to do with clipping coupons.

"All right. I'll burn the midnight oil. If it breaks Friday, that'll give the stock market boys heartburn all weekend." There was smugness in the thought. Call it inspiration. It was tough worrying about your millions over a two-day weekend.

"Be careful. And keep an eye on your syntax."

I hadn't heard that word since the last Scrabble game I played in 1961. I knew he was nervous. It brings out the vocabulary in a writer.

"Sure."

I hung up the phone, sweating profusely. I wasn't nervous until he warned me to be careful. It goes like that.

Gypsy made lunch. It was delicious. At least, I told her so. I never tasted it, don't know what it was. It didn't give me acid indigestion. That was all which mattered.

I wrote like a man possessed, while Gypsy broke the code. She had to get out her astrological charts to do so.

The stars were on our side.

I was on a high, a writer's Cloud 9. This was the Big One, the career-maker. What I had been waiting for all my life. What I had been born for.

We worked through suppertime without stopping. Around midnight, when the muscles in the back of my neck were about to snap, we broke for sandwiches. I offered to help, but with my hand shaking so badly I dropped the kitchen knife. Abandoning the attempt, I slumped into a chair to wait.

I must have dozed for the next thing I remember was Gypsy shaking me awake. I felt refreshed and ready to go. I sleep like that, in catnaps. Fifteen, twenty minutes and I'm wired. We ate hurriedly. I was eager to go back to work.

When I got up to stretch my legs for a walk down the hall to the "little room," Gypsy read what I had written. When I came back, we went over the salient details. She had a quick mind and, I flattered myself, we thought along the same lines. We would discuss a point, go back to the notebook, check it out, then revise where necessary.

Her syntax, I discovered, was excellent. I made a mental note never to play Scrabble with her.

Cross-referencing the facts as we knew them with the notebook, the Mystic Seer's scheme to convert millions into hundreds of millions was clearly revealed to us. What didn't make any sense to me – numbers and dots (I forgot Europeans use periods instead of comas to separate numbers), translated into opening and closing times for markets around the world, price quotes, stock calculations.

But it was worse than that; far more complicated than a clever man influencing a few wealthy investors into buying certain stocks. Not all the details were in the notebook, of course, but what was there was staggering enough.

Mr. Jason Holloway did not just influence a few men. He had tentacles all over the world. He was more like a guru with a religious following than a financial counselor. He sought men who worshipped money, sold them on his Divine Plan and made converts. He made Reverend Moon look like an old-time soap box, backwoods preacher.

When I finished typing the third, interrelated article, I leaned back and looked at Gypsy.

"OK," I began. "Let's go over where we are and where we're going."

"Do you want to start, or shall I?"

"I'll start. You stop me if I get off the track."

She nodded and settled in beside me.

"I am ready."

For two lovers, we were the most work-oriented people anyone ever saw.

But if you can't share work, sharing a bed is only a pastime.

"Our friend, the Mystic Seer, sets himself up as a gateway to the stars – he promises to read the astrological charts, calculate what planet is in who's pocket –

"What planet is in what house," she corrected.

"What planet is in what house, then interprets his star charts into cold, hard, earthly promises of stock market ups and downs. He's not only predicting which individual stocks will rise, so his clients can make a fast buck – he's giving them the whole ball of wax. What days are better to invest on, what markets will be depressed on any given day, where the trends will go. On a daily, weekly, monthly and probably yearly cycle."

"Yes," she agreed. "But, we were not thinking on a large enough scale. He started by influencing single investors, but one of his goals was to control all the markets in the world."

"By manipulating investors?"

"By manipulating money."

"But money is controlled by men."

"It is really the other way around." I waved her to continue while I took notes on my pad. Writing helps me to think. "It is like the old story of rolling cheeses. Do you know it?" I shook my head. "I first heard it –" She stopped, hesitated then rephrased the sentence. I let it pass. I shouldn't have, but she was on a "roll."

"It is an old fable. Elizabeth I often quoted it. Send one man to do a certain task. When he does not return, you send a second to look for him. When he fails to come back, you send a third. Like rolling cheeses down a hill." I got it. "The stock market goes up in Tokyo. It rises in London. Wall Street opens to positive overseas news."

"Like cheeses."

"Wall Street closes on a down trend. Tokyo opens depressed. It does not always work that way, but it often does. When dealing with the international market, a run on the London Exchange means lower prices on Wall Street. If you could falsely depress one market, you could buy on another for low prices. Then you raise the first market when it reopens and sell what you bought on the second market for a profit.

"If you do this often enough, you not only make a great deal of money, you are actually controlling trends. The man who can do that is the most powerful man in the world."

"Why haven't others tried it?" I asked. It sounded simple enough to me. "Given enough money, some Arab sheik should be in the same position."

"But you must always be correct, or you stand to lose vast sums. And so do those you influence into following your lead. Remember, Kimbo, the Mystic Seer cannot do it all by himself. He needs others."

"So, what's his game?"

She scowled at me and I withdrew.

"It is not a game." Then softer, but no less emphatically, "I have already told you."

"He really does have mystic powers." She nodded. Her head went one way, mine the other.

"I don't believe stock market trends for this, or any other millennium, is written in the stars."

"Then what do you believe?"

"He's a wizard." I frowned. "Poor word choice. He's gifted; he's making educated guesses."

"You must believe me when I tell you he has powers."

I rolled my eyes, not so much for her benefit as for Sweet's. I could see him now, his beady little eyes scanning my brilliant work, getting excited, blood pressure rising, neck veins distended. "Good, Andy, good! Very good. Excellent. This is the story of the – Hey! Wait a minute! What's all this about 'dark powers'? What do you mean, he gets his inside information from the Zodiac?"

I had his ulcer to think about.

"I showed you some of my gifts, Andy. I proved I can read your mind. I revealed my crystal ball to you. I gave you information I could not have gotten by conventional methods. The hiding place of the notebook; the combinations of the doors. How do you think I did that if not by occult means?"

I cringed at the word. I shook my leg. It would be easier to go to bed, work on this problem with a clear head in the morning.

"You do not really want to make love," she replied to my unspoken thought. I instantly flared.

"Don't tell me what I want and don't want to do." As though what she said was a slur on my manhood.

"You want to understand."

"Not if it has anything to do with the occult."

"Then we will go to bed."

She stood up. I remained rooted to my chair. It was that damned reporter's instinct. I couldn't let it go and she knew it.

"All right. Tell me. Go slowly."

"I cannot tell you all; I do not know it all. I do not know the full extent of his gift. Only that he is growing more powerful every day."

"The *Incredible Growing Man,*" I quipped. "Radiation did it."

"Some people are born with the ability. Most never know they have it, or are frightened by it and never use it. Some few are like me; some few are like the Mystic Seer."

I held out my hands. They were steady.

"I can believe in mind reading because that makes sense. When I use my brain it generates electricity. Someone with the key to that energy ought to be able to interpret it. I can even buy the concept of people reading the backs of playing cards because the latent energy surrounding the cards probably broadcasts colors or shapes.

"Maybe plants do communicate with each other, and maybe cabbages do scream when you cut them open. If I had a plant, I would talk to it.

"I've read about auras and seen demonstrations of how healers can manipulate the body's life force to take away headaches. I can even believe, just barely, Tibetan monks can lay hands on broken bones and knit them back together. All of those phenomena have explanations based on the interpretation or manipulation of energy.

"But I cannot buy mysteries written in the stars. I mean," I added with no small amount of exasperation, "Who would write it there? God? Why? So some phony could manipulate the stock market and bring on Armageddon? Isn't it just easier to let some power-hungry Third World leader push the wrong button?"

She was patient with me. I admit that freely. She let me rant and rave, carry on, flail my arms, hurtle spittle into the atmosphere. She waited for me to finish with the calm serenity of a Buddha. When I indicated I was through, she spoke.

As her mouth opened, I cringed. It was an instinctive reaction, one honed by long years of working for men who thought you wouldn't understand them unless they shouted. Raising the voice an octave or two ensures compliance. That's Business Ed. 101.

She did not shout and in not doing so, I totally failed to process her sentence. With a humiliation bordering on hysteria, I humbly beseeched her to repeat it.

I was trained.

"He is not a phony."

I was sorry I asked.

Taking in several deep breaths to calm my nerves, I inadvertently hyperventilated, making myself lightheaded. I was compelled to pause a moment for control. As I did, I naturally dropped my head down, bumping my chin on my chest. When my eyes cleared, I saw my feet. They were firmly planted on the floor.

I was a rational man.

"Are you trying to tell me he does read the S&P index futures in the stars?"

"Yes."

I felt like a little boy who has just been told his real, honest-to-goodness pony needed another quarter to make him go back and forth on wooden rockers.

Without conscious volition my hands patted my pockets. No change.

"Gypsy, I have to ask this. I don't want to. I have to."

"Ask anything you wish, Andy." Her voice was sad, resigned.

"Are you a nut?"

She brightened immediately. She had beautiful eyes. The kind of eyes a sentient man could fall in love with.

"No."

I felt giddy. I assumed it was my blood sugar. I threw up my hands and did a little gig around the room. I whistled a tune. I started to tell a limerick but couldn't remember the punch line. No matter. I had worked in the news-gathering business so long I knew no one would notice. They were used to leaving things dangling.

It had something to do with participles and anonymous sources.

"You're not a nut!" I cried. She smiled at me. It was the sort of smile those white-coated attendants get before they slip one of those jackets which lace up the back over your head. "Wait a minute!" I protested, feeling my arms get pinned to my chest. "I'm not a nut, either!"

"I am relieved to hear it."

She said it straight. I couldn't tell if she were joking or not. I repeated my protestation.

"I know you are not a nut, Kimbo."

I was relieved, then instantly annoyed. How had the tables gotten turned? Why was *I* the one trying to prove *my* sanity when she was telling me mystic seer's read the stars for stock market updates?

"Let's sit down," I suggested. She readily agreed. Perhaps she thought I was less dangerous that way. We went into the living room and settled ourselves down on the couch. "Gypsy," I began.

"Kimbo," she countered.

"Gypsy."

"Kimbo."

This was getting me nowhere. I smiled. She smiled. I thought it would be much easier just to take her to bed and forget the whole mess. But I had written the story of a lifetime. Pulitzer prizes dangled before my eyes.

Prize first, bed second.

OK, so I wasn't making a case for my sanity.

"You obvious believe the Mystic Seer divines information from the stars."

"Yes."

"How?"

"I do not know."

"Can you do it?"

"No."

"Then how can you be so sure? So certain? Don't you have any reasonable doubt?"

"No."

"Then how do you know?"

"I read his mind. It happened when you were in his office. I could feel him probing the room. He did not sense me, so I took advantage, when his guard was down. He is very angry, Andy. He will do everything in his power to punish you."

"My stories *will* be printed. And when they are, he'll never be able to work again. Not in the mystic seer business. Not in the stock market."

"I am frightened for you."

"Never mind that." I wasn't able to absorb her concern. That was not one of my better social skills. Being an Outsider meant taking care of oneself and occasionally others. But never, ever, letting anyone take care of you.

At any rate, no one had ever offered.

"You must believe me," she tried.

I almost laughed. A noise came out, but it more closely resembled a cry. *You must believe me.* It was the Classic Line, the oft-used plea a sincere, well-meaning character makes to the hero of cheap detective fiction, just before he gets his head lopped off.

"Gypsy, nothing in the world is more important to me than this story. It's what I've waited all my life for. It's the reason I'm alive. I *will* take it to Sweet, he *will* send it out, it *will* be picked up and carried by thousands of newspapers, worldwide.

"It's a natural, Gyp. Some guy works out a scheme. He presents himself as having sure-fire, can't-miss information on the stock market. He sells his advice to millionaires. They invest every dime they have and hit it big. They're hooked. The Mystic Seer could tell them to put their dough into grape-flavored bubble gum and they'd do it. When he gets the stock where he wants it, he sells off at top dollar.

"It's all a cheat, a scam, a carefully manipulated takeover. It works, because he literally has every dime of his investor's money at his disposal. There's nothing mysterious about that. In fact, if not on paper, he controls a score of fortunes. With those kinds of liquefiable assets to play with, he's ten or twenty times a billionaire.

"Only, it turns out he's not really working for his clients at all. He's in it only for himself. For all we know, he siphons off some of the profits. When you're dealing with that much loot, no one can keep up with it. At least not without a time-consuming audit.

"As this thing snowballs, he's maneuvered a certain amount of Ted Turner-look-alikes' money into his own portfolio. Then BOOM, he sells out at top dollar and runs.

"It's a natural, baby. Don't you see it?"

I leaned forward, almost touching her. It was the biggest pitch of my life.

"Yes, I do see it. But I see so much more."

"Like what?"

"Until now, we have been working on the assumption the Mystic Seer made his 'killing' and abandoned the stock market."

"And now?"

"I realize," she said, tapping the ledger, "that is hardly the case."

"Explain."

"He is still heavily invested – albeit under aliases, corporations, trust funds. The stock market crash was not an end – it was a beginning. He 'pulled the plug' on five men to prove to his other clients just what he can do to them."

I gulped. I had an Excedrin headache #469.

"Go on," I urged. "Just who are his other clients?" Like I really wanted to know.

"Heads of State. Highly placed government officials. Policy makers."

With all due respect, Excedrin wasn't going to cut it this time.

"He now has proof he can run any individual – or country – which has holdings in any stock market. He can bring on world chaos by bringing down Wall Street."

"Unless –?"

"Unless he gets what he wants."

"What does he want?"

"Oh, nothing much," she assured me. I painted a smile on my chalk-white face. "Just world domination."

Bozo the Clown died an inglorious death.

"World domination?" I hissed. Forget the Pulitzer. Now I just wanted to live long enough to collect Social Security.

"Oh," Gypsy sighed. My head snapped up in typical knee-jerk fashion. "Social Security. Are those not the funds politicians want to allow private citizens to invest in the stock market?"

I nodded, envisioning myself hunched over my typewriter, waiting for retirement which had been pushed back ten years – to the age of *85.*

"We have to warn people – investors," I clarified, forgetting, in my excitement, they were people, too. "We have to make certain no Big Players invest in the stars."

"Oh, Andy, you are so gullible."

I felt as though I had just been caught walking into the shower fully clothed.

"I am the most worldly man I know," I stated with conviction. "The most hardened, the most jaded –"

"And yet, your innocence has blinded you to the salient truth."

Take your clothes off, stupid.

"Me? Blinded to the truth?" I scoffed, hardly believing my ears. "Truth is my middle name." I went through a mental chick list.

Did I believe in Santa Claus? No.

Did I believe in the Tooth Faerie? No.

Did I believe in the innate goodness of human nature? No.

"Yes, you do," Gypsy somberly corrected. "You may go through life with a scowl on your face, but deep inside you do believe that if given a choice between right and wrong, most people would –"

"Walk a middle road?" I interjected as damage control.

Somewhere, on a parallel planet, Andy Kimbo began smearing soap all over his shirt.

"Consider," she began, speaking softly as though to a child. The hair on the back of my neck rose in warning. "Jason Holloway, the Mystic Seer, has proven he can manipulate the international stock markets."

So far, so good. I nodded.

"He has made hundreds of millions of pounds for those who follow his advice."

"The Lord giveth and the Lord taketh away," I blasphemed, feeling on safe ground.

"Exactly," she agreed to my surprise.

"So, all we have to do is expose this false god and he's out of business."

Working in the Bible Belt had been good for me, I smugly concluded.

From somewhere, a cat meowed. I looked around, startled. I had not seen a cat before. I did not see one now.

Gypsies.

Mystic Seers.

Crystal balls.

Familiars.

I had a feeling I wasn't going to like what I heard next.

"Imagine you're a millionaire," Gypsy began.

I regretted not having taken Occult 101 in college.

"All right," I agreed. "I'm a millionaire. I have money to burn. I'm sitting on top of the world."

"You dabble in the stock market. You win some, you lose some."

I grimaced, acutely feeling the loss of my pretend money.

"You see other investors having the same luck."

"Tit for tat," I agreed.

"Then you see others making money. Big money. They never lose. How do you feel?"

"Mad. Jealous."

"You hear they are being advised by a mystic seer. You laugh. They make more money – at your expense."

"I get madder; more jealous." My blood pressure was rising.

"Then, there is a stock market crash. All those investors who followed the word of the Mystic Seer go bankrupt."

"Serves them right."

"You continue to invest. You lose some, you win some."

"The world goes on," I stated with a smirk at those dummies who had fallen by the wayside.

In that alternate universe of mine, where A. Kimbo was bathing fully clothed, someone turned off the cold water.

"And then you are approached by the Mystic Seer. You remember all the millions those other investors made. Mr. Holloway offers you a hot tip. What do you do?"

I was suddenly plunged into hot water.

"I think that I might play along with him awhile, make a fortune, then get out before the Mystic Seer dumps on me."

My skin was getting scalded.

"Naturally. Because you are so much smarter than those other fools."

The drain plugged and water started rising so fast I missed her clever use of the word "other."

"That's right. To be forewarned is to be forearmed."

The water was up to my navel.

"At first you invest carefully. Nothing untoward happens. So you commit yourself a little more. Then a little more."

The water was up to my armpits.

"Your friends are doing the same thing. You all pat yourselves on the back you have gotten the best of the Mystic Seer."

"Ready to jump out at a moment's notice."

Water cascaded over my head.

"All the while without realizing that your 'moment's notice' is no longer a moment, but a day or a week or a month."

I drowned.

"You're saying I'm not as smart as I think I am; that although I think I can outwit the Mystic Seer, he's always one step ahead of me."

Gypsy nodded thoughtfully.

"But you understand, Andy, we are only speaking of a hypothetical you."

My head suddenly popped above water.

"That's right!" Somehow I had forgotten I wasn't a millionaire. Thoughts of Rolls Royces and Crystal Louis Roederer fizzled with the pop of a cork and I didn't even care.

Which just goes to show you Doubting Thomas's, money isn't everything.

It isn't worth a plug nickel without pride.

"All right," I babbled, making a good imitation of water draining down the shower pipe. "The Mystic Seer may be clever – and he may be able to read the stars – but he's met his match. He thinks he's throwing a perfect game, but he just made his first mistake. E1 – error, pitcher. He's underestimated a crime reporter, late of St. Louis, and a Gypsy, temporarily residing in London!"

"It ain't over 'till it's over. Yogi Berra said that," Gypsy quoted with a smile.

I rolled my eyes and pulled my head back.

Yogi never played for the Cardinals. Thus, I could be forgiven for not having thought of that quote myself.

"Well, hang on, Gypsy, because we're about to steal home."

The White Rat would be proud.

CHAPTER 11

I wrote my stories. I named names; gave facts and figures. Followed the money trial; built up the suspense, as I took my readers through the years, beginning with the Mystic Seer's first tentative ads and progressing to the current day. I stated his clients believed he was reading the stars. I threw in a lot of background of historical references to such things. With an air of skepticism I questioned whether it was actually possible, but I didn't come out and say it was true.

That would have been professional suicide.

Sweet took so long to read the articles, I wondered if there were something wrong. When he reached into his pocket and put on his readings specs, I began to sweat. When he sent out for coffee, my stomach turned. It was only when he licked his finger to turn a page that I dared relax.

An editor never puts his hand to his mouth while he's touching something he's going to throw out. Would you eat garbage?

I was crossing my legs by the time he looked up. His breath smelled vaguely of Coffeemate. That was another good sign. If he was going to dump on me, his exhalations wouldn't have the distinct odor of brimstone.

He was quiet, too. Real still, like a mediocre representative of a taxidermist's art. My heart was beating fast enough for both of us.

I was perspiring for him, he was breathing for me. He took a moment to wipe his brow before speaking. He never let the papers out of his hand.

I should have seen what was coming.

"I suppose you'll expect a raise after this?" he asked in a monotone. "Turn in your resignation, go back to New York? Take up your career where you left it all those years ago?"

It was better than I thought.

"Who, me?" My voice sounded funny. High pitched. Sort of hysterical. Usually when I sound like that I'm already out the window, thirty floors to go before I hit.

"This is big, Kimbo. Really big. The Big One," he continued.

His voice sounded funny. Sort of like it had respect in it. I wondered if he'd been spending his evenings on Theatre Row, absorbing the acting techniques of the British thespian aristocracy.

"Yes, sir."

He looked at his watch. Newspaper people always look at their watches. It had nothing to do with telling time.

I think his watch stopped in 1947. Mine needed the battery replaced. I had a watch once that was self-winding. I gave it a nervous breakdown because I never stopped moving.

"Right on time, too. Friday. Just like you promised."

It made me wish he'd start yelling.

"Yes, sir."

He stood up. I straightened, but not too far. I was afraid to uncross my legs.

"I'll send it out myself. This sonofabitch will put CANS on the map."

"Yes, sir."

He left. I came close to saluting him.

As soon as the door shut, I hightailed it into his private restroom and was back in time to have the soap smell dissipate from my hands before he returned. No sense pushing it. Rank hath its privileges. I didn't want him to think his private CAN was already on the map.

When he didn't come back, I peeked out through his window. He was on the phone, talking long distance. I could tell because he was drumming out the seconds with his fingers. He was calling the Old Man. When I saw him hang up the receiver, I ducked back and stood, staring at a photograph of the Queen, when he came in.

"It's a scoop, you know," Sweet said. I didn't turn around. I hate to see grown men cry. "The Old Man –" He cleared his throat and began again. That's when I knew he was affected. *"Mr. Poxie* wants to know how you did it."

My temper flared and I spun around.

"What do you mean, how I did it? I did it by honest-to-God hard work, research, cunning, guts, brilliant writing – and the help of a stringer."

"A Gypsy," he said.

"A Gypsy," I agreed.

"We'll have to pay her." He didn't sound nearly so pained as I thought he would. My natural suspicions arose faster than... than you know what.

"I already paid her."

I realized how that sounded and blushed. I had to get the rest out fast. "For her services. I mean, for her help. I mean, for her tips. Oh, shit! For collaborating with me on the exploration – I mean, investigation of –"

He sighed in a fatherly sort of way. "I know what you mean."

I was afraid he did. I half expected him to ask if I were going to marry the girl.

"This ledger – the one you got from the Mystic Seer's office. It will have to be turned over to Scotland Yard."

"Yes, sir."

"We'll make a copy of it, first."

"Already thought of that."

He scowled at me. "I didn't hear that."

"No, sir."

His right hand came at me. I jumped back like he had a snake in it. Then I realized he just wanted to shake hands.

"Am I fired?"

He feigned innocence. It was a newsroom ritual. Like giving the condemned a last meal or offering a blindfold.

"What makes you think that?" I looked at his hand. He removed it. I mean, he withdrew it.

No sense going overboard.

"Go home and get some sleep. I'll expect you back here at nine, sharp tomorrow. We have other stories to cover, you know. You're a reporter. Never knew a good reporter to rest on his laurels."

It was the best compliment I had ever received.

Or ever would receive.

A Pulitzer was one thing but a compliment from Sweet McGraw was another. Anyone can win a Pulitzer. They're not so rare, after all. They give them out every year.

"I'm not going to New York," I said. I don't know why I said that. It was a moment of madness. New York was all I ever talked about. Working for a real newspaper, not a ragtag news service was my dream. Rubbing newsprint in the faces of those who said I wasn't cut out for the Big Time. I don't hold grudges, but I never forget an insult.

He got something caught in his eye. There must have been a leak in the roof because I got something wet in my eye, too. Neither one of us wiped our faces, though. Real men don't rub where it hurts. He blew his nose. I coughed into my hand.

"Get out of here," he ordered. "And don't think this changes anything."

"No, sir."

"And don't think I didn't see you sneak into my washroom. I'm charging you for the paper towels."

"I didn't use any."

"Then I'll charge you for the water."

"I didn't flush it."

He picked up a paperweight and threw it at me. I felt a lot better. Like old times. I ran out with my tail tucked between my legs and everybody in the newsroom thought I had been given the axe. That made me feel real good. I love to disappoint.

The story, under my byline, made the headlines all over the world and in New York, too. It was the first of three interconnected articles. The others ran Monday and Tuesday. By that time, dozens of editorials had been written on the safety of the stock market, long term investments and diversified portfolios. Sermons were preached on the theme, "If it's too good to be true, it is."

Talk show hosts discoursed on the idea of absolute power corrupting absolutely. The editor for Oxford Dictionary was petitioned to add "mystic seer' to their thesaurus under "power-hungry." (Note the hyphen. This is England, after all.)

Bond interest rates fell two percent in anticipation of the rush out of stocks.

My phone never stopped ringing. When a reporter is the target of interview calls, he's really hit onto something big. From schmo to celebrity in forty-odd easy years.

(Excuse me. That last was an editorial error. The line should read, "From schmo to celebrity in thirty-odd easy years. You just can't get good help these days.)

I could hardly wait to see my autograph auctioned off at Christies.

I declined most of the offers, telling the poor slobs on the other end of the horn I didn't see any point giving interviews until I had finished the story. I intimated there was much more to come. They sounded disappointed, intrigued and jealous. I didn't blame them.

Prime Time television anchormen from the States called, pleading with me to drop into their foreign offices and have a chat. Nothing formal. I was one of them; I knew the ropes. They wouldn't pressure me into taping an interview. And by the way, don't wear seersucker. It bleeds.

It was heady. I was walking on air. And I hadn't even played my trump card.

Gypsy and I worked on it all week. Still professing disbelief, I was forced to the conclusion she might, maybe, just could possibly be correct. The Mystic Seer *had* been right. One hundred percent of the time. Every stock he picked to raise, rose. We traced his early start where he only manipulated the market for his own benefit into trial runs with select clients and then on to the Big men with the even bigger money.

"Then why?" I asked Gypsy, "If he's so in tune with the celestial happenings, didn't he foresee his collapse?"

I sounded like a pitch man for afternoon herbal tea. She looked at me with what I thought to be a temperate expression. The sort of look one would give a child.

"You are the random element, Andy."

"I am the *what?"*

"The random element."

"I heard you. What is a random element? It sounds like something out of *Star Trek.* You know: Dr. McCoy sending the *Enterprise* back in time."

Her voice was gentle, patient. I made a mental note never to play Trivia with her.

"The *Enterprise* did not go back in time; Dr. McCoy did. He changed history by preventing the death of Edith Keeler."

"Never mind!"

"I just wanted you to get your reference correct. I should not want you to be embarrassed if someone questioned you on it. Star Trekkers are very protective about their show."

"You have them in England, too?"

She grinned and my heart sank. She had set me up and I had warp-speeded into her trap.

"I know a Gypsy caravan which displays the command insignia on its canvas wagon covering."

"Is it driven by Captain James T. Gypsy?" I asked with a tad too much sarcasm.

"No," she replied matter-of-factly. "It is navigated by Gypsy Sulu, of course."

I was not only collaborating with an honest-Injun Gypsy, she was a Trekkie.

"Trek*ker,"* she sternly corrected. "And I am not certain 'honest-Injun Gypsy' will fly, either."

I put my hands to my head. I knew what had happened. *I* was not the "random element." It was Sweet. His very presence in her flat had thrown us all into a parallel, opposite universe. Once where everybody loved editors, no one appreciated writers and we all wore beards.

Well... half a parallel universe, anyway.

"Please explain." I was trying to be logical, unemotional.

"Your connecting with me, to be precise." I blushed and coughed into my hand.

"Go on," I urged. Perhaps "connecting" did not have the same connotation in "Gypsy" as it did in "American."

"I think the Mystic Seer's guard was up; I believe he was warned something would happen, but he did not see precisely. I never said, nor did I imply, his powers were unlimited."

I plunked down on the couch and she sat beside me. I moved back a quarter of an inch. I was a professional, after all. There was work to be done.

"You better tell me about 'powers,'" I suggested. "I guess I don't understand. Where I come from, people call psychic hot lines to ask about their boyfriends fooling around on them, the status of their finances, and whether their kids will have the same color hair as their husbands'."

"I know all about that," she sighed. "I am in that line of work, you know." I knew. "The Mystic Seer has different powers than I have, although we are both gifted. I do not read the astrological charts. Mine is more purely psychic. I think about a problem, put my concentration out into the universe and wait for an answer. Sometimes I get one, sometimes I do not. I have heard it referred to as Divine Divination.

"The Mystic Seer does not have that type of gift. Or if he does, it is limited. It is obvious he works out his predictions using star charts, ancient texts and numerology."

"Right. So I'll never tell him when my birthday is."

"I am sure he already knows."

"How?"

"Give me your wallet." I gave it to her. She flipped it open, found my driver's license and pointed. "Your birthday is a matter of record. Like you,

Mr. Kimbo, the Mystic Seer has his stringers. It would not take much to check you out."

That made me feel cheap, vulnerable. It almost made me feel sorry for those criminals I had used the same tactics against.

"That's not fair," I stammered. She did not reply, sparing me the old chestnut, "All's fair in love and...," which I had inadvertently laid the groundwork for. "Go on," I urged.

"By yourself, I do not think you could have disrupted his plans. Not so completely. But when you came to me for research, together we became a force to contend with."

I was offended but only briefly. I was used to working alone. I had always been by myself. I was not, as I had been told often enough, "a team player." What I wrote belonged to me. The cases I cracked, the leads I tracked down, the credit for my talents had all been solo jobs. I suppose in that sense, I was selfish, although I do pride myself on the fact I was generous with acknowledgements (where applicable and safe for my informants), and money. That's one of the reasons I'm usually broke.

But this series of stories had been a true collaboration. I had written them, but the guts of the work had been hammered out together. She had every right to remind me of that.

"You're right, Gyp. I'm sorry. I couldn't have done it without you."

She was instantly startled, shaking her head.

"I do not want your glory, Andy. Credit for the reporting belongs to you. I only wish to help. The Mystic Seer is a bad man. He needs to be stopped. And I like you," she shyly added.

Wrapping my arms around her, I gave Gypsy a quick hug, thinking as I did so, that Sweet would never believe any of this.

"We work together," I promised. "I should have put your name on the byline with mine."

"No. Never. I am not a writer. But I do enjoy the – investigative reporting?" I nodded. "I think you and I will have an interesting time 'in the field.'"

God help me, I blushed again. Then dropped my arms as though they had become lead weights. This was no time for a testosterone high.

"It's too risky for you to go into the field! You said yourself this Jason Holloway is dangerous. I don't want him hurting you."

"What people want and what they get, are often two different things."

That scared me.

"You implied that if you got too close, he'd hone in on you."

"Yes."

"Then even my being here is a danger to you."

"We are both in danger."

"I don't care about me."

"I will ask you that again when you are dangling over a fire, your bare feet toasting."

Her image was so vivid, I stamped my feet on the carpet to put them out.

"I don't want to place you in danger."

"We were speaking of the Mystic Seer's powers. He has gone underground for the moment, waiting to see what will happen. The fallout from your articles, the information you supplied the authorities will keep him quiet for now. But he will be back. Better armed."

"With an unlimited exchequer," I added, remembering her story about the millionaires.

"He will be looking for revenge."

"Can't you put blinders over his eyes? Create a cloud to obscure his vision?"

"You are speaking of witches' powers, not that which Gypsies possess."

She was right. I had been carried away. I was caught up in the spirit of the moment. Like that old ad, "You can't eat just one." I had gone from mind reading to supernatural diversions. I had lost my virginity of skepticism.

"Rightee-o," I agreed, scratching behind my ear. "But, here's my problem."

"I am listening."

"Astrology and mysticism was Holloway's hook. I get that. Hocus pocus and the promise of a guaranteed result brings people to his door. All well and good. He goes through his act, makes mumbo jumbo over the stars and their alignment and he suckers men to invest. We played that up in the articles we wrote. Unusual, but not illegal. He invests their money, so he's still on the up-and-up. It's then he starts tinkering with the market by making certain companies look better than they are. Their stock shoots heavenward and he sells out before everyone realizes they were pie in the sky. That much is down-to-earth manipulation."

"Yes."

"It looks like magic, but it isn't."

"As far as you have gone, that is true."

"I went to the end of the line." She remained quiet. "The gobblygook is just window dressing."

She sighed. From the heart.

"You did not believe what you wrote?"

"I believed the sales pitch." No answer. She sat and stared at me. "If I had written it any other way, Sweet would have pitched me out a window. No one's actually going to believe a bunch of numbers written in ancient times, correlated with the position of heavenly bodies, can be interpreted to reveal the future of the modern-day stock market."

"I do."

"Why? And don't give me that old chestnut, 'there are many things in heaven and earth' crap."

"I will not say it, as you already have. Mysticism is as old as the human race, Andy. Older. It predates history."

"Are we back to aliens instructing the Egyptians on how to build the pyramids?"

"I will not answer that because you mock me."

I held up my hands.

"I'm sorry." They started to shake. "Alchemy? That, I understand. It has a solid foundation: transmute metals into gold. But, no one's ever been able to make it work."

"Not in your reality."

"In yours?" I challenged.

She blinked. I took it for a yes. Fortunately, she went off on a different tack.

"Let us stick to the facts as we know them. Jason Holloway, which is not, of course, his real name any more than it is 'Mystic Seer,' did not always raise the value of companies merely to sell off his shares before the deceit was discovered. If that were his only skill he would have been found out before now and stopped."

"So, what is his power?"

She shook her head.

"That is not power: it is what I might consider a mere parlor trick. A game he played. For money, to be sure, but it required no… artistic flair. It was the other stocks where he made his greatest –"

"Killing," I filled it, remembering his late clients.

"If you will. I am speaking of those small, inconsequential companies which he suggested – strongly suggested – his clients invest it. Those which weeks, months or even years later developed breakthrough technologies, vaccines for deadly diseases, items of pop culture which rose to the top of the charts."

"Well, yes, there were those," I guardedly admitted.

"Many of those," she reiterated. "In all your research, did you ever find he had given bad advice?"

"Not for investors I was able to definitively trace to him. No."

"These were the real proof of his power; his ability to –"

I put my hands over my ears.

"Please don't say read the stars."

"Then, you prefer 'read the future'?"

I reluctantly dropped my hands.

"All right. How does he do it? I'm ready to listen."

She inhaled deeply so I knew I wasn't going to like the answer.

"I will begin by saying there are no accidents, Kimbo. Whatever happens on this plain of existence was meant to be. I do not mean to suggest there is no free will," she hastened to explain. "There is. But, not in the way most people think of it."

"Free will is doing my own thing. Becoming a reporter. Quitting a job. Having bacon and eggs for breakfast."

"Yes. That is so."

"Then, what's the mystery?"

"It is *when* you decided on these things that makes the difference."

"Thirty years ago, three years ago, this morning. Or, thereabout," I added, least she hold me to specifics.

"Perhaps not."

"No, no, no. Now, you're talking of pre-destination."

"Might they not be the same thing?"

"I don't see how."

"If your spirit has free will and decides how your life will transpire, that explains it."

"Now, you're talking in riddles."

She was patient with me.

"Everyone on Earth is here for a purpose. We are all in possession of certain gifts. I will not say as corporeal beings we are fully aware of how we will live our life. If we knew from day-to-day what was going to happen, there would be no challenge. No pleasure… and no pain. We would not learn but rather stand still. That is where they mystery of life enters. While our spirit may be aware of what we have chosen, our human mind does not. It is up to each of us to use the talents we gave ourselves to the best of our ability."

I was concentrating so hard I could feel my freckles begin to fade.

"Are you suggesting Jason Holloway has given himself the ability to translate obscure passages of ancient texts – which may not have any significance beyond 32 BC – into data he can then correlate with which House Venus is in on Thursday, June 23rd, 1974, and use it to determine which companies are going to hit the jackpot in 1990?"

"That is my explanation of it. I do not say it is his."

"And therefore, it follows you gave yourself the gift of reading minds?"

"Yes."

"So you could work as a Gypsy fortune teller living barely above poverty level in a London flat?"

"No. So I could place myself in a position where you could find me so we may combine our talents to can try and stop a great evil from being perpetrated on the world."

"You do realize what you've just said is outside the realm of Judeo-Christian belief and therefore is unpublishable in any country outside Tibet."

"I see no problem."

I threw up my hands.

"Why not?"

"We shall lie."

She dumbfounded me.

"What'll we say?"

"Jason Holloway believed in what *I* will acknowledge as his real power. There have been others throughout history. Rasputin is a good example. There have been men – and women – who hear voices which direct them to perform certain heroic tasks. Those with a religious association have been believed without question and become saints. Those who are associated with the dark arts are more often linked with some mythological devil and dismissed. But, not without fear. Their accomplishments have withstood the test of time, since they fit nicely into the concept of God's universe at war." She sadly shook her head. "Human beings are very fond of war." Her voice strengthened. "Angels bringing Mary the Word; fallen angels tempting Mankind to go against their faith."

I finally started laughing. Not because it was funny but because it worked for me. She had provided the perfect answer of how I could transmute gold into lead and sell it to the masses.

Before I was reduced to sobbing, I steadied myself for what was to come.

"What do we do now?"

"You finish writing your articles, presenting what we have just discussed. Emphasize our speculation about Holloway's craving for power, not just money. State our own 'presentment' he is not through. Then we wait."

"For Holloway to make a move?" She nodded. "What will it be?"

"I cannot say. I am not privy to the future."

I didn't even think to groan.

I went back to work, slaving over the typewriter. Or, was that slavering over the typewriter? It was hard work but it was my kind of work.

I investigate, therefore I am. I write, therefore I am. I am in love, therefore I am not that which I once was.

I did not fail to smile at the simile. Which. Witch.

It was written in the stars.

I spent my entire two-week salary on condoms. The pimply-faced clerk died of envy and I never saw him again.

CHAPTER 12

It took a long time for the stock market sensation to die down. All sorts of rules and regulations were discussed, money was moved up and down like working elevators and every advisor whose name even remotely sounded like "Jason Holloway" changed their names, or capitalized on the astrological craze. One of the American networks put together a rush job biopic on Rasputin. PBS advertised future plans for a televised play of "The Devil and Daniel Webster." The BBC rehashed the story about the curse of King Tut's tomb. Fear was good for business.

I got a raise and a cushion for my desk chair. I kept the money and gave the cushion away. Never let it be said success went to my head or my tail.

Peculiar events started happening. They began early one morning when Gypsy and I were lying in bed together, listening to the thump of each other's hearts and breathing in the warmth of each other's bodies.

There was a faint, erotic scent to her I couldn't place. Nuzzling under her breast, I kissed her and murmured faintly.

"What is that perfume you're wearing?"

"Do you like it?"

"Very much. It's extremely stimulating. I can't place it, yet it smells familiar."

"I like it myself," she confessed. "Here."

She took a bottle from the shelf built into her headboard, opened it and placed it under my nose. I inhaled deeply.

"That's it," I agreed. "But what is it? Some exotic type of flower? Some mad Gypsy love potion #9?"

She laughed as I meant her to.

"So, I have put a spell on you?"

"Yes."

"With this?"

"No doubt," I contentedly murmured.

"Then you are a very little boy and easily won over," she teased. I was instantly alert and suspicious.

"What is it?"

"Try again," she urged.

I sniffed, ran the memory over in my mind and still failed to place it. The odor was sweet and compelling, yet not nostalgic.

"Tell me," I demanded.

"It is an ancient Roma secret," she began and I knew she was pulling my leg. I could have wished for more.

"Tell me!"

"It is vanilla."

"Vanilla?" I was mortified. What grown man is stimulated by the smell of vanilla? Therefore, I denied what was now obvious. "It's essence of edelweiss and poppies," I protested.

"With just a touch of lettuce and a drop of swamp rot," she agreed. My throat constricted. "And don't forget the bat's wings. Powdered, of course."

I gagged.

"It *is* vanilla!"

"Congratulations! You have guessed it."

"What's so erotic about vanilla?"

"I did not wear it to be erotic. I put it on because I like it. Do you not like it?"

"I like what's underneath it." It was a feeble protest, at best.

"Let me put some on you."

"No!" I cried. Wearing a woman's scent was in the same category as being asked to hold her purse. It had something to do with cooties.

She smeared it all over me. I thought I was going to lose consciousness. Like most men, I would rather stink like underarm hair than smell like a frilly boutique.

"There!" she declared, proclaiming me a success. Like most women, she preferred me to smell like ice cream rather than gym shorts.

Therein lays the great difference between the sexes.

It was a mystery of the Universe not even the Mystic Seer could explain.

I think it goes back to Creation; the fact men have one fewer ribs than women. (Which, of course, they don't. A morgue attendant proved that to me once, in my green days as a rookie reporter. He thought it was damned funny when I barfed into the chest cavity. But I learned my lesson and grew up a lot that day.)

"I also have vanilla lotion," she offered. "Would you like some for your hands?"

"No, but if you give me some, I'll rub it on you."

Gypsy produced a tube of vanilla-scented lotion. Unscrewing the cap (if you will excuse the expression), I squeezed a generous amount on my hands, then proceeded to rub it into the bare skin of her back and legs. If I died and went to heaven, I could think of worse things than serving as Gypsy's masseur.

It was as much an excuse to get my hands over her body as it was to relax her. It was a testimony to our relationship that we both enjoyed the exercise. When I had loosened her muscles and subsequently covered us both in a thin sheen of lotion, we lay for a moment, side-by-side, smelling like a Baskin Robbins outlet. It was then the second peculiar event happened.

"She has passed her test," Gypsy said. I assured she was speaking of herself in the third person and was referring to my consent to wear vanilla perfume.

"Good." I was sleepy and tingling pleasantly.

"Passed the boards. Is that what you call it?"

"You're board?" I was somewhat insulted.

"To be a police captain. She has passed the examination." Gypsy seemed pleased. I presumed because she had worked through word choices until finding the proper expression.

"She? Who she?"

"Lieutenant Chandler. Also, she has been promoted. She is now Captain Chandler."

I groaned. Not from the heart but from the very fiber of my being. "Now, I'll never get my apartment out of quarantine!" Then, with a firmer voice, I demanded, "Did she cheat?"

Gypsy laughed. "No."

I was disappointed. How could Helen Chandler expect to aspire to political office, the next natural extension of her career, if she hadn't cheated? How would I ever be able to do some investigative reporting and get the goods on her? Life wasn't fair.

"She is very intelligent." That went over like a lead balloon. If she were that smart, how come she hated me? "She does not hate you," Gypsy helpfully supplied. I turned my eyes back from a contemplation of the ceiling to confront her.

"Yes, she does," I replied in a stilted, superior manner. "She thinks I'm a troublemaker and an idiot."

"That is not the same thing," Gypsy informed me. I detected a trace of glibness in her tone.

"What do you know about all this?"

"I am reading your mind."

"Are you reading hers, too?"

"I am getting certain impressions."

I pulled myself up onto one elbow. "What else are you getting?" All the male vanity in the world was wrapped up in that one, less-than-subtle, question.

"She is madly in love with you."

"Really?!" I was shocked.

"No." I was deflated.

I fell faster than a speeding bullet. "I told you," I gritted incoherently, placing a woe-begotten hand to my head. "I'll never get back into my apartment. I'll never get my notes back. I'll never get my car back. She's probably already sold *that* at auction."

"Not yet."

I was so relieved I could have swallowed bits of recently ground-off teeth.

"She's a corrupt cop," I protested.

"She is not corrupt."

"All right. She's a cop. And now she's a captain. Hurrah. Good for her. Bells and whistles. It must have been an easy test."

"She was the only one who passed it."

"Her score must have been on a curve." That sounded obscene so it behooved me to laugh. Some things are simply gender-necessary.

My laugh was hollow. It made me feel like a creep. I regretted it, but real men don't say they're sorry.

"Say you are sorry," Gypsy prompted. I repeated her phrase before I knew what I was doing. And then I knew there was a spell on me.

But I didn't take it back.

Anyway, Captain Chandler would never know. It didn't matter if Gypsy knew. She could read my mind, anyway. It saved a lot of *posturing.*

"Say!" I said, popping up in bed, my vanilla-scented skin gleaming white in the darkness. "Do you have some more of that lotion?" Gypsy nodded. I smiled. Call it inspiration. "I'll send a bottle of it to Captain Chandler. As a sort of 'Congratulations!'"

"I think that is a very nice idea."

My mind was working overtime.

"When she sees the postmark, she'll remember I'm in England. That will make her happy. Being in such a good mood, she'll order the release of my apartment and my car. I'll be able to get my notes back."

"And your underwear," Gypsy reminded me.

I kicked with my foot. I came up with a pair of light blue shorts.

"Yes," I admitted. "That would be nice. But then, on second thought..." I tossed the boxers aside and engulfed her in my arms. "Who needs them?"

The rest of the day, night and in-between times were given over to what we, in the news business, refer to as Rest and Relaxation. I did neither, of course, which is where the joke comes in.

When I was nominated for the "**D**uke **o**f Edinburgh (Excellence in Journalism) **A**ward" I nearly had kittens. Then one of the natives told me it was an "honour," and my throat constricted.

"The DOA is the highest honour an English journalist can ever receive. It's like winning an Olivier, if you're an actor, or becoming a Dame if you're a retired politician. Congratulations!"

Who says the British have no sense of "humour"?

I had never been nominated for anything before, much less won an award. Since I had never heard of it, the first thing I did was research the entire process. I may have been giddy but I did not want to be taken for a fool. But sure enough, it was a Big Deal. I was duly impressed. Excited, even. But I was afraid someone back in the States would hear I won a DOA.

I would never be able to run a single stringer, if they did.

Every cloud has its black lining.

Sweet slapped me on the back so hard he burped me.

"My God, Andy, I knew something like this would happen. You've worked hard enough for it."

I looked under his desk for the seed pod.

"Thank you," I modestly replied.

Then he added, "So did I," and ruined the effect.

After the announcement was made (and run via our own wire service, by the way, although not as an exclusive), the CANS newsroom was as silent as if Ronald Reagan had left the Screen Actors Guild to announce he was turning politician. Smiles were wooden, handshakes perfunctory.

"Good boy!" Rita praised. "When you leave, can I have your desk?"

I told her I wasn't going and she went back to work.

"Jolly good, old chap!" Jimbo drawled in his best imitation of Alistair Cooke. He had watched reruns of *Masterpiece Theatre* before CANS was uprooted from St. Louis to London, in order to "fit in" when we arrived. He wasted his time but did manage to absorb some history by the effort. He learned Henry VIII had six wives. Before then, he thought it was Henry VI who had eight wives.

Who said you can't learn anything from the telly?

This new knowledge, I had pointed out to him, was useful in case Charles ascended the throne and changed his name. To Henry.

For reasons obvious to me, but lost on Jimbo. But then, if the Price of Wales didn't adopt a new name, that was all right with me, too. As a name for a British monarch, Charles was a bummer. I could see the copy, now.

"Cromwell Has Last Laugh."

Concerning my award nomination, of all my friends (one) and all my associates (three), Gypsy was the most excited.

"We will celebrate with a dinner!" she declared. "And I will bake you a cake."

"I thought I'd take you out," I protested. In all the time I had known her, I had never enjoyed the pleasure of her company in public. I thought we would make a handsome couple.

"No, no. Please. Let me do this for you. I have been wanting to make a special dinner. Hungarian goulash. I have excellent paprika from home. You will like it."

"Thank you." I was strangely touched by her offer and readily acceded. "But what if I don't win? You'll have gone to all that trouble for nothing." She winked at me and my heart fluttered. Something chronic was happened to my internal organs.

"You will not lose."

"Did you look in your crystal ball?" Just getting my facts straight. If I really were going to win, I needed to write an acceptance speech. If she were just hopeful, I was only going to write half a speech, so as not to be completely disappointed when I didn't have to deliver it.

Of course, she didn't answer me. I had a sinking suspicion she wouldn't and I was right. To punish her for withholding evidence, I promised myself I would not write any speech.

For luck.

When I was told there was a ten thousand pound "honorarium" for delivering the acceptance acknowledgement (which really meant for accepting the award), I went to work. With that kind of money I could take a sabbatical and write my novel. That is, if I could get my notes back from my quarantined apartment. Which made me hope Captain Chandler put some of that vanilla lotion I sent on her feet, slipped and fell and bruised her keester. Her successor would undoubtedly be a man. Someone with whom I could communicate.

With ten thousand pounds in my pocket, we would have a lot to talk about.

Not being superstitious in any way, sharp or form, I asked Gypsy to make her special dinner the day *before* the awards ceremony. That way, I could be assured of proper digestion and a good night's sleep. She obliged me so readily I could only suppose the expiration date on her meat was up yesterday.

I requested two days off and Sweet gave them to me without arguing. I consoled myself by reasoning he figured I would be too nervous to work.

When I arrived at Gypsy's flat at five o'clock, the door was unlocked. I let myself in. She had given me a key but I was hesitant to use it, so was relieved to leave it in my pocket. I don't know what my problem was; I had exchanged keys with women before and never felt awkward about such a ritual. It meant no more than a mutual physical attraction and convenience. Not in that order.

I would have to reason out the puzzle when I had more time.

"Hello," she greeted me from the kitchen. "Come in and sit down."

The whole flat smelled delightfully of spices, fresh baked bread and simmering beef. My mouth began to water, prompting me to think I needed a drink. She kept liquor on a side table but this was not an occasion for scotch. For some odd reason, the sound of ice tinkling in a glass reminded me of being alone.

"Here," she said, coming into the living room. "I have decanted a bottle of wine. Will you have some with me?"

I nodded and she poured the dark-red liquid into two Star of Edinburgh wine glasses. We held them up to toast.

"The blood is the life, Mr. Renfield," I said in a Hungarian accent. It was the only Eastern European salute I could think of.

Gypsy pulled a long face and I thought I had murdered the dialect. But then I realized I had set her up for the wrong line.

"It is very old wine," she quoted, waiting for me to try it.

"Aren't you going to have some?" I queried.

"I never drink... wine," she finished and we laughed. It was good to laugh with her, even better to share a memory of a cherished film. It was the first time in my life I was drunk without tasting a drop.

She asked me if I wanted some music and I agreed, requesting – what else? *Swan Lake.* She held the record in her hand before the words were out of my mouth.

While we listened to the London Philharmonic play the theme to *count*less Universal horror films, I acknowledged the usefulness of Public Domain while she finished her preparations in the kitchen. By the time the last strains were playing (it will never sound right to me unless the finale is slightly sour, much as *The William Tell Overture* is never complete without hearing the familiar, "Hi Yo, Silver!"), dinner was ready. We sat at the table to eat.

"I hope you like it," she said. "It is more highly seasoned than you are used to. If it is too much, you must tell me, so I can use a lighter hand next time."

I did not tell her the only Hungarian goulash I had ever eaten was either prepared by a consumptive chef in a greasy spoon, or had been massed produced by Dinty Moore. I suppose she guessed.

Feeling like an American who thinks cucumber sandwiches are the prelude to Beef Wellington, I dug in with a ravenous appetite. With a tip of the hat to Dwight Frye, I sighed in hedonistic sincerity, "It is delicious." And so it was. I wouldn't even care if Dracula's three wives came after me when I was finished. Especially not if one of them would be a Hungarian Gypsy in a future life.

I ate like a wolf, devouring all she put before me, then politely requested seconds. With my plate filled again, I set to, this time savoring the exotic flavors I missed the first time around.

"Perfect," I sighed, demurring wiping my lips on a linen napkin. I didn't think they made linen napkins anymore and rued their lack of common usage as I carefully replaced it on my lap. In a "time is money" culture, where fast food is called "budget gourmet," I had forgotten the meaning, if I ever knew it, of Old World charm. And for the first time regretted my lack of culture.

"Will you teach me your ways?" I asked, with as much reverence as though I had said, *Will you marry me?* "I want to learn; I want to get to know you. There's so much of which I am ignorant."

"You want to know?" she replied in a tone suggesting fidelity for all eternity.

"I do."

No further comparisons required.

"Then I will teach you. There is much wonder in tradition."

"Wonder" was not a word I used or heard often. "Wonder," in my world, was reserved for processed bread without air holes. I was beginning to realize what I had missed from life.

I prayed it was not too late to be reborn.

"Prayed" was another foreign word to me, symbolizing no more than an act performed after near-misses between two cars, or before opening my monthly bank statement to see if any checks had bounced.

When the meal and the hot bread, replete with air holes and melted, unsalted butter had been consumed, the *wine* drunk, as opposed to the imbibers, and the heart content, we retired to the living room.

"You are not too full for desert?" she inquired as we sat.

"No. Never."

Desert, to American men, was a red flag word. Like quiche. Real men did not eat desert. Without knowing it, I had turned in my membership card at the door.

"I have made a chocolate cake. You like chocolate?"

For someone who had never had a childhood, the idea of chocolate cake stirred old memories from deep within my soul.

"Yes. I like chocolate."

"You will have some now, with coffee, or you would rather wait?"

"Now, please." I did not want to postpone anything. Time was eternal, but moments went by too quickly. I didn't want to spend what could no longer be bought; I wanted to experience.

Gypsy rolled out the cake on a small pastry cart. It was, by my inexperienced eye, a four layer cake, iced with dark frosting of a highly polished sheen, testimony to real butter and high-content chocolate liqueur. Written on the top were the words, "Andy's First Cake."

I would have wept like a baby, if I knew how.

She offered me the serving knife and I cut us both huge pieces. She poured the coffee. We made no further communication until our plates and cups were empty.

"You're making a new man out of me," I sighed, patting my bulging stomach. "Or, is that two men?"

She reached over with an innocence bespeaking her nature, poking a finger into my midriff.

"Full," she acknowledged.

I started to say, "Chock full O'...," then bit off the words. I did not want to parrot something out of the 50s. And "nuts" sounded out of place.

"Satisfied," I agreed.

She put on another record, this time *The William Tell Overture,* and we sat on the couch holding hands. When it had played through, I requested *The Blue Danube,* and drifted off to sleep, my head on her shoulder.

I had to rent a tux for the occasion of the **D**uke **o**f Edinburgh (Excellence in Journalism) **A**ward. I can't bring myself to use the initials because of a quip Jimbo made as I was leaving the office this afternoon.

"So, he said. You're off to the banquet. Don't get drunk."

"Thanks," I smiled thinly. "It's pretty hard to, on the watered down booze they serve at those kinds of functions." I knew he was jealous. That's why I could afford to poke fun at my own ceremony. Otherwise, it would have been, "Are you kidding? They serve only brand names at this type of ceremony. The kind that have little symbols on the labels, like castles, and initials like QE II."

"Those aren't castles, and the only initials you'd recognize are 'big W, little g,' for Walgreens," he would say in my imaginary conversation, followed by a juvenile laugh. "I saw that brand of bourbon in your apartment once. It was beside the Welch's grape jelly glass and filled with the ice you siphoned out of the soft drink you bought at lunch."

I struck myself on the forehead. Geez, why do I do this? I can't even make up dialogue and have it turn out right.

Or, I had gone into a parallel universe (again) and Jimbo had started reading my mind. How else would he know I had grape jelly glasses in my cupboard?

"And, by the way," his doppelganger called as I hurried away, eager to get to a mirror and see whether I had given myself a bruise. "Be careful."

I *had* given myself a bruise. Worse, he had seen it.

Be careful?

I was compelled to ask, "Why?" It was some perversion in my nature.

"Well, it is called the **D**uke **o**f (Edinburgh) **A**ward, isn't it? The DOA? Dead on Arrival?"

I shriveled. I had better win this thing. Then I could hit him over the head with the trophy.

Sweet was waiting for me downstairs. We piled into my car and I drove to the tuxedo rental store. They had two black suits waiting for us.

"I hope nobody thinks we're going to a funeral," Sweet nervously laughed, admiring himself in the mirror. I didn't laugh. I figured he was in on it with Jimbo.

"Not when we're paraded through London in a limo," I articulated somehow, through gritted teeth.

I did cut a handsome figure, if I say so myself. The only thing out of alignment was my hair. I meant to get a haircut for the occasion but Gypsy talked me out of it. She likes long hair. I suspected her of being a hippy. But, I was forced to admit, my red locks, touching my starched white collar, made a nice contrast. Red, white and black. White for paper, black for ink and red for the blood and sweat it took me to earn this nomination. Just the proper look for a man about to receive (I hope), Europe's highest journalistic *honour.*

Sweet was fussing with the lapels. I glanced at him out of the corner of my eye. A tailor, or a fitter, or whatever they're called, was hovering nearby, but I knew Sweet wouldn't summon his help. That was tantamount to asking for directions.

"There's something wrong," he complained. "Do they button their shirts on the wrong side?"

"Why would they do that?" I asked, surreptitiously glancing down at my French-cuffed shirt.

"They *drive* on the wrong side, don't they? Maybe when drivers had to reach across with their left hands to get their coffee mugs, they kept bumping it against their shirt, so European tailors switched the whole style around."

I didn't want to pursue that. Not when *my* shirt had button holes on the right.

"Never mind," I reassured him. "No one will notice."

"I don't want to look like a girl," he moaned.

Sweet is five-foot ten and weighs about the equivalent of 16 stone. (Did you know 1 stone = 14 American pounds? And one British pound equals anywhere from twice to half an American dollar? I think that's where the expression, "penny wise and pound foolish" originated.) He has short, jet black hair (which he can't accuse me of turning grey unless he stops going to the "hair dresser"), and a five o'clock shadow at eleven A.M. He couldn't look like a girl if he were dressed in a "two-two" stuffed with falsies.

I say that with a quick shudder of guilt because it reminds me of the scene in *Fantasia* where the hippos dance. It was supposed to be amusing but I never liked that routine and always thought it was cruel. Women have enough problems without Disney making fun of them for their body shapes. Ol' Walt wasn't exactly Johnny Weissmuller, himself, but no one would ever think of drawing him as a fat animal. Actually, when you think of it, cartoons can be very hurtful.

"You look fine to me," I reassured him, changing one mental image for a physical one. "Very masculine. I have some Old Spice in the car. We'll splash some on you and everyone will start whistling sea chanteys."

He was appeased. I knew he would be. Make the slightest concession to an editor and he's happy. That's because they're so used to flat-out refusals.

It was as well to know your enemy's weaknesses.

We paid a staggering deposit, neither of us having any first born children to leave as a promissory. I drove to Gypsy's, where she was waiting outside. She waved madly as she saw the car coming. We both waved back. It did my heart good to know we were so warmly anticipated. As we disembarked, she whispered in my ear.

"Next time, don't drive down the right side of the road. Someone not familiar with your point of origin may hit you."

"Because I look Irish?" I hurriedly inquired, missing her larger and more obvious point.

She didn't answer. I guess she didn't want to hurt my feelings. I did look as though I'd missed a few meals. I guessed it had something to do with the Potato Famine way- back-when.

The chauffeured limousine picked us up at her place. All three of us sat in the back. Sweet thought it behooved me to sit up front with the driver but I didn't trust him alone with Gypsy. Besides, I didn't want to be mistaken for the driver. I suspected his getup of being more expensive than mine.

Mr. McGraw got me on one point, though, and I seethed all the way to the Awards Centre. I let Gyp in first, then quickly followed her, expecting Sweet to get in behind me. But he simply shut the door like a good footman, crossed in front of the stretch limo and got in the other door, thus positioning the lady between us. She seemed to appreciate the gesture. I hoped he was sitting on bubble gum.

"Are you nervous?" Sweet asked as the car took off. Just because my teeth were chattering was no reason to ask if I were scared.

"No," I lied. "What do I have to be nervous about? I wrote the best series of newspaper articles to hit GB since Canary Wharf sank into the ocean," I bragged. "Where is this ceremony, anyway?"

Neither one of them answered. I guess they didn't know, either.

At exactly seven o'clock our transport pulled up in front of a multi-*storey* tower. I didn't quite catch the name of the building. One of the letters in the neon sign was burned out. It was _anary Towers. I didn't have time to play Hang the Man.

Our credentials were checked, I gave them our passes and we went through a metal arm that rose to admit us. It was like being admitted for jury duty.

"This way, please," a guide informed us. She was about twenty years old and looked sixteen. I surmised she was a college student making some money on the side.

We were seated in a large ballroom with about seven hundred other people. As we sat, Sweet poked me in the ribs.

"I don't see anyone else with their shirt buttoned on the left," he complained.

"You're starting a trend," I placated. I did observe there was one guy about three rows ahead of us with a shirt buttoned on the wrong side, but he also sported a purple crew cut so I refrained from pointing him out.

Gypsy was wearing a flowing gown of silken material. It was an earth-brown color, with streaks of yellow and green interwoven through it in a sort of non-pattern pattern. She had a scarf of the same hues and wore a simple necklace of gold weave. A small charm hung from it, but I could not make out the figure and didn't want to stare.

They had seated us toward the front. I was placed in a chair on the outside. That was a good sign. It meant they expected me to get up. They do the same thing at the Oscars, I hear. If you've won (although no one knows the outcome until the seal is broken, of course), they seat you on an aisle. I immediately started checking out all the others who were on the ends of rows. I didn't know any of them.

There were a lot of speeches and a large number of minor awards, commendations and back-patting before the DOA was given out. After the first ten minutes, my stomach growled. In half an hour I looked for an Exit sign, wondering if I could make it to the Men's Room and back before my name was called. Naturally, I didn't budge.

After two and a quarter hours of excruciatingly boring "programme," my back ached, my foot was asleep and I had consumed a two-month supply of Pepto Bismol tablets. I decided the best thing that could happen to me would be to make it to the john intact. I guess they do it on purpose. Even if you don't win, you're so happy to get out, you'll cry anyway.

Gypsy squeezed my hand for comfort. Tears of excitement came into my eyes. I cursed myself for not putting lifts in my shoes.

"I hope you're taking notes," Sweet whispered.

"Why?"

"So you can write about it for tomorrow's edition."

I remembered why I hated him. He was probably mad because I hadn't offered him any of my pink chewable tablets. If he realized my mouth tasted like wintergreen and felt like sawdust, he would have felt better. I didn't enlighten him. It was a payback for maneuvering Gypsy into the middle.

By the time it came to give out the main award, I had a headache that would have staggered a buffalo, I had ripped off a hangnail and gotten blood on the cuff of my shirt. I tugged on the sleeve of the rented tux, trying to cover it. I remembered I had forgotten to put on deodorant.

"Bla bla bla." It was the Duke, himself. He sounded like he had toured too many widget factories, trailing three steps behind his wife. My sympathy runneth over.

"... Andrew Kimbo, of the Cover All News Service," he finally and excruciatingly concluded.

I had won.

The worst speech makers in the world are people who write for a living. I am proud to say I lived up to that tradition. I have no idea what I said, why I said it, or even if I were speaking English. It didn't matter. I figured no one was taking notes.

I shook a lot of hands. I babbled. I thanked everyone, including Sweet. That's when I knew I was delirious. I had my picture taken. I could feel the hair standing up on the back of my head, like a cowlick. I'd ask for the photo to be airbrushed before it went out on the wire.

After it was over, Sweet and Gypsy came and took me away. There was a banquet. I guess it was a very nice dinner. The wine was decanted so I couldn't tell if it came with labels with castles and QE II's endorsement. I'd lie if asked.

There was a line five thousand, three hundred and sixty-two men long line at the toilet facilities. I counted. I didn't have anything else to do. I was gone thirty-nine hours. Gypsy was back after five minutes. I guessed it was reverse potty parody. Who was I to complain? I had won.

It would take a long time for that realization to sink in.

"You were right," I told Gypsy as we escaped from the bevy of well-wishers, dignitaries and dukes. "It was written in the stars."

"I was correct about you winning," she replied.

"Look up there," I said, pointing into the night sky. "My lucky star. Shall we make a wish on it?" I was so excited, I almost broke into a few bars of "Twinkle, Twinkle Little Star." "Come on," I urged. Nothing could go wrong now. "If that's my lucky star, which one is yours?"

"I do not have one," she said. "You are the only star I wish to have."

I told you my luck was running hot.

"What about you, Sweet?" I continued, oblivious to the old wives expression, *Whom the gods destroy they first make starry-eyed.* "Which one is yours?"

"When I was a kid, I always thought the dark side of the moon was lucky. I used to wish on that."

I looked at him to see if he were kidding. He wasn't. Now I knew why he had grown up to be an editor.

"You can't see it," I protested.

"But I can imagine it."

"What could you possibly wish for, using the dark side of the moon?"

"A pair of glasses. I was myopic as a kid but my parents didn't believe me."

"What happened?"

"I grew out of my myopia."

I laughed, thinking he was making a joke. I winked at the lady.

"Let's drop Sweet off at his flat, then go back to your place and open a bottle of champagne." I was bubbly, soaring through the heavens of uncharted heavenly bodies.

"We do not have to drop him off," she protested. "I think he should share the wine with us."

"Why?" I flatly croaked.

"Because he gave you a job when no one else would. Because he cares about you. As I do."

"Not exactly in the same ways," I dryly stated. I was beginning to wonder about Gypsies.

"I'd love to have a glass of champagne with you," Sweet announced. I decided I would like to send him to the dark side of the moon.

As we got out of the limo and wished the driver Godspeed, I was struck with a sudden burst of inspiration. I fumbled for something in my pocket, pulled a long face and opened the front, left side door. In my haste, I had forgotten in England, *almost* everything is backwards. I had to whisper my instructions to the driver across the expanse of rippling seat covers.

"The gentleman with me changed his mind. He wants to go home. He's had too much to drink."

I winked, hoping that universal signal between bosom buddies would be comprehended, as I had no idea how to wink from the bottom, up.

"Here," I continued, thrusting a wad of folded bills at him. "Take him anywhere. Around the park. Across the Chunnel. Drop him off at NASA."

"Where's that, gov?" the chauffeur inquired in what even I, a lowly American, could tell was a put-on accent. I pegged him as having come from Wales, which, to the English, was the equivalent of originating from Jersey.

"Never mind. Take him to see the Queen. He has an appointment. Very hush-hush."

"The Queen is at Balmoral," he protested. But not too strenuously.

I should have figured, her husband being in London.

"Take him to Scotland." He stared dubiously at the money. I didn't have time to quibble. "Take him as far as this will go."

"What about me tip?"

"Take the tip off the top."

He gave me a flop-eared grin and gunned the motor. He understood fast getaways. With a smugness born of possessing a DOA, I coughed, drew back, then held my stomach.

"Oh..." I groaned. "I think I'm going to be sick." I had to react fast because I knew Gypsy would respond first. "Sweet," I specified, calling on his manhood, "Hold me up."

"What? In a rented tux? What if you puke all over me?"

I had forgotten he had a maiden aunt in his family tree who had hailed from Scotland in the time of Robert the Bruce. Since coming to the British Isles, that distant heredity had blossomed.

"Not *that* kind of sick," I muttered, like a curse, through gritted teeth.

"What kind, then?"

My God, now I was required to be a medical dictionary. Fortunately, I was up on my diseases.

I said the first thing that came into my mind.

"Down's Syndrome."

That sounded about right. I was threatening to fall down.

Fortunately he didn't know any more about medicine than I did, for he rushed to me, arms spread out like a second baseman backpedaling into the outfield after a shallow pop fly. As swift as Willie McGee charging in from center field, I dodged to his right, striking him in the midriff. He plunged, head first, into the front passenger seat.

Pushing his legs inside the cabin, I slammed the door shut and waved at the driver. He gave me what I wanted to believe was a thumbs-up and drove off. Not knowing how much he was going to take as a tip, I hoped he would at least get Mr. McGraw out of the neighborhood.

As the car sped away, Gypsy sidled up to me, a tender, reproachful expression on her loving, soft, beautiful face.

"That was not nice."

"Neither was his offer to invite himself up for a drink."

She made a sad expression, then finally grinned.

"I hope you did not tip the driver too much."

"Oh, don't worry," I assured her. "He's from Wales. They won't get far."

"I meant," she interrupted, an elfin twinkle in her eyes, "I hope you did not give him all your coins."

Puzzled, I reached into my trousers pocket and withdrew the contents. Holding the assorted articles out for inspection, Gypsy studied them a moment, then made a low "Ah ha!" and plucked out a large, shiny gold "coin."

"This is what I was searching for," she announced with a smugness equal to mine. I looked at it. My jaw fell seventeen centimeters.

At that moment, I could have auditioned for P.T. Barnum and gotten the white-faced, red-nosed job.

What Gypsy held between her thumb and forefinger was a condom.

I laughed and she laughed. We interlocked arms and started for her flat, anticipating a cold bottle of France's best and a commingling of fluids not commonly served in a wine glass.

We hadn't gone more than four or five steps when a car roared down the street. I groaned, cursed Welshmen and turned with an authoritative, "keep on going" gesture when I realized it was not the limo. Nor did the car have its headlights on.

Some sixth sense I had hitherto denied the existence of started at the back of my neck and grew goose bumps down my spine. Croaking a warning to Gypsy, I flung my arms around her just as something was thrown from the speeding motor vehicle.

I don't know if it was my off-balance weight which brought us down, or the force of the explosion.

I never will know, this side of heaven.

CHAPTER 13

If the expression "scared shitless" means what is sounds like, then I was that frightened.

I was also in pain. At first, I just assumed my entire body had been blasted away, reducing me to a skinless hotdog. I dared not move for fear of discovering my not-so-flattering analogy was correct. When I tried to move and found I couldn't, I started to holler. It wasn't fair. This was supposed to be "A Hard Day's Night," not "Baby's in Black."

It was not until I opened my eyes and saw only darkness that I started screaming. Being unzipped from my outer covering was one thing; losing the power of locomotion another. But adding blindness to the equation equaled hell on earth.

Unless I was dead, already, and this was Hades. I hadn't figured to end up there. I guess no one ever does.

"Sweet, sweet, sweet Jesus," I moaned. I would never scoff at death bed conversions again.

Little did I know, "sweet" was the operative word.

"It's Sweet," I heard a voice saying from far, far away. "It's Sweet, Andy. I'm here."

"Sweet is in Wales," I mumbled. My brain was all mixed up.

"I'm here, boy. Right here."

For a fleeting moment, I thought I had been so evil I had condemned him, too. That choked me up, big time.

"It wasn't his fault," I prayed. "He only gave me a job. He's not responsible for my actions. Jesus, it's not like he was my godfather." In fact, I never had a godfather. Or, a godmother. That saved two other souls from rotting with me. For the first time in my life, I was glad I didn't have a family.

Relieved to be an Outsider.

Scared to death I had died and no one cared.

And then I remembered. With a scream of pure agony, totally incomparable to the physical pain I no longer felt, I cried for *her*.

"Gypsy! Gypsy! Where are you, baby?"

"Andy, Andy, listen to me, Andy."

I could hear words being mumbled over me, but they made no more sense than all the prayers in the word mean to an infant being christened.

"Gypsy!"

When she did not answer I knew, categorically, without a smidgen of doubt, where I was. The *why* had suddenly turned inconsequential.

"Kimbo, will you listen, you dumb ass."

It was then I responded to the voice.

"Where is she, Sweet? Don't lie to me. I can take it." The Great Fib. Like good father-figures the world over, he told the truth. Sort of.

"She's all right."

"Really?"

"Really."

"Where am I, what happened, and when can I see her?"

I heard his tongue click.

"Kimbo, Kimbo. Always the reporter. Who, what, where, when and why."

My mind wasn't that dull.

"I only asked where, what and when."

"Don't be petulant."

He had that tone in his voice which caused an instant flare-up of suspicion. Totally unfounded, but persistent, nevertheless. My rear end was so inflamed with pain, the thought paddled through my brain that he had wholloped me several thousand times in the traditional, misguided form of discipline commonly referred to as "spanking."

"What did you do to me?" I whimpered.

"Picked you up off the street and called an ambulance." I thanked whatever gods there are he was not reading my mind. "It's a good thing you were so cheap," he thoughtfully added, and I knew the thoughtfulness had nothing to do with my being cheap. "The cabby was taking his time and we'd only gone a block or two when we heard the explosion. At first, I thought it was your champagne cork hitting the ceiling, or something."

I knew he reasoned the noise was somehow connected to me, but doubted the first thought he had was a champagne cork. I groaned and wondered if *that* part of my anatomy was still attached.

"The driver was Welsh." He laughed. He wasn't making a joke.

"Where is she, Sweet? Can I see her?" And then I remembered I couldn't see. This was turning into a grandiose night of revelations. "I'm blind," I added in a divinely penitent whisper.

"No, you're not," he informed me in his editor's voice, so I knew he was telling the truth. It was the "cut to the quick and forget the Dickensian writing" tone I knew so well. Never before – or ever again – would I be so glad to hear that out of his mouth. "The lights are turned out."

"Are we having an air raid?"

I wasn't in England for the Big One, but I knew the Cold War pretty well. Like all the others, I had crawled under my desk at school in mock preparation for Red Airplanes to bomb Manhattan.

"No." Succinct. No wonder he had grown up to be a blue-pencil man. "Your eyes were hurt by the flash of the bomb. But the ophthalmologist examined you and said there was no damage to the optical nerve."

"Optic nerve," I corrected. Every good show in the '60s had at least one episode where the main (male) character suffered temporary (usually hysterical, although they seldom used that word, it being derived from the Greek *hysterikos,* or "womb"), blindness, so I knew the correct terminology. Maybe TV series still do that. I wouldn't know. I stopped watching episodic TV around 1974.

"Turn the lights on, will you?"

It wasn't that I didn't believe him – I *had* to believe him. I just wanted to be able to see his sweet, dear, grumpy, prematurely-aged face.

There was a lot of fussing and grumbling. It took, what seemed to me, the humble blind wretch, an inordinate amount of time for the blaring, two-zillion watt overhead candescent light to come on. I figure Sweet didn't know where the light switch was and guessed wrong the first fifty tries as he fumbled in the dark.

Hospitals never make it easy for patients to find anything. That's so "927-bed-2," the miserable bedridden, pain-tortured "customer" has to use a call light, and the overwrought, overworked, underpaid nurse has to answer it sometime before change of shift.

It's always amazed me that hospitals, like major corporations (which they are, now-a-days, although nobody likes to admit it), do "discharge interviews," when they already know they're going to consistently score low on "promptness." Realizing what they do, you would think they would rectify that problem (other than through in-services and tacit threats), but they don't seem to. That might require hiring more staff, or something.

I groaned as the light blinded me, bringing home with crystal clarity the oft-used expression, "damned if you do and damned if you don't." I was sightless in the dark and visionless in the light.

"Are you all right?" McGraw fearfully whispered. "Shall I call a doctor?"

I am not what they call a professional patient, but I did know the only place you will never find a doctor is in a hospital. The only place you're less likely to find a physician is at his office when you have a regularly scheduled appointment.

But I forgave Sweet for asking. I know he knew better, but he was hysterical.

"No."

Twenty minutes later, when my pupils had contracted to the size of my last raise, I could make out his concerned mug staring down at me.

"Move back. Give me some air," I complained. I didn't want to see a grown man cry. He jumped back with alacrity.

"Can I get you anything?" he asked helpfully. "Some ice water?"

I groaned again. After physicians, the scarcest item in a hospital is ice. No, make that, after physicians and pain medication.

"Please, Sweet. Stop trying to be my nurse and tell me about Gypsy. Was she hurt? Did she get burned from the heat of the blast?" He stood at attention, mute as a statue. "She didn't try going after that bastard by herself, did she?" I demanded, horrified. That would be like her. She was a crusader, cut from the same cloth as Eleanor of Aquitaine, who fought in the Holy Land before women were banned from all the fun.

My living statue twitched, shuddered and remained mute. My world caved in.

"You lied! She's dead! I knew it!"

"No!" He unfroze for one word, a glacier moving at an infinitesimal pace.

I tried to be calm. I put on my reporter's face. It's the same one police officers and ambulance attendants learn to assume after staring tragedy in the face day after day, night after night, year after year. The same face which allows ICU personnel to eat on the job and postal employees to show up at work.

"Tell me."

He swallowed, tried a smile. It made him look ghastly.

"She's gone."

Only twenty-odd years of training allowed me to refrain from shouting.

"Gone?" He nodded helpfully. "Gone, where? Grocery shopping? Star gazing? Back to palm reading?"

"Gone," he reiterated. I had gotten that the first time. His work face was slipping. He really did need to get back into the field. A little combat, a few murder stories, a high- rise suicide and he'd retrieve his stoicism. He was a pro, like me.

"When you came back and found me lying on the ground, was she missing?"

He nodded. Any more nodding and I'd stick suction cups to his hands and put him on my rear car window.

"Yes."

"Then it's safe to assume she was taken by whoever threw the bomb. She couldn't have just gotten up and walked away. Not without me," I added, to save an argument.

"That's what the police think. They'll find her, Kimbo."

"Sure they will. And when they do, you and I can go down and identify the body. *Now, Mr. Kimbo, this isn't going to be pleasant for you. Have you ever seen a dead body before?* 'Yes, officer. Lots of them. I'm a crime reporter.' Relief. *Good. Now, did she have any identifying marks, scars, moles, that sort of thing?* 'She had a life force strong enough to sustain *homo sapiens* on Mars.' *Now, when we draw back the sheet, please try to remain calm.* 'I'm calm.' *If you feel as though you're going to faint, raise a hand and we'll take you away."*

"Shut up, Andy. They'll find her alive."

"She has to be hurt, Sweet. She couldn't have survived that blast without sustaining some serious damage. She may be bleeding to death at this very moment."

"They're doing everything they can to find her."

"They told you that?" I asked. He nodded hopefully. I might as well have been back in St. Louis. I could hear Captain Chandler's voice now. She was a master of deception.

I tried to make him see reason. "I know what that means. That means the police don't have a clue."

"I never realized how cynical you've become. England has one of the best police forces in the world."

"Get me my clothes."

"What for? Nurses see naked men all the time. Nobody cares if you're undressed. You're in a hospital, for goodness' sake."

I had to say it. "Goodness has nothing to do with it." He flinched. "I can't sign myself out of here without my pants."

"You're not leaving. You left half your butt on the sidewalk. All the skin was seared off by the tremendous heat."

Which explained why I felt as though I had been flailed alive. It was a sickeningly familiar feeling. It reminded me of being a helpless kid, at the mercy of "caregivers."

"I have to get out. I'm the only one who can find her."

"You mustn't think like that."

"The Mystic Seer has got her, Sweet. We both know that."

"We don't know that. If it was Jason Holloway and his people, why would they have left you behind?"

Good question. Too bad I had the answer.

"Because they want me to come after her; they want to torture me, letting me get close enough to see her, maybe, then whisking her away. It's called retribution, my friend."

"Let the authorities handle it. That's what they get paid for. They're professionals."

Deafness suddenly replaced blindness as my number one affliction.

"And maybe he wants to find out how much power she really has. She was linked to him, you know. Psychically. She read his mind and told me things. That's how I found the ledger and the money."

"What money?"

"If she's alive, she'll be trying to contact me. I can't hear her inside these walls. I'm stifled. My brain won't work right. I need to escape, to be outside. Go to her flat, maybe."

"You're not psychic."

"No. But she is. Believe me, McGraw. Her life is at stake."

"What about yours? Doesn't that mean anything to you?"

"Not a hell of a lot. Not at the moment. I'm scared, sure." I remembered how scared, and cursed myself. I had messed the bed. That scared. Scared like a kid is frightened of monsters in the dark.

"Please, Andy. I don't want anything to happen to you."

I could have said, *Nothing will happen to me.* That's what all the movie stars say. On film. That's because they know the ending. Mine was far more uncertain. I wasn't a franchise.

"Sweet, I'll cut you in on it."

He wavered. He wasn't looking for glory. He was scared, too. But he cared. I could have kissed him but my lips were chapped.

"I have orders from Mr. Poxie."

"Yeah. I bet. He'll take a loss if my nearest and dearest collects on my insurance policy. He owns that company, too." He flinched. The truth always hurts. I tried my ace. "Tell him he's my beneficiary. Then he'll be sure and let me go."

"Is he?" Sweet gasped.

This wasn't real life, this was a Three Stooges short.

"No. You are."

I knew he wouldn't believe me. Anything to bring him around.

He was saved by the bell. A nurse, or a sister, or whatever they call those white-clad females with the caps and the perpetually cheerful faces, arrived.

"Time to change –"

"No!"

"– your bandages, Mr. Kimbo. Will you please leave, now, sir?" she demanded of my friend.

"Yeah. Sure. I'll be right outside," he told me, walking out backwards. Never turn your back on someone wielding a dressing tray.

I'm not a big man, as men go, but I'm not exactly tiny, either, yet she flipped me over onto my stomach as though I were a three-year old. I don't think she broke sweat. I guess they get a lot of practice.

At least I could hide my face in a pillow. It smelled of disinfectant and starch. Before I passed out I wondered how many dying heads had rested on it before mine.

I knew too much.

When I awoke, it was day and someone was changing an IV. The damned IVAC had been beeping for so long, I had incorporated the sound into my dreams. When it was suddenly shut off, I felt as though something precious had died.

Silence in a hospital is never golden.

There was a large, easy-read, single-day calendar on the wall across from my bed. I watched the pages being ripped off and died a little inside at each passing day. Gypsy was out there, all alone, held hostage by a devil d/b/a the Mystic Seer.

She might think I was dead. On the whole, that might be a comfort to her.

The way you know you've been asleep in a hospital is when they wake you up to ask if you want a sleeping pill. The nurse assigned to me was very nice. She came from South Africa, and spoke like a Colonist. I was relieved. In Los Angeles, you communicate with the help via hand signals.

After declining her offer, I repositioned my pillow and stared out the window. At least, I stared toward where the window was physically positioned. I couldn't see out because the blinds were drawn. I think they did that from habit. Block all signs of life, like in the blackouts during the WWII. Don't let anyone know you're alive.

I thought the "hangover" from the Big One a bit inappropriate for a hospital, but no one asked my opinion, so I didn't give it.

I had just counted the slats for the tenth time when the door opened. I assumed it was an orderly, coming in to take my temperature, pulse and respiration, so I didn't bother breaking my concentration. When the interloper didn't speak, didn't turn on the light, didn't rattle a bedpan, my curiosity was aroused. I turned and stared into the darkness.

"Who's there?" I felt compelled to ask. No answer. "What do you want?"

I heard a noise, which might have been air, being sucked in through front teeth. The ones most kids have a gap between. Orthodontists love those spaces; the braces parents inevitably buy equate to a Mercedes payment or two.

I don't know why everyone has to have perfect teeth. You'd think we were all going to grow up and be movie stars. Personally, I think parents ought to save their dough. Christopher Lee has pretty crummy looking teeth, and he's done all right for himself.

Playing Dracula.

Which is who I could believe was standing in the shadows. My hand went instinctively to my neck.

"Que pasa?" I inquired. Spanish was the only other language I knew, and I learned most of that from old Westerns.

I could have played either the "good," or the "ugly." What was standing in my room had already cast himself as the "bad."

"Your time is running out, Mr. Kimbo," the voice said. It had that slick tone, reserved for used car salesman and insurance adjustors.

"Sure," I replied, a bit too flippantly. "If you want me to leave, I'll go."

"You know what I mean."

I did, but I didn't want to admit it.

"Would you care to be just a tad more specific?"

"All the pieces are in place. Soon, the world will be mine."

"You've made a lot of money," I agreed, sinking into the mattress like a bedbug. "But money isn't everything. Money can't buy happiness."

"Oh, but it can," my visitor snickered. "Have you ever thought to consider what I can do with it?"

"Pay off your Master Card bill?"

"How much does uranium cost? How much smallpox disease can two trillion dollars buy? Or what about funding experiments in genetic manipulation? With an unlimited exchequer, scientists can create super men – or super idiots. An invincible army, or an army of drones. Take your pick."

"You're going to do those things?" A chill of horror ran down my spine. Spittle rolled down my cheek.

"Not I," he scoffed. "There are already world leaders in place who would... kill... for the chance to destroy the Civilized World. Why should I replicate their most worthy efforts? All they lack are the funds. Which I intend to supply."

"Why?" My question came out sounding as though it emitted from a plastic squeeze toy; hardly human. Which put me on a par with Mr. Jason Holloway.

"For excitement. Thrills. Kicks," he hissed in pleasure.

"You're the – devil!"

"Tut tut, Mr. Kimbo. What is Satan, after all, but an angel cast from heaven? No one would ever accuse me of being one of God's chosen."

He had a good point.

"I... don't understand." And then braver, for I had nothing to lose, "Why tell me?"

I could feel the sneer.

"You are the random element."

I shuddered. He had been privy to more than we suspected.

"Life isn't a theatrical release, Holloway. You're not going to get your name above the title. You may think of yourself as a hyphenate: produced by Jason Holloway. Directed by Jason Holloway. Written by Jason Holloway. But, it's not going to happen that way. This time, you've overextended yourself."

"How so?" he leered.

"Think of all union dues you're going to have to pay."

He had the gall to laugh.

"I can afford them."

"Unless I make you pay the piper first."

"Alas, I can dance to whatever tune you play."

"You're read your ancient texts and charts wrong this time. Mistook the meaning of an obscure hieroglyphic. Added an extra star into your calculations."

"I am never wrong."

"He who laughs last, laughs best," I threatened.

"I assure you, Mr. Kimbo: you will have nothing to find amusing from now until… the end of your life." Without able to see details, I noted he brought a hand to his head. "Ah, but I see it is *her* life of which you are concerned. You will find no humor there, either, for you are both doomed."

"You won't get away with it."

"Who's to stop me? You? You are not a leading man; you are only a character actor."

I should have taken that for a compliment.

"Step into the light so I can see you."

"Not now. For the moment I prefer to remain anonymous. But the time will come when we meet face-to-face."

"When?"

"Soon. But you must hurry. I grow impatient. And – Gypsy – misses you so."

"If you've harmed a hair on her head, I'll smash you and your empire to smithereens!"

"A lovely thought." I had the sick feeling he meant it.

"I'll be out of here in a week," I tried, making my best guess.

"You do not have a week. Or should I say, *she* does not have a week. Do you take my meaning?"

I "took" it with pretty-please and sugar on top.

"How will I find you? At Mystic Towers?"

In my excitement, I forgot that was not the name of the building. I imagined I could see him smile.

"You will be summoned."

"Phone call? Western Union? Radar love?"

"Something like that."

I heard the door open and he was gone. A blast of cool air washed over me. I was vaguely disappointed he hadn't turned into a bat and gone out the window. And then I remembered it was closed.

It was as well to know one's enemy's weaknesses.

The day they removed the tubing from my arm with the needle long enough to suture an elephant after a Caesarian section, I knew my chance had come. I hadn't eaten much and I felt as weak as a kitten, but now that I was free from entangling alliances, escape was possible.

As soon as the graveyard shift reported for duty and made their rounds, I maneuvered myself out of bed and stood on my two legs. The world went topsy-turvy but I waited, willing my head to clear. It did. My clothes were in a drawer. Not the ones I had been wearing, of course, but a fresh set. I knew Sweet had brought them and sent a silent "thanks" his way.

When the nursing staff looked for me again at 7:00 A.M. and I was gone, Sweet would be the only one who wasn't surprised.

Dressing wasn't easy. My backside still had a dressing on it, making it appear as though I were wearing nappies. I was in no position to quibble about my appearance, however. Since I was in London, I could assume people would think I was just trying to look hip. The idea of being taken for an old man wearing diapers for his inçontinence didn't occur to me.

I opened the door to my room and stared out. The corridor was dimly lit by evenly- spaced night lights, simulating a home atmosphere. I don't know why they bother. They do the same thing in prisons, I understand.

Maybe it's supposed to help the graveyard staff find there way, but everyone who's ever worked the late shift knows a healthcare professional can walk down any hospital corridor in their sleep.

I cocked my head (no jokes, now, please) and listened. From somewhere down the corridor I could hear a television playing. It made my skin crawl. They do that for the comatose ones, the ones with brain death, those patients they're waiting for the insurance to expire on, so they can ship them out to a "rehab facility."

No one knows what goes on in the subconscious of someone who's out for the count, so in those facilities where the TV is free of charge, they leave the set on. I think it's meant kindly.

I said a prayer as I passed that room; the one with the grey, flickering lights emerging from the black and white film starring long dead actors. I didn't know who was in that room and I didn't want to know. It didn't matter.

It was meant kindly.

Remarking to myself that I was growing maudlin, I hunched my shoulders and clipped my press pass onto my shirt, face toward my chest. I wanted to look like I belonged, that I was One of Them, a brother hospital worker, possibly from X-ray, or one of those vital but unseen departments. Adopting a hurried, snail's pace shuffle and a look of extreme importance finished my disguise.

I've been in enough hospitals to know you can't walk out the front door at midnight. Security locks those doors so the staff won't smuggle office supplies into their cars. That required I leave via the Emergency Room. I didn't think anyone would stop me, but I didn't want to take a chance.

Patients who get caught leaving Against Medical Advise often have a hefty dose of MOM and a series of tap-water enemas prescribed for them the following day. That keeps them too occupied to plan another escape.

The Nurses Station was empty as I passed it. My eyes scanned the small, shabby, "home away from home," looking for something which would prove to the most skeptical guard I was an employee. That way, I could pass without having to be frisked.

I was hoping to find a lab coat, or a scrub shirt thrown carelessly over the back of a chair, but my luck was only running so-so. The sole article of clothing I found was a pair of high heel shoes left under the chart table. I didn't think they would be of much use.

I settled for a clipboard and the fourth "No Carbon Required" copy of yesterday's diet list. Inasmuch as the paper was utterly illegible (the nurse, obviously did not comply with the "Press Hard, You Are Making Four Copies" advice), I felt there could be no breach of confidentiality and took it with a light heart. I felt worse about the clipboard. It would probably require an Act of the Governing Board to requisition another.

I made a note to return the clipboard by mail, no return address on the outside of the envelope.

They probably get lots of such packages, containing used patient gowns, paper slippers, plastic bedpans and telemetry monitors.

I made my way to the elevator and tried to guess on which floor the E.R. was located. It had to be accessible to ambulances, which meant the first or second level. There was what looked like a "You Are Here" information guide by the service elevators, but it turned out to be a fire escape plan and covered nothing but the stairwells. There were lots of red, yellow and blue dots, but I hadn't attended the staff-only in-service and didn't know what they meant.

I guess the employees could get out, but the patients and visitors were on their own. Which reminded me of a seminar I attended once when I worked in Los Angeles. One of the city firemen was giving an Earthquake Awareness Program. He said to keep a plastic bottle of water, a cache of non-perishable food and blankets in your car at all times, and to count the number of over- and underpasses on your route home. Any one of them could crumble and block the highway.

It was good advice and I still do that.

I guess that's why people call me cynical.

But I digress.

I was too weak to take the stairs in any case, so I pressed the elevator button and waited. It being a little after midnight, I only had five minutes to kill before the car arrived. I pressed "2" and hoped for the best.

The doors slid open and I baby-stepped out, not for the sake of silence but because my rump was on fire and that was the longest stride I could manage. There were directional signs everywhere. The "E.R." was marked in blood-red ink. I followed the arrows with religious precision and got utterly lost. I almost gave up and went back to my room.

When everything else fails, follow the worn tiles on the floor. That path will either lead you to the E.R. or the cafeteria. I lucked out.

Walking into the glare of a busy staff room, I clutched my clipboard and accosted an orderly.

"I'm a temp from the Extra Arms and Legs Registry. My shift ran late and I'm on overtime if I don't leave in the next ten minutes. Can you tell me how to get out?"

He blanched. I'm not sure it was the "temp," or the "overtime," and didn't stop to ask.

"Sure," he said, in a thick East Indian accent. "Everyone gets lost. When you finally learn your way around this place, they lay you off."

I laughed and clasped him on the shoulder. I had said that a time or two myself about the newsroom.

He took me to the Security Exit and introduced me to the guard.

"This man is from the Agency. He's on overtime."

The guard stood up so fast and so straight I thought he was going to salute me. He pressed a button and a sliding door whisked open. I was almost through when his expression changed. I thought he might be suspicious of my diaper-padded buttocks, so I thrust the clipboard out toward him.

"Can you authorize my time?" I asked in a plaintive manner. "I was supposed to have the supervisor initial it but she was busy in a Code."

If I thought the Indian had paled, that was nothing compared to what the guard turned.

"No, no," he stammered. "I can't do that."

"But then I'll have to come back in the morning." I had him on the run. "Do you validate?"

He waved me through and I was free.

As free as a patient on the lam from the Sisters of Mercy. As free as a lover in desperate search of his kidnapped Gypsy. As free as a hack reporter on the trail of a bomb-tossing Mystic Seer.

I put one threat behind me as I scurried down the ambulance ramp and into the night air. Surely Jason Holloway could not be more formidable than what I had just survived.

Once on the street I paused long enough to glance up at the stars. I didn't have a chart. I simply had to believe Aquarius was ascending into the right House.

CHAPTER 14

I didn't have my wallet, my car, my flat keys or any money. Those personal items, I presume, had been confiscated in the name of saving the patient from himself, otherwise known as locking them up for safe keeping so the staff couldn't steal them. It was a wonder my press pass had been left in the drawer. I guessed no one thought it had any value.

At any rate, there was no point going back to my own pad because that's the first place they'd look for me. I seriously doubted the hospital would mount a manhunt. True, my disappearance would be a legal nightmare and lots of memos would be written about it, but I could make that right by returning when this fiasco was over and freeing the staff from any wrongdoing.

Maybe I could send my absolution in the same package as the clipboard. That would save me the parking fee.

I had no idea where I was, what part of the city, but had to presume that if I had been injured close to Gypsy's flat, I would have been taken to the nearest hospital. That meant I couldn't be more than four or five miles from where I wanted to go.

As I shuffled along the street, I regretted the fact I was not in St. Louis. In that city, there were major medical centers on every street corner. I probably could have seen Gypsy's place from any half dozen of them.

England, employing socialized medicine, was more frugal. Under their system of health care, a man needing a non-emergency cardiac catheterization could wait eight months before finally having his coronary arteries unplugged. In the States, doctor's send a cab for him. Employing a for-profit health care system, the US is near the bottom of the world in life expectancy. I don't know if they figure strokes and heart attacks in the equation which result from a patient seeing the bills for his procedure, but they should.

I couldn't very well stop a bobby and ask directions, even if I saw one loitering about. That meant trusting to my innate sense of direction. I seldom get lost but that's because I frequently don't know where I'm going.

Each step brought with it a new agony. It felt like a 4th of July wienie, while my muscles had weakened from an enforced, prolonged stay on my face. I hadn't eaten anything to speak of and my blood sugar had probably bottomed out.

My blood sugar was undoubtedly *low*.

I tried whistling to take my mind off the pain but when I found my lips wouldn't pucker, I tried humming. I got through several songs, then abandoned the effort because I couldn't remember more than a few bars of any one song, and the constant refrain of "Band of Gold" got on my nerves, big time.

Like a prisoner undergoing Chinese water torture, I tried reciting poetry ("Ode on a Grecian Urn"), Shakespeare ("Once more onto the breech, dear friends"), then chit-chatted back and forth to myself as Kelly and Scotty (*I Spy*), before collapsing into a heap on the roadway.

Fortunately, I fell to my knees, for if I had toppled over backwards, that would have been the end of me. I waited until my ragged breath slowed and my pulse returned to a semblance of normalcy before attempting to stand once more. If I had not been so afraid for Gypsy, I could just as soon have curled up and died. But she was out there, somewhere, and I had to find her.

That much, I knew, the Mystic Seer was counting on.

I couldn't feel dawn coming – you never can in a big metropolis – but when the traffic noises picked up, I knew it must be nearing five-thirty or so. If the shift at the hospital changed at seven o'clock, that gave me two solid hours before I was missed and someone placed a call to Sweet.

Lots of unfortunates were declared dead between seven and seven-thirty in the morning. That's not when they died, just when they were found.

The more you know about hospitals, the less you want to go to one.

Personally, I had always fantasied about dying under a bush. If I didn't look livelier, I might end up under a double-decker.

By six-thirty, I found myself in a neighborhood I recognized and quickened my pace, like a good bird dog. Or, I guess I should say, considering where I found myself, *like a blue-blooded fox hound.* I was on the scent. Any moment Prince Charles and his heirs would go galloping past me.

There were some advantages to being an American. We only keep our leaders for eight years, max. England is stuck with theirs for a lifetime. Or, until they abdicate, whichever comes first.

Another quarter-hour of forward movement took me to Gypsy's flat. Mounting the steps proved an exercise in character, for the upward lifting of one leg after the other stretched the muscles in the back of my legs and buttocks. There was a hand railing, but like the lifts, one learned not to trust them.

As I reached the landing, a devastating thought occurred to me: I had no key. I decided if the door were locked, I'd melt on the spot and slide beneath it, like tigers turning into butter.

"Please, God, let the door be unlocked," I beseeched. I know all about free will. If the door were locked, then it would stay locked. I turned the knob, gave a desperate shove and found myself standing inside her entranceway.

The journey of a thousand miles starts with a single prayer.

I shut the door and barred myself against the world.

"Gypsy?" I called. It was hope, nothing more. "Gypsy?" No answer.

I checked the bedroom and the bathroom, just to be on the safe side. Empty. Deserted. Abandoned.

As long as I was in the Facility, I opened the medicine cabinet and removed the bottle of aspirin. I swallowed the little white pills down with a glass of water. The recommended dose being two, I took six, knowing the increased dose would work better and faster. I wasn't a layman for nothing.

Gypsy had some petroleum jelly and I took that, too. If nothing else, I could rub it on my burns. It was better than butter and didn't cost as much. Ever since Mad Cow Disease, who trusted dairy products, anyway? In a pinch, margarine might have done the trick, but the way my luck was going, it would have been manufactured with genetically-altered soy beans or something and burned my ass off.

After making a complete circuit of the flat and determining without a shadow of a doubt she was not there, I found some bourbon and took two more aspirin. For medicinal purposes, only, you understand. The bourbon, not the ASA.

I wanted a shower and I needed a nap. I had been up all night and my nerves were beginning to jangle. I knew all the warning signs my body gave. When I was over the edge, there was little sense ignoring them. To do so was asking for trouble and I had enough of that, as it was.

Truth be told, a bath would have suited my needs better, but I could not sit or recline for any length of time, and the thought of immersing my back in hot water was frightening. In the hospital, I had taken care of my sunny side, while the nurses and orderlies had attended to the rear. Now I was alone, hurting like hell and shaking like a leaf.

The old fear, the creepy-crawly shakes stole over me and I backed away from the tub as though there were a nest of snakes holed up there. Nothing could induce me to raise a leg and step into the bath.

"Be reasonable," I warmed myself, in the old tried-and-true, patience-wearing-thin lecturing voice parents around the world employ on balky children. As though a five-year old could be expected to understand.

"But I am not five years old," I said aloud to the ghosts of What Might Have Been. "I am a grown man. I can take care of myself." Yet, for the first time in my life, I doubted the veracity of that bold assertion. I did not feel grown up, wise or brave. I was scared and there were monsters lurking in the drain.

If only Gypsy were here, she would know what to do, what to say, how to take care of me. She was not afraid of monsters.

As soon as I thought that, my body went into a fit of shuddering and I clasped my arms around myself. I was not used to having anyone take care of me. In fact, I can think of no time in my life when I felt relaxed enough to trust my decision-making, or the well-being of my person to any other soul.

The fact that in my hour of need I thought of Gypsy was tantamount to a metaphysical trauma. What was happening? What was this woman to me; just how much did she mean? I was an Outsider, I reminded myself; a man resigned to life as a solitary being. It was not that I was anti-social. Far from it. I had always considered myself a boon companion. Not in the style of Brom Bones, perhaps, but enough of a social animal to keep away the lonlies.

Now, as I stood by myself, naked and hurting in the Gypsy's bathroom, my face contorted. Damn it. This was unacceptable. I *would* take a shower, I *would* get some sleep and I *would* wake up strengthened for the ordeal ahead.

She loves me, she loves me not. She loves me, she loves me not.

I felt as though I were a lad of sixteen pulling daisy peddles off a flower while reciting a lover's chant. It was a trick, a subterfuge, which actually translated into, *I will take a shower, I will take a shower, there are no such thing as monsters.*

If only that were true.

Feeling every inch a craven coward, I backed out of the bathroom and shut the door. I made the rounds of the flat, turning on all the lights, then crawled into bed and pulled the blankets over my head.

Drawing the pillow to me, I fervently kissed it, then slept atop it, in the missionary- method position. I did not stir for ten hours.

When I woke, unrefreshed, feverish and with a mouth burning from acetylsalicylic acid, I knew I was in trouble. The evil lurking in the bathroom had not dissipated and my hidey-hole was no longer safe. Sooner or later Sweet would find me here and take me back to the hospital. Or worse, the Mystic Seer would come and cram me down the drain.

I had the awareness I was not completely rational, yet that knowledge did not comfort me. It reminded me of a line from a Poverty Row movie.

"Try to be sane, Dr. Vollin."

How can you ask a mad man to be sane? It was like requesting the dead to rise again and live. I was not Christ, nor even Christ-like. I was only a reporter, for God's sake.

Taking a bath or a shower was now out of the question. I could not even bring myself to open the bathroom door and use the toilet. I was Don Quixote, afraid of a commode. The windmills were everywhere, trying to strike me down. I had become the anti-hero of my own novel.

If I could not go here, then I would be reduced to making an attempt outside. Even if I found a place of total privacy (which was unlikely in London), I had two thousand years of civilization bred into me. I was not Joe Mountain Man, I was Andy Kimbo, crime reporter. Exposing oneself in a briar bush, even on a mission of desperate need, was not conducive to success.

The New York *Times* bestseller list faded from memory. I would never make it.

I did not dare drink coffee, so settled for a shot of whisky. It turned my stomach and further soured my mouth. Jack Daniels could never use my testimonial in an ad.

Time was running out, the sand going pit-pat in the overturned hourglass.

Open your mind, I ordered myself. *You will be summoned.* That was what Jason Holloway had said. But he had not said how.

That was for him to know and me to find out.

I wandered through the flat, trusting to inspiration. I was a writer, after all. It would come.

I felt her most strongly in the little area where we had sat together, consulting her crystal ball. I did not dare duplicate that position for fear of further exacerbating my throbbing buttocks, so I stood, head bowed, arms clasped in front of me. When that did not work, I opened my hands and held them up, palms open.

"Gypsy. Gypsy. Tell me where you are and I will come to you. I am here, Gypsy. One word and my faith will rekindle into the fire of righteousness."

I did not hear her and I did not sense her, but an address came into my mind. I wrote it down on a piece of paper, not daring to trust my memory. Impressions, like dreams, have an annoying tendency to fade. After I had written the words, I stared at them with a dull, blank expression. They meant nothing to me. No inspiration there, no feeling of connection.

I had almost convinced myself I had done no more than remember the address of some tea shop taking adverts on the side of a bus when I heard a voice. It was so sharp, so crystal clear I spun around, thinking someone had come into the room without my knowing. I was alone.

Kimbo. Andy. Do you hear me?

I could have answered in my head but I spoke the words aloud.

"I hear you."

It is Gypsy, Andy. Come to me. I need you. I want you.

God forgive me, my heart quickened and my pulse leapt erratically.

"Gypsy!" I cried. It was a false hope and I knew it, but I needed the facade. "Where are you?"

I have sent you the address. Come quickly. You have not much time. Come to me, my darling, before it is too late.

"I am coming. Wait for me."

Come to me soon, my beloved. I need you. I want you.

Images came to me, swirling, twisting, half-formed. Gypsy and I in bed. Gypsy and I entwined in passion. My lips met hers and we were making love, oblivious to the world and the dangers lurking outside the closed door.

I am here, she said. *Do not fear. Trust me. I trust you.*

My mind was desperate, my body pleading. I wanted to believe, needed to comfort and be comforted, yet in the back of my mind, I knew it was a lie. It was not Gypsy talking to me, caressing me, loving me. It was another mind sending the images, another soul worming its way into my subconscious.

I had never seen a photograph of the Mystic Seer, but if he were in a crowded stadium, hidden among a million other men, I would know him. It was Jason Holloway, the evil scourge, to whom I was making love, not my Gypsy. He was sending me the images, trying to lure me into a trap, blunting my senses, confusing my brain.

It was false faith he was feeding my fervid body, lies he was feeding my burning flesh.

"I love you, Gypsy," I lied, willing myself to believe, so The Mystic Seer would believe. "I am coming, my darling. Coming to you. Coming now, coming without reserve."

I was too sincere, too desperate. I could sense Jason Holloway believed me, but I had fooled myself, at the same time. She wanted me, needed me. She was safe, she was warm, she was willing. The weaknesses of the body were falling away and I knew I would go to that address, find her and match wits with the Devil in human guise.

The bottle of bourbon fell from the table, breaking as it hit the floor. I must have brushed against it as I careened, unknowingly, around the room. The sound startled me, jarred me from the trance, but it did not break the images.

I ran to the radio and turned it on, loud. I snapped on the telly, changed the channel until I found a game show with a money-crazed audience, then cranked up the volume. I needed distraction, noise, something on which to concentrate.

When the connection snapped, I reeled backward like a fish breaking the line. He was gone, exorcised from my thoughts by the discordant agony of Sergei Prokofieff's opening notes of *Romeo and Juliet,* and the greed of studio participation for a thousand pounds and a trip to Northern Ireland.

I had met the enemy and repulsed him. But not nearly as much as he repulsed me.

Jason Holloway was a dirty, wicked, perverted being. He had wormed his way into my inmost thoughts in the guise of another. He had cheated my heart and by so doing, had come close to stealing my soul.

I thought my enemy was a man of flesh and blood, a man susceptible to earthly laws and mortal judgments. I had been incorrect. The stars *were* on his side. They guided his actions, protected him from paying the penalty for his crimes.

The police could not catch him because he was always one step ahead of the law. He had no conscience. He was accountable only to a higher authority. One I knew nothing about.

He was not a human being as much as he was a fiend, drawing life from other men's sensations. I had underestimated him, believed the accumulation of money was how he got his jollies. That was true, but only in that money was his aphrodisiac. The consummation was domination of spirit.

Those investors who went to him for advice did not know, had no way of knowing, the Master Game Plan. They were pawns, not in the Mystic Seer's quest for riches and power, but as a means to another, far more nefarious end.

Jason Holloway had salivated over their passion for gold. After sating that need, he had gone for other, deeper sensations. As the stock market teetered, Holloway ate their growing fear, supped on their developing desperation, dined on their destitution. For desert, he had consumed their utter sense of loss, then terminated the relationship by living their deaths.

Suicide was the ultimate high.

After his unnerving foray into my hospital room, he had inadvertently granted me insights into his psyche.

With infinite patience, believing in his ultimate superiority, Jason Holloway had set out to blow his own mind. If that had been all, the consequences of his actions might have been overlooked. After all, society had survived stock market crashes. Who would grieve if another wealthy investor took the plunge? If the Ultimate Star Gazer wanted to go "pop goes the weasel," who would really care?

Jason Holloway would. Like a drug addict, he craved a more powerful "fix" before he was through. With all the money in the stock market at his disposal, he had already threatened to pay for World War III.

Suicide bombers. Germ warfare. A few well-placed bombs. I could see it now. Congress up in arms. U.N. resolutions. The might of the United States and the Free World pitted against the Evil Genius.

How long would it take for corrupt scientists to make the Master Race he spoke of? Or worse, the Automaton Army? German scientists had experimented with all sorts of derangements. In a few years, two billion troops, unafraid to die, unconscious of pain, could be unleased. Being bred for nothing but war, they would be unstoppable.

He was right: he didn't need to perform the actions himself. He had plenty of accomplices to do it for him.

I bet even those who don't subscribe to cable TV could name a dozen without straining.

But, here I came to a screeching halt. Why me? What role did I have to play in his scheme? Gypsy, I could understand. She had power. She was a threat. I was just a schmo. A transient with a typewriter. What was my place in all this?

I tried to reason. It wasn't easy. Me, myself and I. Alone, I had no value.

Think!

What had led me to this place in time?

As it was in the beginning....

When did all the weirdness start?

My butt throbbed. That helped me concentrate.

I traced my life. It was oddly mundane.

And then everything cleared up. Like I had been given a shot of penicillin.

It all began when Mr. Poxie decided he needed a news service in England. For a man as cheap as he was, it hadn't made any sense. CANS was losing money in St. Louis; it wasn't likely it would flourish in London. Why throw bad money after good?

What did London have to offer? I snapped my fingers. The Mystic Seer, of course! Maybe the Old Man was a client of Jason Holloway and he had put the suggestion in his mind. To bring us all together. Since this was supposed to look accidental, Mr. Poxie gave Sweet the investigative assignment on the Mystic Seer knowing he'd give it to me. If the Old Man had ordered me to take it, I would have been suspicious; on guard. This way, I entered the scene figuring it was nothing more than an overworked Sunday supplement.

Then, Holloway fed me just enough information to give me that reporter's itch. Without doubt, the stars had forewarned him someone dangerous to his plan was lurking in the background. When he couldn't find that person, he hoped I would. I checked the phone book for leads on psychic phenomenon and followed up on the most bizarre of clues, something only an oddball like me would do. That's how I found Gypsy.

My insides shriveled.

Once we hooked up it was inevitable Holloway would realize I had struck pay dirt. How much of what happened after that was contrived? Did he intend for me to find the ledger and the cash? That would make sense only if he wanted me to expose him. Had he? Gypsy and I didn't think so at the time but now I was beginning to wonder. He certainly had his escape well-planned. He was never in any real danger.

So, I wrote my articles and became famous overnight. I won the DOA. An abbreviation that should have meant more to me than it had. Anything I put out on the wire after that would be headline news.

Jason Holloway wanted to see his name in print. He craved infamy. And I was the one hack writer who could give it to him. He killed two birds with one stone: eliminate the one real threat he faced in Gypsy and see his name in 50-point bold type.

Ironically, it reminded me of Ewing Kauffman, owner of the Kansas City Royals. His manager at the time, Whitey Herzog, was a winner. He was also a character. Fans loved him. His name was always in the newspaper. Whitey this, Whitey that. As the story goes, Kauffman counted all the times the White Rat's name appeared and then contrasted it to how many times his name was mentioned. No contest. And that's the real reason he fired him. Not because he lost to the Yankees in the playoffs but because he was *more famous.*

Life imitates baseball.

Jason Holloway may fiddle while he destroys the world, but he didn't want to play second fiddle to anyone.

And he wanted me to write about it. I could envision it now. Andy Kimbo of CANS, at the front, madly typing out my firsthand account. Defeat after defeat; death and destruction on an un-paralleled scale. And in every headline the words, "Jason Holloway, Mystic Seer."

Maybe in the end, he would leave a few of us alive. We would regroup, hide in caves. Raise children who would never see the light of day, praying for a chance at revenge. All so it could start again.

How much torture would it take to overdose a megalomaniac?

I didn't know. I hoped to God I'd never have to find out.

The Mystic Seer wasn't angry at me because I exposed him to the world. On the contrary, I had played right into his hands. He *wanted* publicity, craved it, needed it to live. His attempts to take my life were not meant to succeed. To scare, yes. To fire me up, yes. To inflame my passion, hell yes.

And now he had Gypsy. In my egotistical naiveté, I had assumed he merely wanted to draw me into the open and torture me. I was right, but hadn't taken it far enough. He wanted me to look for him, to make his capture my sole, all-consuming quest. I was the Amusement of the Moment, the current Name of the Game. And my name wasn't even Gene Barry.

Which begged the question: what was I supposed to do now? Answer: play into his hands. What else could I do?

He had the Gypsy.

If I had been well, I would have marched out the door, address in hand. I would have stomped to my car, jerked open the door, inserted the key with masterful precision and driven like a bat out of hell, thinking that if this phony wanted to experience some emotion, I'd give him a taste of ones he never dreamed possible.

But I was not well. Surprisingly, the aspirin had done little, if anything, to quell the burning in my forehead. Nor had it alleviated, even slightly, the pain in my stern which was growing worse by the minute, matching my black mood.

My muscles had stiffened. I could feel the jangling in my nerves. My hair was sticking up in an unflattering cowlick. The last so annoyed me I began my journey of a thousand thoughts by marching into the bathroom. I was looking for Brylcream.

It was not until I jerked open the door and began rummaging through the cabinet that two things occurred to me: it was extremely unlikely Gypsy would stock anything even remotely similar to Brylcream and I was in the bathroom.

No monsters assaulted me; no slimy creatures slithered out of the drain pipe, flickering tongue over pointed teeth. I gave a boyish whoop of delight, thrusting my fist into the air. Anyone seeing me would have thought my team just scored a cricket.

Conquering the loo made me feel in charge once more. I could do anything. I'd damned well let my right-handed reliever face that right-handed slugger. It was only the bottom of the eighth, after all, and the opposing manager had nothing on his bench but good-glove, no-power pinch-hitters. His pitcher was due up first. I was Whitey Herzog, perched on the steps of the dugout, calm and unconcerned.

Good pitching nearly always defeated good hitting. That's why no one will ever come close to hitting .400 again.

Besides, once we struck this poduka out, we batted in the top of the ninth. We could score five more runs.

Better make it ten to be on the safe side. Think big. This was the Seventh Game of the World Series and there was no tomorrow. A ring was in the balance.

Do it right, do it fair. Make your own luck. Always stay one step ahead of the enemy. No one ever caught Whitey without any lefties on his bench. We'd save the MVP for John Tudor and get the Rat into the Hall.

Jason Holloway was a formidable enemy but he had met his match.

There was the Brylcream, shoved in the back of the medicine cabinet. Why not? More improbable things had happened. Gypsy was a mystic, herself. She knew one day it would be needed. Everything was making sense.

I fussed with my hair, laughing at the memories of old ads and grease heads. The girl was gonna love me and the rival was going to find himself unhorsed. A little dab "did me."

I emerged from the facilities considerably relieved and almost ready for a photo session.

I drank some milk, shoved some cheese down my gullet and pocketed six Cadbury milk chocolate bars. I would have preferred dark chocolate but no one ever said this was a perfect world. Besides, I didn't think Cadbury made dark chocolate. I'd take that point up with their board of directors when I got back, reminding them what a new product could do for their stock.

And wasn't "stock" where it all began?

My motor was where I left it. I didn't bother inspecting it for tamper marks. Jason Holloway wanted me to find him. He had sent the address, hadn't he? There was no point in his wiping me off the face of the United Kingdom with a car bomb.

"I'm coming," I threatened with a deep-throated growl. "I'm going to blow you away."

It didn't take long for my confidence to erode. Pain has a way of making even a sure-thing-bet seem risky. Sitting was a torture and shifting my leg to accelerate or brake was nothing short of agony. Why did I have to be injured? Why couldn't I affect a miraculous cure?

The White Knight ought to face the Black Knight on an even playing field. But that was faerie tale and this was reality. I would have to "endure with dignity."

I drove out of the city without bothering to ask for directions. I didn't need any. Along with the address, Mr. Seer had supplied the route. He was as eager for a confrontation as I was. Eager-er. (Is that a word?) Besides, he probably figured if I was reduced to inquiry, I'd end up in Yorkshire, the last place on earth God made.

When my hand started to shake, I ate one of the candy bars. It had melted and I was forced to lick most of it off the foil. I told myself I needed energy, that my blood sugar was low. A shot of sugar would quell my raging insulin and steady me. I didn't work, so I resorted to the tried and true: I ate another.

"I'm coming, Gypsy, I'm coming."

In an hour I found myself out in the boonies. If Jason Holloway were really hereabouts, he had smuggled himself back in the country. No surprise there. He had probably disguised himself as a little bag of white powder. No knock on England. Little bags of white powder can get in anywhere. It's the nature of the beast.

Where there's a will, there's a way. Good words to live by.

After another quarter of an hour I pulled over to the side of the road and rested. I was just too weak to go on. The pain had crept upward and down, spreading into my arms and legs until it was an effort to move. I didn't want to hit a hedgehog because I was too sick to swerve out of the way. The innocent had suffered enough, already.

Resting my head against the steering wheel, I closed my eyes and envisioned Gypsy. She could not have escaped the blast unscathed. Any plans for escape I made had to take into consideration the fact she was injured. Not seriously, of course. I had to believe I had shielded her from the worst.

Sacrifice without success was pretty damned unrewarding.

I must have dozed off, for the big hand on my watch had jumped twenty minutes when I stared at it again. This was getting me nowhere. I fumbled for the ignition key with my right hand, couldn't find it, and was forced to stare down. It's disconcerting to be forced to use your eyes when performing a task you could do in your sleep. It has an oddly unnerving effect on the psyche, as if your world has suddenly changed and no one bothered to tell you. Deprive a man of his habits and he comes unglued.

Of course, the key was on the left, not the right. I had forgotten. That was a danger sign to me, a warning my mind was not sharp. I was running on auto-pilot, not functioning on all cylinders. I was going to have to do a hell of a lot better if I hoped to beat the Mystic Seer.

The loonies were running the asylum and Don Denkinger was umpiring at first base. The odds didn't look good.

I started the engine and drove toward hell in a heavenly cause.

CHAPTER 15

When the car chugged up an incline (which, to my foreign-made auto meant a hill), and perched at the top, I knew I had come to the right place. Sitting across a broad expanse and settled into a shallow basin was an olde English house, or more correctly, a "park." Chimneys on the dwelling were evenly spaced, two to a side, while the whole was encased by a well-trimmed hedge, no doubt originally planted by a lord from Queen Mary's reign.

Everything in Britain, one learns quickly, was planted, constructed, decorated or once occupied by someone noble. History is as alive here as it was in your seventh grade text book.

There were no cars parked out front, no sign of life, save a pencil-thin wisp of smoke from one of the rear chimneys. It reminded me that by coming alone, I had burned my bridges. No one knew where I was; the Lone Ranger was dead and the frontier heroes had perished at the Alamo. I couldn't expect the cavalry to come to my rescue.

She was there. I could feel her. At least, I thought I could. There was always the possibility the Mystic Seer was putting those impressions in my mind. But if he were, then I had unknowingly joined the grey ranks at Gettysburg.

But then, Hopeless was my middle name.

A.H.K. I'd have to remember that monogram the next time I ordered towels from Lillian Vernon.

What to do? I could always drive up to the gate and request an audience from the gatekeeper. If there were no gatekeeper (good help is hard to come by), then I could always call up on the intercom affixed into stone, first quarried by the Druids. Neither approach seemed practical.

I might as well wave a flag and run naked through the hedge.

I shifted the auto into reverse and rolled down the hill until it was out of sight from anyone in the manse thoughtful enough to be staring in my direction. Parking it along the side of the road, I got out, remembering to leave the door unlocked. I wasn't foolish enough to believe locking it would keep anyone out. In today's world, even Mystic Seers kept picks in their breast pockets. Don't leave home without it, and all that.

Besides, if Gyp and I were on the lam, we'd need to get in, in a hurry. And knowing England, the key would have to be inserted upside-down and we'd never get the door open.

So, brave hero. Now what?

If I had my wits about me, I could have searched my didactic memory for implausible rescue missions. I'd skip the modern military ones, naturally. Those guys don't even know helicopter blades stir up sand when they land in the desert.

I began walking. Right or left? It was a toss-up. I chose right, because I was on the Side of Right.

Just left of the angels....

Stands of old wood lay in the distance to either side and the back, while the hedge, rising to the height of six feet, covered my approach. I picked my way carefully, trying to make as little noise as possible. It would be ignoble to be mistaken for a quail and shot by Holloway's gamekeeper.

I could feel the wounds on my back blister and bleed. My shirt stuck to me like a second skin and the bandages on my rump slipped out of place, starting a retrograde movement down my legs. I paused long enough to rip them off, then deposited the bloodied mass under a shallow pile of leaves.

That left me considerably lightened, but the rough fabric of my pants had an immediate sandpaper effect on my buttocks. If I ever lived to write by autobiography, this was one chapter I'd blue-pencil myself.

When I figured I had walked far enough, I made my way through a convenient break in the hedge and took an accounting. I had come out about one hundred yards from a rear entrance of the house. There was no one about. I noted an empty kennel off to the side. I sniffed the air; no dog scent. I guessed dogs weren't overly stimulating companions for the Mystic Seer.

I bet the neighbors didn't appreciate it, though. A squire without hunting dogs? What was this realm coming to? No wonder they were thinking of putting the monarchy up to a vote.

Covering my eyes with a trembling hand, I employed the temporary shade to help me clear my mind, then summoned Gypsy with a quick blastoff mental power.

"Gypsy! Are you there?" No answer. Perhaps she didn't trust what she was hearing. How to send her a private code so she would know it was me?

"Gypsy," I concentrated. "Andy's first cake." I felt a subtle alteration in the air. Radar love. "I'm out back. Where are you?" I thought.

Go away. He's waiting for you.

"I know. Where are you?"

She was longer in answering this time.

In the cellar.

"Are you all right?"

Yes.

"I'm all right, too." That made us even.

Andy, you cannot get me out. Go away. Save yourself.

"Not on your life. Or is that a bad pun?" Miss Kitty said that to Matt Dillon once, when they were in the hands of a mad woman, played by Bette Davis. They had escaped. I took courage.

I could hear Gypsy laugh. She was reading my mind. It was good to "think" her laugh.

It was a first year color episode but you never noticed, she transmitted. That *had* to be my Gypsy. No one else could have ever known. She was alive, she was within my grasp and she understood my eccentricities. How could a man ever fail a woman like that?

"How do I get in?"

Through a lower window.

That made sense.

"Which one?"

The texture of the air changed once more and I had the eerie feeling we were being eavesdropped on.

"I'll go in the back door as you suggest," I quickly sent.

There was no answer, nor had I expected one.

I walked boldly across the well-manicured lawn to one of the ground-level windows. I tried it. Locked. No problem. I removed one of my journalistic tools (aka a maxed-out credit card), from my breast pocket, inserted it under the sill and jiggled it. The latch snapped up. I raised the window just to be certain I could, then slipped away.

The rear door, too, was locked. I repeated the above procedure and opened it. Looking inside, I saw it led to the kitchen. I tiptoed inside, touched a table, left my impressions on the counter. I told Holloway I was coming in this way; I had to make sure he found traces of my passage. I opened a drawer and removed a paring knife, then took a butcher knife, as well. Let him think I was armed.

Going back outside, I re-locked the door and ditched the butcher knife. It was too unwieldy and far too conspicuous. Then I located a cellar window, dropped to my knees and poked my head through. It was a long drop into nothingness.

Oh, joy. My back crawled with the thought of the pleasures I would encounter landing on my butt in a pile of paint buckets and garden rakes.

With a semi-dramatic gesture of holding my nose, I plunged into the depths, feet first. The fall was not as steep as I anticipated, and I crashed into cement, or hand-laid rock with a soft plop. Something had broken my fall. Daring to use my pocket torch, I stared around in disbelief. I had landed in a pile of dirty laundry. A laugh welled in my throat.

"I never said I wanted to get into the Mystic Seer's shorts," I grumbled, kicking away a suspicious-looking piece of dark silk cloth and extinguishing the light.

Enough levity. I had work to do.

There were three doors leading from what I supposed to be the wash room. Like the Lady and the Tiger, I was faced with a dilemma. Behind one was my Gypsy. Behind the other two might be anything from a closet filled with Wisk and Downey to a storage shelter filled with gold and silver coins. Of the spending variety.

My hand shook as I held it out. I had a dire presentment of doom. Make the wrong choice now and a fate worse than death might befall us both.

Don't ever let anyone tell you death is the ultimate failure. Living with loss is the greatest grief humankind can ever have. No one asks questions of the dead; no corpse ever bemoans the fact it died. Once the silver cord is broken, it's an entirely new ball game.

Suffering, my friends, is for the living. They're the ones who know pain. They're the true lost souls, the tortured wretches who cry over harsh words, un-retracted points driven home in anger, opportunities for gentleness ignored from a surfeit of pride. It's the ones condemned to live who beg for forgiveness and receive no reply; those of mortal composition who question decisions, bemoan long absences, missed birthdays, ignored holidays.

If there is a God, then Heaven is a place for rest and renewal. Earth is the learning ground, based on the principle, "Spare the rod and spoil the child."

I was not at all confident but I had come this far. If the Mystic Seer got me, I'd make him pay. Just let him try to put me on the rack. I'd croak the entire anthem, beginning with, "Jose, can you see," while he was disjointing my arms and legs. Then we'd tell who had the highest breaking point.

I couldn't toss a coin, for there were three choices. Being a logical man, I headed for the one on the right. It seemed the least likely and therefore my best bet. Then, in the back of my mind, I remembered an old magician's trick. Ask someone to pick a number from 1 to 3. You had to guess the number.

It's a well-known fact among prestidigitators that the vast majority of people will chose the number 3. When the odds are overwhelmingly in your favor, you chose "3" and you're right the majority of the time. Bingo! You're a mind reader.

I was the wrong person to play that game with, because I always chose number 1. The reason is simple. I like to be on top. It ruins the party-piece but never fails to make me feel smug.

I had a feeling I wasn't going to feel smug no matter which door I went through, but I wasn't going to pick the obvious. Two was my least favorite number. Logically, then, Gypsy had to be behind it. At least, I hoped so.

Door Number 2 was unlocked. Surprised, I paused, considered, then tried Door Number One, to my left. It, too, was unlocked. Only the door to the right was fastened. Behind that, I decided were the plate and valuables. I dismissed it immediately.

I don't know why. Usually, when a door is locked, that means keep away. It thus becomes the center of interest. But not in Jason Holloway's house. This jerk was just screwy enough to lock up his Mumbo Jumbo robes and fright wig, while leaving unguarded what I had come to find.

I went back to the middle door, opened it and shot a thin beam of light from my torch (flashlight to Americans) into the gloom. As expected, there were no lights or windows of any sort, so the downward-spiraling tunnel gave no indication what it cradled within its realm.

Moving within, I gently brought the door to an almost closed position, then had a sudden burst of inspiration – my first, since coming onto the property. I backtracked, dug my hand into the pile of laundry and removed a sock, stiff enough to have belonged in a high schooler's gym locker. Not quite long enough for a club, it would serve as a door jam. I hurried back, placed it between the door and the wall, leaving it open no more than a crack and proceeded into the depths, feeling slightly more confident.

The floor of the corridor, for, in fact, it was no wider than the outstretch of my arms, sloped downward so gradually it was barely perceivable. I had gone one hundred yards, maybe further, by the time I felt "deep." If that were the case, then the floor had dipped more rapidly as it descended and I had been unaware.

Sensory deprivation. Pitch blackness, total silence. There wasn't even the customary dampness associated with a basement. Curiously, I placed a hand against the wall and felt the cold stone. There was no indication of long-standing condensation. In a country with a high water table, that meant there had to be dehumidifiers working. If, after all this trouble, I ended up in the Mystic Seer's wine cellar, I swore I'd break a few bottles of 1855 claret in my frustration. The Glenlivet whisky I'd save for myself.

If I didn't drown in a vat of malmsey.

I kept going down, down, down. I was aware of the descent, now. The floor of the tunnel was more sharply depressed. As best I could tell, no corridors or hidden doors led off in either direction, although I could have missed one, if it were flush to the stone walls.

At the end of what seemed like a mile, I came to a door. In my surprise, I almost jammed my nose into it and withdrew so fast you'd have thought I was bitten by an asp. I had come to the end of the trail, partner. There was no door knob. I tried pushing it open. No dice. I tried sliding it. Nothing. Immovable. I started searching for hidden levers, depressed buttons, springs or touch pads.

I found what I was looking for on the floor. It was a tiny, weight-sensitive pressure plate, of the type Jason had installed in his desk at Mystic Towers. I placed my foot on it and the door slid back. I was instantly assaulted by light. Not that it was department store bright, just a radical alteration from the darkness of the tunnel.

She spoke before my pupils dilated enough for me to see her.

"Andy."

Behind Door Number 2, the contestant had revealed the Major Prize. I silently applauded for myself.

"Gypsy!"

As a long-lost welcome, it was brief, but aptly expressed my sentiment. She was seated on a chair in the middle of the floor. Her hands were tied behind her. Dried blood caked her face.

"What in God's name has he done to you?" I demanded.

"Nothing." I was relieved. "In God's name," she completed.

I ran to her, arms outstretched. Just before I reached her, I collided, head-first, into some invisible force. I ricocheted off, staggered, then caught my balance. Barely.

Undaunted, I tried again. It was only after being repulsed a second time that I realized Gypsy was behind a glass partition. I banged on it with my fists. Nothing.

I tried shouting, but she didn't answer. I presumed she was trying to keep the conversation short.

Scuttling around like a rat in a maze, I realized the entire chamber was a big Fun House. The enclosure had been cordoned off into glass-enclosed paths, with mirrors set at odd angles to make it appear Gypsy was never more than a few feet away.

Running back and forth, I must have repeated my mistakes a dozen times before the pain and frustration got the better of me. With my breath coming in ragged gasps, I tried to summon "calm."

"Calm" did not come. Instead, a vision of Diana Rigg appeared before my eyes. Looking into her serene orbs, I knew she would be calm for me.

"Remember that episodes of *The Avengers."* Gypsy's voice reverberated in my mind. "When Mrs. Peel was lost in a creepy old house. The walls kept revolving, so she always ended up back at her starting point. What did she do?"

"She took out her lipstick and began marking the doors," I promptly replied.

That sounded like good advice. I expectantly patted my pockets before remembering I didn't carry lipstick. (I don't think Mrs. Peel did, either, but at least she had an excuse.)

I did have a pen, but it wouldn't write on the glass. I was about to implode at the thought the "talented amateur" of my mind's eye had steered me wrong, when I deduced a simple solution to my dilemma.

Unscrewing the pen, I removed the ink refill and snapped off the tip. A pool of black formed at the break. Using that, I began marking the walls, leaving a trail so I wouldn't continually repeat myself.

I may not have been as smart as Algernon, but by avoiding all the crisscrossing I had done earlier, I slowly worked my way through the puzzle.

At the end I found Gypsy.

My first thought was to throw my arms around her, but I had seen too many Westerns to fall for that old chestnut. While the guy and the gal were smooching, the villain sneaked up behind them and clobbered him on the head.

I decided to untie her first and kiss second.

"Those wounds on your face," I observed. "Did he beat you?"

"They are from the bomb."

"Are you badly hurt?"

"I am... all right. But you. I felt your pain as you drew close." Her voice was quiet, yet I sensed the tears in it.

"No, no," I hastened to reassure her. My answer was purely spontaneous, although, in truth, I had forgotten about the agony in my back until reminded. "Tell me quickly. Are you well enough to stand?"

She gave me a sad smile.

"I have some blisters, but nothing like you suffered. You saved me when you threw yourself on me."

"We'll exchange Vaseline later," I promised. "We have to get out of here."

"I believe we do," she agreed. I was ecstatic to see she was going to be cooperative. I was in no mood for noble sacrifices.

I worked rapidly, cutting the straps with the paring knife I had stolen from the Mystic Seer's kitchen drawer. Starting with her hands, I then worked on her feet. I had almost completed the job when I heard a deep, rumbly laugh. My blood froze.

I finished what I was doing and casually turned.

Jason Holloway, a/k/a the Mystic Seer, was standing beside me. I had not heard him come up. Even though I had received a psychic impression of him, and therefore thought I knew what to expect, he was disappointingly trite-looking. One expects the great nemesis of your life to be tall, dark, swarthy, or perhaps deathly pale-skinned. Evil Geniuses are generally depicted as larger-than-life, beady-eyed, long-finger-nailed monsters.

My personal devil looked vaguely like Clarence, the inept sub-angel from *It's A Wonderful Life.*

I felt cheated. It was totally irrational, yet irresistible. This man might have played the leading actor's best friend, or worked as a pitching coach for a minor league baseball team.

I expected him to say, "Welcome to my castle," in an Hungarian accent, but knowing his physical limitations (he was playing the part of a British count), he wisely refrained.

For all of that, he more closely resembled a Hollywood producer.

That hackled the hair on the back of my neck. Now, those people are *really* scary. I was glad I didn't have a script to peddle, or a part to audition for.

"But you are wrong, Mr. Kimbo," he said in a mild, almost kindly voice. "You *have* come to audition for a role in my little production. Not the one you hoped for, alas. I am not casting for a hero. Not even one as unlikely-looking as you. Be fair, sir. I may look disappointing to you, but you are twice a disappointment to me."

"How so?" I asked before deciding silence was the best policy.

"A freckle-faced, red-haired crime reporter of no more than average height and capped teeth. Like you, I anticipated... someone more formidable. You, Mr. Kimbo, look like a writer. Those cretins better read than seen."

I knew what he meant but failed to appreciate it. I, too, had seen pictures of Famous Authors on the backs of dust jackets. They all looked so – plebian. Normal, even. Like your next-door neighbor.

Or an axe murderer.

"Stand back," I warned. "I have a gun in my pocket. I'll shoot you dead."

"Really? You would shoot a man in cold blood, thus going against the application of Judeo-Christian values? Show the weapon."

I tried the tobacco-pipe-pressed-against-the-cloth-of-the-pocket routine. He laughed.

"You have no gun, Mr. Kimbo."

"If I had one, I would place a bullet between your eyes." I knew it was far safer to shoot a man in the chest, where there was less likelihood of missing, but I went for dramatics. It was a moot point, inasmuch as I had no gun, but it made me feel better, imagining his head blown off.

For a moment he paused and I had the uncomfortable feeling he, too, was savoring the idea of his own destruction. Creepy bastard. Sick soul.

"I have been waiting for you," he said as his fantasy subsided. I wondered if I had kept the image up, he might have melted into a puddle of puke, so I tried again. This time, he deflected my thoughts with his mind and sent them back to me. I let out a frightened cry, putting my hands to my head.

Never let it be said anything dies without knowing. In that split second, I discovered that "truism" to be an ugly falsehood.

One which would never protect me again, when I covered mob shootings and massive traffic fatalities.

The human mind is faster than a speeding bullet, more powerful than a locomotive, able to comprehend tall finalities with a single bound.

I felt ill.

"You had better let us go," I threatened. Like a bird fluffing its feathers, I tried to make myself appear larger, more formidable. "The authorities know where I am. If they don't hear back from me within a certain time, they'll storm this place. Save yourself," I urged, "before it's too late."

He clicked his tongue. "Do not try to bluff me, Mr. Kimbo. I can read your mind. Remember? You told no one where you were going. Not even that overblown, underrated editor-friend of yours. Tell me," he continued, eyes merry with anticipation. "Is he really the beneficiary of your life insurance policy? I do hope he has the decency to spend some of that twenty-thousand on a good, old-fashioned Irish wake for you. I might even go, myself."

I started to protest, then sidetracked myself with a sudden thought. It was true, he could read my mind, but the sincerity of his question about whether Sweet was actually going to inherit my insurance payoff held my tongue in check. His powers, then, were surely limited.

As limited as the height of the Empire State Building.

Well, standing on the moon, no one could see the Empire State Building. The only man-made structure visible from our satellite was the Great Wall of China. As an edge, it was better than nothing.

"You have caused me a great deal of recalculating, Mr. Kimbo."

I made a slight bow. "My pleasure."

"Nothing irreparable, I assure you. But now, you may, in some slight measure, repay me."

"My paycheck is already garnished." He smiled. I wondered if it were meant to be endearing. "I know. You want me to expose you to the world. You want your photograph hung in all the grade schools by those of George Washington and Abraham Lincoln."

"Adolph Hitler and Genghis Khan would be more like it." I was in no mood to parlay. "Your lady – Gypsy – you call her. Kindly persuade her to be reasonable."

"Be reasonable," I repeated, turning to face her. The Mystic Seer ignored my sarcasm, proving, I suppose, he had been bred as a gentleman.

"I desire her... crystal ball. If she passes control of it to me, I shall let you both go... without further damage. If she persists in being stubborn... then I shall be forced to settle for another kind of... ball, or two, if you catch my meaning, sir."

I frowned. "What do you want her crystal ball for?"

"To warn me of random elements."

I started to speak, but Gypsy interrupted.

"You know I cannot give it to you. Nor is it within my power to grant you permission to use it. The crystal ball is a living entity. It makes its own choices."

"It has some – feeling? – for you?" he asked. She gave no indication of hearing. "Then I suggest you communicate your plight to it. Surely, it will reconsider." The Gypsy remained mute. "If you will not save yourself, consider your would-be rescuer. I can do terrible things to him."

He was preaching to the heathens.

"What you ask is not possible."

"We shall see." The Mystic Seer raised a hand. A hidden door slid open. Two men emerged from the darkness. Both wore hoods over their heads, in the style of executioners. "If you will not petition the crystal ball, then perhaps A. Kimbo will do it for you."

I never said I was the bravest man in the world. Before they laid a hand on me I crumpled to the floor like a used Kleenex.

When I was roused from my unnatural slumber, I heard Gypsy speaking.

"... cannot do it from here. I must hold it in my hand. I must physically pass it to you."

"Tell me where you keep your crystal ball and I will go myself and retrieve it."

"You cannot touch it before I transfer it to you. You know that." There was obvious haughtiness in her voice. I applauded with my toes. "I must go myself and get it."

"I cannot allow that." My feet went numb. "I will send one of my men."

"No foreign hands may ever touch that crystal, or it will go into hibernation. It will be of no use to you if that happens. Nor, do I have the knowledge to wake it from sleep."

"You know the spell," he insisted.

"That incantation may only be used once by any chosen person. I have already used it when it was first presented to me. It will not hear me again. If you know so much, you are aware of that."

"I will never release you until I have that... *mystic seer* in my hands." He smiled at his own joke.

"Send Kimbo for it," she suggested.

"No. I won't go!" I don't think I spoke the words aloud, but my thoughts were understood.

I had a dull awareness someone picked me up from the floor.

"Gypsy," I pleaded. "Don't ask me to do this thing. You love that crystal ball."

I had not thought to say that, didn't know where the words originated, yet I knew them to be true. As she was my one true love – and I hadn't known that, either, until this moment – I sensed her deep affection for that round, mysterious crystal ball. They went together as surely as Gemini shining in the night sky. Separate one from the other and lose both.

And that didn't even cover the horror of placing it in Holloway's hands, giving him the wherewithal to protect himself from the likes of Carl Kolchak and Andy Kimbo.

"How touching," the seer snarled. My hatred of him evolved into a living passion.

"I will do this for you, Andy."

"No.... No. I won't allow it." I made a valiant effort to lift my head. My eyes were on the level of Holloway's kneecaps. "Please," I begged. "I know how you live. Torture me, then, and exist in my agony, but don't separate her from what is her life."

God help me, I meant it, and finally understood the meaning of sacrifice.

"It is all right, Andy," she said, and I knew she understood. I gasped and slobbered. It was all so very unfair.

I began to slump forward. Invisible hands held me, suspended between hell and limbo. In my misery, I had forgotten "limbo" and been consigned, like Saint Christopher, to Never-Never Land.

"You will go and get it," Holloway decided. There was erotic delight in his voice.

"Screw you," I decided.

I had already passed out when the blow came, depriving me of the chance to thank God for small mercies.

CHAPTER 16

When I woke, I was sick... sick onto death. The constant jolting of the car (for this is where I found myself), made me want to vomit. As my vision cleared, I realized there was nothing in my stomach.

To add insult to injury, I became aware we were all crammed into my tiny Czech Republic automobile. Under the circumstances, I expected to be in the boot of a Rolls Royce.

I groaned, inadvertently alerting my captors to the fact I had arisen from their imposed sleep. Jason Holloway was sitting in the front. He was not driving. A henchman I hadn't seen before was at the wheel. Gypsy sat beside me, unusually pale in the moonlight. As I turned my head to face her, she bravely smiled.

That made one of us.

"I'm sorry, honey," I mumbled through cracked lips. "If I had never come into your life, you'd be safe and your crystal ball would be safe. And the world would be safer."

Take courage, she thought back.

"Take it where?" I asked.

Our conversation brought a smile to the Mystic Seer's thin, aristocratic lips. At least, that's the way his type of facial feature is always referred to in Gothic and pseudo-Gothic novels.

"Yes, Mr. Kimbo," he agreed, thus earning my ethereal abomination. "I do have you to thank for bringing me together with this woman."

"Lady," I corrected.

For my trouble I received a jab from his walking stick. I just bet it had a silver wolf's head as a handle, but I didn't ask to see. None of my orifices had eyes.

"Shall we settle for 'Gypsy'?" he agreeably inquired. I nodded. It seemed a reasonable compromise, although in retrospect I believe he meant it as an insult.

It comes from living in different worlds.

No one, in their wildest imagination, would ever accuse me of having aristocratic lips.

"I knew she existed, of course," Holloway prattled, "but it was not until recently I sensed she was in London. How convenient."

"You should have looked her up in the phone book," I spat, knowing full well her number was unlisted. Apparently it was an esoteric joke for he didn't laugh.

"It has long been known among a… select few that there existed a… 'person' with a crystal ball. The subject of a very ancient prophesy, shall we say? The light, compared to my dark. An enemy," he underscored. "Who would try and prevent me from achieving my destiny." He arched an eyebrow. "World domination. And to her would come a… familiar. Not a cat or a hunchback," he sneered, "but a man. Years ago when you were a child," he addressed to Gypsy, "I became aware the crystal ball of exotic, undreamed power had been transferred into your hands. When you – activated it," he added, seductively rubbing together his hands.

"That is not the word," she corrected him.

"Awoke it from hibernation," he casually clarified, then laughed. It was a cruel sound. "What did you do – kiss it?"

"If I did, then my crystal is one up on you," she retorted. "For I do not believe any woman has ever kissed you."

"I have had many such encounters."

"Willingly."

A light flickered behind his eyes. His answer was remarkably soft.

"You mistake. Women have loved me quite willingly. Even eagerly."

When Gypsy addressed his statement it was not as I expected. There was no bitterness in her tone, but rather a sad commiseration.

"Then it was not you they loved, but another; your alien mind stealing a familiar body."

"Is that not the same?"

"No."

His right hand twitched as he dismissed her with his left.

"No matter, so long as *I* received the benefit."

Gypsy hissed, though not in recrimination. I could not understand why not.

"I thought to encounter you in business," Holloway began anew, although his voice remained soft.

"We are *not* in the same business," she replied. For the life of me, it appeared they had just joined a mutual admiration society.

Holloway nobly shrugged. The man's veins just coursed blue blood. I'd like to see some of it spilled, just to be sure. I guess it was my journalistic fervor.

"I fail to see the distinction. I predict the future of the stock market for greedy men and you tell love-sick clients where to look for wealthy spouses. The only difference being, I consult the stars while you peer into a crystal ball."

"I have never used my crystal ball for mercenary purposes."

"And neither shall I," he heatedly agreed. "I am a philanthropist. Have I not made men wealthy? Given them great joy? You have unprofitably used your talent, Gypsy."

"And you have let yours corrupt you."

"An interesting word, coming from one whose ancestry boasts child stealers and petty thieves."

She articulated a word which sounded like "Roma," and Holloway shrank back faster than if he had just discovered his Cracker Jack box held no free toy.

"You waste your time, Jason Holloway," Gypsy continued. "I shall never allow the crystal ball to reveal to you anything which will hurt others."

"Hurt?" he asked, as though the statement offended him. "I? Hurt? Nonsense. My hands are clean." To prove his point, he extended his lily-white digits.

"You recruit others to do your evil."

"True. But I am merely an agent, not the perpetrator. You understand the difference." They were speaking some language of their own. I wondered if it were Esperanto.

"My crystal ball will not bring you the power you seek. It is to be used for good."

He shrugged. "Good. Evil. A question of semantics. With the divinations of the crystal ball, I will become invincible. I will have my way. The world, as you might pedantically write," he addressed to me, "will be my oyster. Elections, wars, plagues, famine, disease – the outcome of the World Series," he laughed, "will be mine to dictate. No one will ever be able to stop me."

He seemed to be on some truth jag. It didn't seem to have anything to do with astrology, or Ronald Reagan would have been a third-term president.

The car took a sharp turn and I fell into the Gypsy. Her hands went around me and a sweet comfort stole over my body. I eased into a semi-trance and woke again as the vehicle stopped in front of her building.

I was helped from the car by the goon. When my legs refused to support me, I was carried across the pavement and lifted up the steps. I counted thirteen before blacking out. It was not until we were inside the flat that my senses returned to full awareness. It must have been the incense. I had worked up an immunity to its poison and now was using it as a stimulus.

"Go into the room and open the hidden compartment," Gypsy ordered me. I understood she could not do this herself, although I did not know why. "Take up the crystal ball and bring it to me. Be certain you do not remove the black covering from the ball," she warned.

And then I knew her plan. It was all so simple, I don't know why I hadn't thought of it sooner. I would bring back the crystal, sidle up to the Mystic Seer and bash him over the head with it. That was why she didn't want me to remove the cloth. With all the blood and brains scattered about, she didn't want the crystal soiled.

Afraid the Mystic Seer would read my thoughts and anticipate our plot, I attempted to fill my mind with other thoughts. None came so clearly as those hours I had spent with Gypsy. Feeling more like a voyeur than a lover, I sought her lips, kissed them, working up my passion. I must think only of her, only of being with her....

I opened the hidden compartment and discovered the hiding place of Gypsy's crystal ball. My fingers worked with a knowledge of their own. It was a phenomenon almost as mysterious as that possessed by people who can type without looking at the letters. A drawer slid open and I found myself taking the crystal ball out of its resting place.

The ball was lighter than I expected and warm to the touch. I thought it made a slight purring sound when I touched it, but that was imagination. I returned, cradling it to my breast, suckling it to my body as a parent would a new born babe. Yet, I sensed it was old, extremely old, and that I was the infant. I failed to work out the puzzle.

I inched forward, pleading with my mind to concentrate on my woman, and thus keep my mind away from murder. Gypsy was with me, we were lying on the bed, we were undressed, we were making love....

Tamely, I handed the crystal ball to the Mystic Seer without ever lifting it above my head, without having the slightest desire to smash it into his skull. As it passively transferred from my hands, I gave out a faint cry and dropped to my knees.

For some reason I could not fathom, I had forgotten to murder him.

"Oh, God, Gypsy, forgive me. I have failed you."

I had played my role too well; substituted love for hate, and in so doing, had doomed me, Gypsy and the rest of the world to certain death.

"Be still, my love," she said.

"I meant, I meant... I meant...." But what I meant was lost to memory. I slumped against her, having failed in this, my greatest test. I would have traded all the Pulitzers and all the DOA's in the world for one single chance to redeem myself.

How could she love me after this?

Accepting my gift, Jason Holloway cradled it in his hands a moment, then slowly raised the crystal ball. His arms began to tremble as he strained under what was, to him, a tremendous weight. By the time he succeeded in extending his arms to full length, he looked like Atlas, holding Earth.

It was not a comforting thought.

After completing this obscure ritual, the Mystic Seer apparently achieved some sort of communication with the crystal. He smiled, then gracefully lowered his ill-gotten treasure.

For a moment the earth stopped rotating on its axis. I expected the furniture to go flying, but strangely it did not.

Getting to my feet, I stood in front of Gypsy, shielding her from the killing blow I expected to come. She made a slight move, then spoke from behind my back.

"Sit down," she purred. I felt my knees weaken, but it was not to me she was speaking. "At the table."

Holloway positioned himself like an obedient child, arms encompassing the glass. He sat in the manner of a man having found religion – that, or he was looking through it to see if, somewhere on the bottom, were engraved the words, "Made in Japan."

I half expected Gypsy to start a recitation on history, or begin a spelling lesson.

Bowing her head, she silently communicated with the crystal. I assumed she was apologizing. When she completed the ritual, her eyes cleared and she stared at the Mystic Seer.

"Remove the black covering," she dictated. He did as ordered, hands shaking with anticipation.

"The mysteries of the Universe," he whispered with godlike adoration. I felt my face flush and my blood pressure rise. This was not what I had expected. "All of time is before me."

"Look into the mist," she ordered. "And observe all which you desire."

From where I was standing, I could see a cloud fill the ball. It slowly dissipated, revealing a miniature of Gypsy's room, a Lilliputian land of microscopic people. It was like watching yourself on a security camera at the bank, only in tiny and in living color.

In Cornwall, the people have a belief that if an elf uses its shape-shifting powers too often, it reduces in size until it turns into an ant. No one ever steps on ants in Cornwall for fear of harming one of the wee people. Staring into the crystal ball, I became a believer. We had all turned into ants.

Perhaps that's all we ever have been.

The Jason Holloway in the crystal ball began giving orders. Henchmen came and went. A telephone was brought in. He began calling numbers. Somewhere, I could hear Red Phones ringing.

I had an awareness of time passing at incredible speed. Through my mental link, I connected with Jason Holloway, who was, in turn, connected with his image in the crystal ball. In that future, Holloway was amassing power the way kids collect baseball cards.

But when he went to trade in his collection, it wouldn't be for a game-used jersey, or an autographed baseball. It would be for a plague of unimaginable horror and a world war.

I was horrified and disgusted. I willed A. Kimbo in the crystal to do something to stop the takeover of the world, but he had no Kryptonite. He was powerless, no more than an ant.

And then, "I" disappeared from the crystal. So did Gypsy. We had been removed from the Larger Picture.

Unbelievably, I had witnessed my own destruction and lived to tell the tale.

What a story this was going to make.

In my mind's ear, I could hear Sweet, his patient voice droning on, just this side of madness.

Andy, you're not Houdini, you know.

Of course I knew. Houdini made more money off his gigs than I did with mine.

Sweet, I know what's going to happen. I've seen the future!

The Sweet in my imagination remained skeptical.

I hope this isn't going to be one of your typical pieces, he began. *Al Gore reinvents himself and wins the presidency. He's going to need more than a beard, you know.*

Bigger than that!

Hillary wins?

I've just witnessed the end of the world As We Know It. With All the Money in the World, ordinary nuts will run amuck. Scientists will create drone armies. Microbes will be brought back from outer space and set loose on humanity. Our destiny will be controlled by -

He threw up his hands, knitting his fingers over his head in the shape of a noose.

I don't want to know, he said. My eyes bugged out.

How could you not want to know? And then, more forcefully, *IT'S NEWS!*

There are some things Mankind is not meant to know.

I shrieked. Sweet was quoting from every 1950s science fiction movie ever made. That was worse than the reviews for *Waterworld.*

I was so shocked, I came to my senses, finding myself once more in Gypsy's flat. She was standing beside me, just as I had left her.

"What's happening?" I gasped.

She pointed with her hand. I tried to comprehend the sight before me. Jason Holloway still sat at the table, staring into the crystal ball. He was utterly transfixed, frozen in time and space, eyes riveted to the future scrolling before his eyes.

I wished I had a tricorder.

"Look!" I pointed in horror. The Mystic Seer had stopped breathing. He was turning into a Purple People Eater.

"He is lost in his own mind," Gypsy explained. "His fantasies have replaced his reality. He is seeing the world that may be. He is self-destructing from too much emotion."

"What do you mean?" I was blubbering, not for Jason Holloway, but from abject horror.

"He wanted unlimited passion; he wished to dominate the minds of others, so he could experience their hopes – fears. He wanted to absorb all the devastation of nuclear war; to live and die with a world at his command. And so he shall."

"You mean he's overdosed on misery?" She nodded. "But it's not really happening. Is it?"

"It is one possibility of the future. That is why it is real to him. Should he regain the present, break away from the images he is seeing, what he imagines will occur. But he asked for too much, all at once. He is held by his own greed."

I turned to him in sick fascination. He had drawn down, nose pressed into the crystal, consuming and consumed at the same time. The beds of his fingernails were blue. "Shouldn't we wake him, or something?"

It was a hell of a time to remember ethics.

"We cannot." And then softer, "Try."

You might ask why I cared. But I hope you don't.

Crossing behind him, I shook Holloway's shoulders. No response. I grabbed a fistful of hair and tugged. *Nada.* Images of myself, performing CPR filled my mind. I couldn't remember the formula. Was it two breaths for every six chest compressions, or the reverse?

Resuscitation Annie did not have aristocratic lips.

I administered a blow to his back. He let out a gasp and toppled over. At this rate, I was never going to pass my recertification.

"He can't simply have stopped breathing," I tried, sidestepping the body with the grace of a catcher sliding into third base.

"He has not 'simply stopped.' He has forgotten how to breathe. Life, in this three-dimensional world, has become inconsequential to him."

"But, where is he? Is he here with us, or is he in there, in the crystal ball?"

"His body is here; his mind there."

All the religious training I never had assailed my consciousness.

"You mean, the crystal ball has his soul?"

I turned to her and saw her smile.

"There are some things Mankind is not meant to know."

Existence, as I knew it, winked out.

When I finally woke, the Men in White Coats were hovering over me. My lips formed a silent protest.

"I meant to return that clipboard. I really did."

They shook their heads, then turned away. I rose unsteadily to my feet, trying to get my bearings. Boris Karloff was by my side. He was wearing a wig and holding a lexicon in his hand.

"I need a word which rhymes with Mortimer," he said. It was then I knew I was being carted off to *Bedlam.*

"Not you."

I turned to see Gypsy at my side. I grinned.

"I love thee."

"Thou art a wonderful man," she replied in her best Anna Lee voice. She pointed across the room. I followed her direction with my eyes.

Jason Holloway, former mystic seer, was lying on a stretcher. There was a smile on his frozen face.

"He's supposed to be bricked up behind a wall," I protested. Gypsy shook her head.

"I used something much more powerful than a mason's trowel."

It was then I remembered the crystal ball. I looked for it, but it was gone. Vamoosed. My mouth went dry.

"Did he use it up?" I asked. "Take it with him?"

"Use what up?" the attendant inquired. "Is that what this bloke did – take poison?"

"Alas," Gypsy sadly replied. "He took nothing." I found myself mouthing the next words with her. "It was beauty killed the beast."

The beauty of unlimited power, corrupting absolutely. Jason Holloway had blown his mind on What Could Have Been. He had reduced himself to a blank page – the kind hammered out on a 1920s typewriter with a dry ribbon.

The man in the white coat took him away. I suppose Jason's thugs preceded him, for they were nowhere to be seen.

"Is he dead?" I whispered. "Really dead? As in kaput?"

"He is no more."

Boris Karloff couldn't have put it more succinctly.

I was in the hospital for a week. Sweet brought me my typewriter. When I went to hack out my Final Chapter, words failed me. What was I to write? The guy who had come so close to world domination was done in by a crystal ball?

No one in the work-a-day world would believe it.

I wasn't sure *I* believed it. The only ones who might remotely be credible had already jumped out high-rise windows.

I tried contacting the remaining financiers – those who had made millions from the interpretation of the stars. One had "retired" and gone on a long vacation to Guam. Another had given his remaining money to charity and gone "in search of God." I bet the author of *I Am Not Spock* would one day end up narrating his life's story.

My article went out on the wire without a hitch. Sweet said Mr. Poxie was pleased with it. A worse insult I've never received.

Ruth and Jimbo forgave me for winning the DOA when they discovered nine-tenths of my honorarium would be lost to taxes.

When I was released, this time with permission, Sweet drove me to Gypsy's flat, where I contemplated a long, leisurely recovery. Inasmuch as I was bandaged from "head" to foot, there was little I could do along any lines of entertainment other than sit and be amused.

"Gypsy," I said, taking advantage of my invalid status. "I never got a chance to watch you work. At your trade," I hastily added.

"You wish me to read your palm?" she asked. When I nodded and held out my hand, she laughed and agreed. "Oh, I see may things," she said, pouring over the lines in my hands. "Amazing things."

"Save that for the tourist trade. Tell me the truth."

"The truth," she warned, looking into my eyes, "means different things to different people. As our Mystic Seer discovered."

"Tell me anyway. I want to know what stories I will cover; if I will ever win another major award."

She peered again at the inscrutable twisting and turning of Fate, as represented by the creases in my palms.

"Yes," she finally agreed. "I see a trip. A long journey on a very important mission."

"Really? Where? Someplace exotic?"

"Most definitely! A place of high arches, a gateway to the world. All expenses paid. A trip which will be fraught with danger, suspense, wonderment, revelations. A journey which concerns high finance."

"Not another stock market story," I protested. "One is enough to last this crime reporter a lifetime."

She shook her head.

"One which touches on the very highest levels of government."

"A political scandal?"

"Only *you* can handle this story."

My brain swelled for lack of any other part of my anatomy being cooperative.

"Will I meet important people?"

"In mysterious places," she readily agreed. Too readily. I should have been suspicious, but I was lost in my fantasy. Fortunately, I missed the similarity with Jason Holloway.

"Will I triumph?"

"You will survive." I mistook drollness for approval.

"This is wonderful!" I joyfully exclaimed. "Tell me more."

"You are about to be summoned."

"Soon?" I was breathless.

At that moment the doorbell rang. I leapt to my feet and wormed my way over to the door. My heart was beating furiously. And to think she had read it all in the palm of my hand. I was a True Believer.

"Mr. Andrew Kimbo?" the uniform-clad man inquired.

"I am he."

"Sign here," he said, shoving a clipboard into my hands. It looked suspiciously like the one I had purloined from the hospital. I scrawled my signature on the dotted line and took my registered letter back to the table, where the light was better. I gave myself a paper cut as I ran my finger under the flap.

I had a sudden feeling I shouldn't have answered the door, should have feigned ignorance of one "Andrew Kimbo," but Gypsy had said she saw a journey. Besides, I was only a reporter, not a man given to listening to voices in his head.

The letter was printed on cheap, official stationary. It looked like a mass-mailing sweepstakes notification, informing me that I and two other people I had never heard of were finalists in the "One-Trillion Dollar Giveaway, All Prizes To Be Awarded. Respond within ten days or miss your Big Chance. Magazine subscriptions optional."

You know the one. The clearing house being sued for false advertising.

In fact, there *was* something about responding within ten days of receipt of this Official Notification. But it didn't say anything about winning money. For a minute, I had the funny feeling I was being drafted. It was *that* kind of letter. The kind which replaced telegrams as the most feared missive in the English language. Or, any other language, for that matter.

"Does it say anything about a trip?" Gypsy cheerfully inquired. I didn't look up.

Uncle Sam wanted me, all right. And she was correct. There *was* a trip in the works. But not the kind I had so happily anticipated only moments before.

"Yes," I croaked in a nearly inaudible, unintelligible voice. "It says something about a trip." I looked up. A smile curled around my teeth. I think it was the beginnings of insanity. I had survived stock market crashes, suicides, Mystic Seers, bomb blasts, hospital incarcerations and the End of the World, for this. Compared to what I held in my hand, they appeared tame.

"Who is the letter from?" Gypsy moved closer, trying to read over my shoulder. I held the letter back. I didn't want to pollute her innocent eyes with such poison words.

"The I.R.S." I explained. I tried to be brave for her sake. It was hard. Inside I was weeping uncontrollably. "My tax returns for the last three years are being audited. I am to appear in person at the Office of the Internal Revenue Service no later than ten days after receipt of this official notification. Failure to do so will result in fines, imprisonment or both."

"In person? Where, in person?"

Why did she have to sound so confoundedly cheerful? Didn't they have tax audits in Great Britain? Didn't she understand this was the kiss of death? That I was reduced to a single, naked, vulnerable citizen, at the mercy of the entire United States government?

"Where?" I slowly repeated, my world crumbling away from me. "Where I filed my return from, naturally. St. Louis, Missouri, U.S. of A."

She beamed with delight.

"Then I was right," she declared. I shuddered. "Declared" was not a word high on my list at the moment. "The lines in your hand foretold your future."

I wondered if it were too late to plunge them into a fire. Images flashed through my mind.

Arches. Gateways. Journeys. The highest levels of government.

Danger. Revelations.

She had seen it all. Right down to the last...

Deduction.

I didn't need a crystal ball to know I was in for it, right up to my 1040EZ.

I had been picked off first base.

My lucky star winked out.

The End

GSFE

ALSO BY: S.L.KOTAR AND J.E.GESSLER

"The Hugh Kerr Mystery Series"..

The Conundrum of

- **I** **The Decapitated Detective**
- **II** **The Absconded Attorney**
- **III** **The Sins of the Fathers**
- **IV** **The Two-Sided Lawyer**
- **V** **The Clueless Counselor**
- **VI** **The Loveless Marriage**
- **VII** **The Executed Defendant**
- **VIII** **The Jettisoned Jury**
- **IX** **The Perjured Pigeon**
- **X** **The Haunting Halloween Party**
- **XI** **The Tuneless Tunesmith**
- **XII** **The Meddling Motorcar**
- **XIII** **The Blundering Bear**
- **XIV** **The Shooting Fish in a Barrel**
- **XV** **The Girl with the Emerald Eyes**
- **XVI** **The Vanishing Cream**
- **XVII** **The Convoluted Confession**
- **XVIII** **The Skeleton in the Closet**

"New Beginnings Series"

- I **The Believer**
- II **The Heretic**
- III **Arrow Song**
- IV **Peas In A Pod**
- V **The Agnostics**

"The Kansas Pirate Series"

- I **Pirate Treasure**
- II **Strawberry Fields**
- III **The Drinking Gourd**

"the ReproBate saga"

I	**Beneath the Rose**
II	**skull and cRossBones**
III	**Redefining Bastions**
IV	**thicker than Blood**
V	**prioR Battles**
VI	**Requited Blasphemy**
VII	**The waR Between**
VIII	**To Richmond or Bust**
IX	**carrying Battlescars**
X	**RamBlings**
XI	**Retrieving Ballast**
XII	**captain's RB**
XIII	**wondeRous Backdrops**
XIV	**ReproBate**
XV	**time and tRouBle**
XVI	**the Road Back**
XVII	**oveR the Brink**

"the Hellhole saga"

- I **First Draw**
- II **Audition for a Legend**
- III **Strange Bedfellows**
-

" The Kimbo – Stop the Presses! – Series

- 1 **Mystic Seer**
- 2 **I am the News**
- 3 **Antie EM**
- 4 **Ashes to Ashes and all that Jazz**

- **Catman**
- **ONE**
- **Shepherd of the Kingdom**
- **Wolf Eyes**
- **I Am the Ship**
- **Blue Moon**
- **Target'd**
- **Star Bright**

Non-Fiction
"The Kepi Magazine," :

- **Volume I and II**
- **Volumes III and IV**

www.ingramcontent.com/pod-product-compliance
Lightning Source LLC
LaVergne TN
LVHW020043110826
845155LV00029B/618

* 9 7 8 1 9 5 0 3 9 2 6 0 5 *